The Postman's Daughter

Sally Anne Palmer

ISBN 978-1-936556-06-9

Published 2016

Published by Black Velvet Seductions Publishing

The Postman's Daughter Copyright 2016 Sally Anne Palmer
Cover Copyright 2016 Breanna Hayse

Printed by Black Velvet Seductions Publishing
A division of Savage Publications

Visit us at:
www.blackvelvetseductions.com

Chapter One

I am dead, my love. The words of his last letter haunted me, whispering through the darkness when I tried to sleep. How did he know? And, more importantly, was he right?

If I hadn't got lost, maybe everything would have been different. I remember I was walking home from the library, via Poplar Park and Charlotte's house, trying to recall the name of every book I'd ever read and thinking about Charlotte's news. The blackout rules had been in place for more than a year so every house I passed had stuffed up its windows and doors with new curtains, old sheets, sacks or bits of rag depending on style and circumstances. But in East London, where I'd lived all of my eighteen years, some of the houses didn't have any windows left and the doorways of others spilled darkness onto the street. The zeppelins had been bombing us for two years, once or twice a month, and I was used to watching the sky.

That night though, it was cloudless, festooned with stars and when I realised I was lost, I wasn't worried. I followed steep brick walls around corners, crossed roads, squinted at illegible street signs and all around me I had the sense of people, pressed in behind the walls, talking, shouting, living, somewhere close by. The East End was like that, everyone on top of everyone else, but it was home and at that moment I was glad of it.

Overhead, but still some distance away I caught the first faint rumbles of thunder so I picked up my pace. A couple more turns and the walls got bigger, stretching further up into the sky and coating the pavements in thick shadow. I began to have trouble seeing my feet and I stretched out my hand to one side, trailing my fingers over the rough walls as a guide.

The lack of windows and a faint, acrid smell told me I was near a factory, although which one, I wasn't sure. I heard the thunder throbbing through the sky above, some way behind me but coming closer by the minute. I buttoned my coat, began a slow trot through the gloom and promptly tripped over.

A hand shot out of the darkness, grabbed my elbow and arrested my fall. "You shouldn't be here," said a voice, overly loudly and with an arrogant tone I didn't care for.

"I'm quite aware of that, thank you," I retorted, and tried to wrest my arm back, but the fingers of my unknown assailant were pinched tight. "If you would kindly stop breaking my elbow and tell me how to get to South Street, I'll be on my way." My mother always said I was blunt, by which she generally meant rude, but I hadn't paid her any attention since I was twelve years old and I usually spoke to people exactly how I wanted.

The man in the darkness did not let me go. "South Street? That's about two miles in the other direction. Are you stupid as well as lost?"

"If you don't let go of my arm I'll be stupid, lost and calling for help."

"You shouldn't be here."

"You've said that already, although it's clearly alright for you to be here, lurking around at night assaulting young women."

"They're coming," he said.

I instantly felt sorry for him, and slightly guilty for the rudeness. I couldn't tell much about him apart from that he was taller than me, older than me and also from London, but I'd seen enough young men back from the front by now to know that the damage wasn't always on the outside.

"Alright," I said, straightening up. "If they're coming, where should I be?"

I could hear an exhalation and the man bent closer as his fingers relaxed. "About two miles in the other direction, I would think. Come on."

He stepped out of the shelter of the wall and in the dim starlight his face was as white as bleached bone, eye sockets gouged out of shadow. Still holding onto my arm, he stepped off the kerb as if he could actually see it, and steered me across the road.

"So, who's coming?" I asked carefully, because the answer might well be flying monkeys or God or something else that I'd have to pretend to believe in.

I glimpsed the turn of his head towards me as he said rudely, "Who do you think?" A long line of shadow snaked down the right side of his face, cutting across a cheekbone, ending in a ragged patch by his mouth.

"Someone with better manners, I hope."

Our footsteps tapped across the cobbles but the noise was muffled by a sudden rumble overhead as the thunder muttered to itself impatiently. We'd reached the corner of the road now, turned right and passed under a railway arch I didn't remember seeing before. The man stopped short, span both of us round and raised an arm dramatically at the sky. "They're coming."

I blinked at the clear night and wondered vaguely where the thunder was coming from since there weren't any clouds. I waited for a heartbeat, two, nothing happened. "Do you think they could come a bit quicker? If you asked them nicely?"

I saw the flicker of movement in the darkness as the man's shoulders straightened, heard his indrawn breath. "You want me to ask them to come quicker? I should be the one shouting for help. Hey you – the attacking German air force. There's a girl here who wants you to hurry up!" he yelled.

Then the most enormous plane I'd ever seen shattered the calm sky with a throbbing shout of noise. The roar it made was immense, deafening, battering the air out of the way with two screaming engines, trailing a curtain of sound that was so loud, so all-encompassing I couldn't think about anything else. I felt the man's grasp on my elbow release, and his fingers creep down my sleeve until he was holding my hand. But the plane overhead held all my attention, all my awareness. I knew I should run. Hide somewhere. Get underground. But there was a brick wall against my back, a man's hand holding mine and a clutching, clenching fear in my guts that wouldn't let me go. The quality of the sound modulated, shifted, differentiated itself into a more immediate low whistle that started quietly, and then expanded and expanded until the drone of the plane was obliterated and the whistle sliced through my eardrums.

The bombs fell. There was a split second of silence, and then the explosion. The pavement beneath my feet shuddered. The brick wall shook behind my back, and then spat dust all over my head. A hot wind licked my cheeks and my eyes were full of fire. Red flame smeared the darkness as the factory against whose walls I had been stumbling not ten minutes before disassembled itself at speed into brick and plaster.

I felt a hand on my shoulder, a rough shake. The man next to me said, "You shouldn't be here."

In the firelight I could see him clearly for the first time. His face was thin, gaunt even, the pale skin marred by a thin thread of scar tissue which stretched from just behind his ear to the right hand side of his mouth. I guessed his age as around thirty, and, apart from the scar, he seemed uninjured, although when he glanced down there was something not quite normal about the way he was looking at me.

"Oh," he said. "That's new. I mean, you're new. That is, I'm sorry. I didn't realise you were going to happen."

I gestured at the burning building, which felt slightly more important than his inarticulate introductions. "Shouldn't we go and help?"

"No, there was no one inside. I already checked."

"But we could put the fire out or something. Maybe. I don't know. How can you have checked?"

"Easily. I got in through one of the doors at the back and had a look around."

"No, I mean, how can you have known to check? I haven't seen German planes over London before. How can you have known there would be a raid tonight? How did you know that the factory would get hit?"

"It wasn't a factory, it was a works. Tanners Steel Works to be exact. Not that I know what the difference between a factory and a works is."

"Is that your best attempt at changing the subject? How did you know that factory would get hit?"

"Lucky guess?"

"Rubbish. Practically the only thing you've said to me tonight is "you shouldn't be here" and "go away". You were lurking around it. You knew it was going to get bombed. How?"

"I didn't tell you to go away. I wanted to, but I didn't actually say it. South Street wasn't it? Come on."

And he jammed his hands into the pockets of the long black coat he was wearing and strode smartly away. It wasn't all that easy to storm off though, because every house now had an open door and every inhabitant of every house was taking advantage of their open door to chat to their neighbours. Amidst the roar of the flames and the odd plink of exploding brick I caught fragments of conversation.

Air raids in London were a regular occurrence, and they usually managed to kill a handful of people, but we were protected now by searchlights, by a smattering of our own airborne defences, but mostly by the great British weather, which had managed to produce enough fog and cloud and even snow during 1916 to keep the Germans at bay.

Besides, someone had managed to shoot down an airship with a new kind of ammunition only a couple of months ago and the parts had been sold to help the war effort, so they weren't unbeatable. That was the sort of thing people liked to talk about after a raid.

I weaved through the street on the trail of the suspicious man in the suspicious black coat who had suspiciously known exactly when and where the Germans were going to strike.

"Are you a German?" I asked his retreating back.

"No. Are you a German?"

"Of course not. Two of my brothers are away fighting them."

"Poor Germans. Turn left."

I got no more conversation out of him all the way home. At the end of South Street, he paused, waited for me to walk past.

"Thank you for bringing me back," I said. "I'm also grateful not to have been killed."

He nodded in my direction and turned on his heel. "We'll meet again," he said.

"Do you know where? Or when? It's just that I'd prefer you not to jump out at me from the dark again Mr...?"

"I know exactly where," he said.

Even back then, I didn't know whether or not to believe him.

Chapter Two

My house was the sixth one on the right from the top of South Street, the only place I'd ever lived. I was born on my parents" bed like my three brothers before me, which made for a strong sense of community, as well as a really stained mattress. Our house was quite large as it had three bedrooms and its own toilet in the garden although we would quite regularly find some of our older neighbours in there using it as their own toilet too.

I ran down the narrow passageway between our house and the one next door, counting off eight steps before reaching for the gate. The alley was dark even at noon on a sunny summer day and in winter in a blackout, memory was the only map. I unclicked the latch, swung the door, stepped down into the brick yard and saw immediately that there was something wrong.

The back door was open and from inside I could see a candle flickering on the kitchen table, doling out slices of light to one portion of the room then another as it guttered in the draft. My mother had let the range go out. That was probably some kind of commentary on the fact I was back so late, since the task of keeping the home fire burning had been delegated to me about six years ago and since then my mother had deliberately forgotten the location of the matches on a number of occasions. I went inside, hung my coat on the back of the door and threw some wood on the fire, lighting it with the candle. This took far longer than it should have done, because even though we had six rooms in our house and were better off under the new coal rationing than lots of people, we were still hoarding it against a cold winter. By the time I'd finished, my mother had opened the door to the kitchen.

"Oh," she sighed. "Ivy. I thought you were your father."

"What's happened, Mother? The door was open."

"Your brother."

"Tom? Philip?" The rush of hot panic was instant and uncontrollable. "What happened? Did you get a letter? A telegram?"

My mother was dismissive, something she had practised extensively. "It's much too late for the post, you know that. Alfie is missing."

That was panic of a different kind, a worn and threadbare alarm that I was always half expecting. My eldest brother Alfie was different to other boys. His difference wasn't something you could name or label, he didn't have a missing hand or two heads and people walked straight past him in the street without a second glance, but if you spent any time with him it became his defining feature. I was sure he loved me, in the same way he loved all his family, and his collection of shells from the beach and the stick he found in the park. His loves were fierce, but easily picked up and just as easily put down again. He spent so much time listening to other people he rarely remembered to speak.

I picked up my coat again and shrugged it on. "I'll go and look. Did he take anything with him?"

My mother shook her head, sighed, and dropped heavily onto the kitchen chair. "He'll be the death of me, that boy." She was always saying that, but it hadn't happened yet, unfortunately.

Alfie was a creature of habit, and that creature was probably a squirrel, because he loved to collect things and he had a special brown bag to hoard them away in. If he hadn't taken his bag, that meant he wasn't out on a forage, so I started next door. I rattled the letter box, which hadn't been polished, and dislodged a few flakes of paint from the door. Mrs Norton would be inside but she was probably already in bed, because with a husband and a son gone to fight she seemed to be finding fewer and fewer reasons to get up. I knocked again, and then called through the letterbox. "Mrs Norton, have you seen Alfie?"

There was no reply so I moved onto our next neighbour, Mrs Carmichael, who was opening the door even as I raised my hand. She had at least six children, most still in shorts, and consequently liked to get out of the house as much as possible. She stepped out onto the pavement and pulled the door to, which didn't quite muffle the odd yell and the stench of drying wool.

"Alfie's missing again, Mrs Carmichael. Is there any chance you've seen him?"

Mrs Carmichael was one of those plump, rosy cheeked women you see on posters advertising the countryside, the sort of woman who always wears a flowery dress and a white pinny, in which she's probably concealing a freshly baked apple pie or two.

"Not as such, Ivy love. But I did hear a big bang a while ago that might have been him."

"That was an air raid Mrs C. A factory exploded. Alfie didn't do it, I promise."

"Of course not, love, of course not. Although I did hear your mother yelling a lot afterwards."

"Do you remember what she was saying?"

"Oh no, I wasn't listening. It was Margery's bath time and Peter was winding her up something rotten so we had a lot going on here too. But I may have heard your mum telling Alfie to eat his potatoes and cabbage because there wasn't anything else, and Alfie obviously didn't and I didn't blame him really because your mother over boils her cabbage, as you know. And Alfie still wouldn't eat it so your mother said she'd been working her fingers to the bone to put food on the table, although she did get that cabbage for a knock down price from Mr Murphy yesterday because it was on the turn and anyway, I think that was when Alfie left. Your dad came round looking - I think he was off to the pub next."

"Thanks Mrs C, that helps a lot."

She watched as I turned right and headed down the length of South Street towards the White Star. The pub on the end of our road served the whole street, in theory, but with the price of beer and the scarcity of supply these days what it mostly served was the solitary few who could afford it, and my dad. Alfie had tried to go there every week since he was ten years old, because once Mrs Reckitt, the landlord's wife, had a leftover meat pie and took pity on his heavy sighs and air of desperate longing. The pub didn't actually serve food, no one could afford to give away that much meat these days and Mrs Reckitt moved out to her daughter's in Folkestone six months ago, but Alfie didn't realise any of that.

I poked my head around the door into what was effectively someone else's front room. The chairs were harder, and there were more of them, gathered around assorted mismatched tables but the room wasn't much bigger than our parlour and back room combined, with a pine table in the corner that Mr Reckitt used as a bar.

"Ivy Drummond, why are you out so late? And on your own too?" Mr Andrews was sitting at the closest table to the door, waiting to find fault with whatever came through it. He was an old style military man, which meant he'd fought in the Boer War and consequently had an unusual fondness for both shouting, and the curl of a luxuriant moustache.

"Yes sir, sorry sir. Have you seen my brother Alfie at all? Sir."

"I saw him heading over towards the school about an hour ago. Your father's gone to find him. You'd best get home and wait. A girl your age shouldn't be out walking the streets late at night on your own. It isn't safe. There's a Hun on every corner."

"Yes, sir. Sorry, sir. Of course, sir. Anything you say, sir."

"Go home, Ivy."

"Sir." Mr Andrews liked everyone to show him the respect he deserved, and I tried, I really did, although every time I said "sir" I was thinking "idiot". I let the door swing shut and then walked deliberately away from home and followed the trail of Alfie's stomach towards South Street School, home of school dinners.

South Street Elementary was a three storey, red brick, no nonsense educational establishment, on top of which some enthusiastic architect had misplaced a white bell tower, too small and off centre, which made the school look as if it was wearing a miniature top hat and was closely associated with the word "jaunty". As I reached the end of the street and rounded the corner I began to hear faint sounds of shouting, or raised voices, bouncing off the pavement, rebounding around walls in little balls of noise. The streets were otherwise silent, and the dark windows of the houses reflected back untrustworthy skies. A few more steps and I could pick out individual voices, a few more and I turned into the alleyway which led to the back gate.

Directly in front of me was Alfie's back, tall, broad of shoulder and great with muscle and in front of him, my small, slight dad, whose eyes widened a bit when he saw me approaching, before he gave a tiny shake of the head. He had his hand out in front of him, a placatory gesture.

"Now, Alfie. Leave it. Come home with me. Leave it, boy."

"Yeah, that's it doggy. Go home with Daddy. Unless you want this." I saw in the shadows, close to the gate, David Andrews, whom I had refused to kiss on the last day of school because he was just too pretty. His hair was blonde, soft and wavy, his lips a glorious rosebud pink and his wide spaced, cerulean eyes were full of a brutal, undiscriminating malevolence of a kind you only find in the very mad or the very stupid. And pigs.

Alfie took another step forward, shaking his head.

"What's the matter Fido? Do you want this? Come on then, come and get it. Come here boy, there's a good doggy." David Andrews was waving something around in the dark but I had a pretty good idea what it was.

Alfie shuffled forward again.

"Leave it son, I'll get you another one." My dad blocked Alfie's path, but it wasn't David Andrews he was protecting. "Come home Alfie, come on."

"Hey, doggy, is this a family outing? Your sister's behind you. Where's your brothers then? Where's your brothers, Fido?"

My dad half turned. "Be quiet David, or I'll have to tell your father."

"They're in France, aren't they doggy? I bet they're having a great time without you aren't they? Beating up the Hun, kissing all the girls without you following them around on your lead. They couldn't wait to get away from you could they?"

"David," my dad snapped.

Alfie didn't react, simply stood still but I could tell he wasn't listening this time, he was waiting.

"Come on then doggy, let's play fetch shall we? I'll throw your stick and you can fetch it back, you'd like that. That's the only thing you're good for. Fetch, doggy, fetch. "

"David." Dad turned a bit more, broke eye contact with Alfie.

"Oh alright, Mr Drummond, I was only playing."

There was a movement in the darkness and then a sharp crack as David broke the stick against the school wall. Everything that happened next was inevitable, everything.

Alfie charged, straight through my father who lurched awkwardly into the brick wall and fell to the ground with a cry. I heard three wet crunches as Alfie's fist met David Andrew's hitherto perfect features and bludgeoned them into a mess of blood, gristle and snot.

I shot to Alfie's side but I knew better than to try to touch him. "Alfred Drummond. Stop." I called loudly, and calmly, because with Alfie, it was all about the tone of voice. Alfie's meaty right arm slowed in its backward arc. "Arms by your sides. Turn around. Go and stand by your father. "

Alfie would have made an excellent soldier. He was very good at following orders. Alfie shuffled backwards towards Dad with one long, lingering look at the broken stick.

David was whimpering to himself, curled in a ball on the floor, blood oozing between the fingers he had clamped around his nose.

I crouched next to him and whispered. "If my brothers had heard any of that you'd be lying there with a couple of broken arms as well as that nose. If you bother Alfie again, I'll break them myself."

He was still crying when I walked away. "Alfie. Help Dad up. Let's go."

Alfie heaved Dad effortlessly to his feet, but Dad was rubbing his elbow slowly. I put my arm around his waist.

"I think he's broken my arm, Ivy."

"I doubt it Dad, he didn't push you that hard. David's bound to go straight to his father, so we can expect a visit tomorrow. Or maybe tonight, depending on how much David cries. Let's get you patched up first."

"Are you alright. Alfie?" called my father with a backwards glance, and Alfie didn't reply, already scanning the ground for replacement vegetation.

"Of course he's alright, Dad. Do you know what he was doing out on his own?"

"Your mother said he wouldn't do as he was told."

"I heard he was told to eat his cabbage. "

"Really? Dear God, that's a disaster. That means I'll have to eat it when I get home. And what were you doing out on your own Ivy? I trust it wasn't cabbage related?"

"I was reading in the park, and then I was reading in the library, and then I went to Charlotte's house to do some more reading, but we got carried away talking about the characters we were reading about," I lied.

"I'm going to assume that "characters" is code for boys," interjected my dad.

"I don't think Shakespeare wrote much about boys Dad, at least, not the sort of boys that you're talking about."

"You should be talking about boys Ivy, at your age. You do too much reading."

"I have an interview for a job, Dad. First thing tomorrow morning right there at that school." I jerked my head towards it. "I'm going to be an English teacher. They will expect me to know how to read."

"And I expect you to be an eighteen-year-old girl, Ivy. Not an old lady with a job who spends all her free time as a nursemaid to her older brother. "

"There's a war on, Dad."

"There won't always be a war on. You need your own life. It's my job to look after you. Alfie is my responsibility."

I shrugged. "Alfie is everyone's responsibility. And I want to work. If there wasn't a war I probably wouldn't get the chance. How's your arm?"

"For me to deal with. Are you alright back there, Alfie?"

The heavy thud of my brother's boots on the pavement was his only response.

I changed the subject. "Did you hear the air raid, Dad? It was a plane. I saw it. Six bombs straight down. It blew up a factory a couple of miles away. Or maybe it was a works. What is a works anyway?"

"No idea. What were you doing a couple of miles away?"

"Well that was the thing. I was so busy thinking about boys that I got a bit lost and ended up walking down a street next to the works. Then this man grabbed me, said I shouldn't be there and manhandled me under a bridge."

"What I said about boys? I take it back. Are you hurt? You don't look hurt. A bit dusty maybe but that's not unusual for you, it comes with the reading. You saw an air raid and you just walked away without even a scratch? That's amazing Ivy. Incredible. What the bloody hell were you doing out on your own in the first place?"

"I told you, I got lost."

"No daughter of mine gets lost. What the bloody hell were you doing near an air raid?"

"That's what I'm saying, Dad. I didn't know there was going to be an air raid, did I? There weren't any zeppelins or anything. No noise except for thunder and then this plane flew out of nowhere and started dropping bombs. But the man I was with, he did know. I was right next to the factory when it exploded, I'd be dead if he hadn't been so rude. 'You shouldn't be here, you shouldn't be here' he kept saying. So when it blew up, I wasn't."

"Who was the man?"

"I don't know. But I was wondering – what sort of person knows there's going to be an air raid?"

"What sort of person manhandles a young woman under a bridge?"

"The same sort of person who's already checked there's no one in the factory. So do you think it's a bit odd, Dad?"

"I think it's a bit suspicious. You say he was just waiting for the factory to blow up?"

"Seemed like it."

"And was he at all…foreign? I mean, that's a stupid question because most of them don't even sound foreign, or look foreign these days."

"He said he wasn't German, if that's what you mean."

"Well he's not going to say he's German is he? No one's going to admit to that any more. And you didn't know him at all, he wasn't from round here?"

"I wasn't round here when I met him."

"Good point. You're forbidden from going out on your own after dark for the next two months. I think I'd better tell Andrews about this."

"Oh no, Dad. Really?"

"Yes. This man sounds strange. Andrews is responsible for civil defence. He needs to know."

"I don't care about Mr Andrews. It's November. It gets dark early. With the daylight saving that means you basically want me home before lunch."

"It's that or eat the cabbage, Ivy."

We turned into the alley next to our house and I stretched out my hand in the darkness. We crossed the yard, finding the back door closed and the curtains drawn, and then my mother in the kitchen, boiling a kettle on the range for tea.

"Jack," she shrieked, as soon as the door opened. "Jack. Did you find him? What's happened to your arm? Does it hurt? Sit by the fire and let me have a look. Alfie, take your shoes off, take your coat off and then sit down at that table and eat your cabbage."

Alfie, hulking in the doorway behind me, breathed out heavily but said not a word. I tugged the edge of his sleeve, bringing him into the circle of light thrown by the candle, still guttering on the table. "Go to bed, Alfie. I'll take you out for breakfast in the morning."

Alfie didn't acknowledge either instruction, but clumped off in the direction of the stairs, his boots still firmly laced.

My mother shot me a sour look as she helped my father take off his jacket. "Excellent work, Ivy. Now he'll think all he has to do is wander off and then he doesn't have to do as he's told."

"He's twenty-two, Mother. He doesn't have to eat cabbage if he doesn't want to."

"Ladies. I will eat the cabbage. I've been looking forward to it. Now, can someone find something to put on my arm?"

My dad sent me to bed with a nod of the head, but I was glad to go.

Talking to my mother was like drinking cod liver oil – it was probably the right thing to do but it left a nasty taste in the mouth.

My bedroom was at the top of the stairs on the right. It used to be Tom and Philips" bedroom before they went away, and it still had that dank, slightly sweaty air about it that boys' bedrooms tend to get if you don't leave the door open. I hadn't moved much around since they left except for pulling Tom's bed away from the window and pushing it as close to the wall as possible. I found if I had bad dreams it helped to have something solid at my back.

I shucked off my boots, tossed my skirts, stockings and my high necked white blouse onto the chair beside the bed and collapsed under the blanket.

Chapter Three

I woke in the morning with slobber all down my face and one of Tom's last letters pasted to my cheek. Tom was the brother closest to me in age, the only one likely to laugh at my jokes, the only one I could really talk to. He had gone to France to fight, of course, but he hadn't wanted to, and seemed to be spending most of his time looking for our other brother Philip. I read through the letter again before storing it safely under the pillow where it belonged.

Dear Ivy, Tom had written a month or so ago now.

24th October: Rain.

30th October: Heavy drizzle.

1st November: Drizzle, sleet and rain.

2nd November: Light precipitation.

Well, what do you expect me to say? Nothing has happened and continues to happen here in France, where the rain falls and the mud rises and someone I've never met decides what I'm doing next. We sleep when we can, and eat what we can but the Germans can't be bothered to aim more than the occasional sniper at us and I've stopped polishing my bayonet.

I met a man the other week who'd been further up the line and he'd seen an actual tank. He said it looked like a big tin on wheels with guns sticking out on all sides. The damn thing had rolled over the top of our trenches to great cheers, had got a few yards through the wire and then got one of its tracks stuck in a tree stump. Apparently it spent two hours going backwards and forwards in the mud and digging itself into such a big hole that the crew had to get out and leave it. And we thought tanks were going to help us win the war! Looks like it's back to pinning our hopes on the Hun running out of wellington boots.

That's the end of the bit you can read to Mum. Tell her I love her etc etc. Round it all off nicely. This next bit is for you.

The search for Philip Drummond - the story so far, some of which you know and some you don't. Phil joined up in September 1914 and went into the Post Office Rifles, I think mostly because it would make Dad proud, and because it was a way out of that job in the sorting office he hated. There are at least two Rifles battalions - the first battalion sailed from Southampton in mid-March 1915, landed in France and went to fight at Festubert (also in France, I know your geography anywhere outside London is terrible) – but don't worry, Phil wasn't with them. He was still back with the second in England. Mum got his last letter around June last year as I recall.

I found a man who was at Festubert (France is the one across the Channel) and he said the first battalion took heavy losses and some of the second came over to replenish the ranks. I think that was Phil and I think that's why he stopped writing home. I think he was here in France by October 1915 and about to fight in the battle of Loos (also in France. See above re: location of France). There's a man here, a chaplain, very nice but utterly useless. I guess once you've been preached at by Father Moran any other religion loses its sting. Anyway, he knows a man I can ask what happened. I'll write again when I know more.

Love to Charlotte, when you see her.

See you soon.

Tom

It was around seven in the morning. Dad had been at work for hours but Mother wouldn't be leaving for her shift at Regent's Park until this afternoon. I laid out my best clothes – a dark blue wool skirt, a clean white blouse and a shawl I'd knitted last winter and went downstairs to heat some water.

The bathroom was off the kitchen but as long as you stayed close enough to the range on the other side of the wall it wasn't too cold, even in winter. I had a flannel wash, and then set the iron on to heat before pressing my blouse on the kitchen table and pulling on woollen stockings, and my flat black leather shoes. I pinned up my hair in preparation for stuffing it under a hat.

After I was dressed, I paced. Despite Dad's comments about the reading my two best qualifications for the position of an English teacher were that I was both available, and alive. And English, of course. So many teachers had enlisted that schools would basically employ anyone, or so I hoped.

At ten o'clock I was knocking on the headmaster's door at South Street School when Miss Bird opened it. "Ivy Drummond. What a very great pleasure it is to see you again."

I smoothed down my skirt with a shy grin, instantly transported back to the time I was ten and Miss Bird had made me stand up in class and recite a poem I'd written to a chorus of sniggers and derisive laughter from the other children. "Hello, Miss Bird. I didn't realise you were still working here."

"I'm part of the furniture, Ivy." I'd have gone with armchair, if I had to choose, because Miss Bird was plump and squashy at the front but had a ramrod straight back and thick, sturdy arms, capable of supporting anything. "They'll never get rid of me. I hear you've come about the job." She patted me on the hand. "Well. Good luck, love. I hope you get it; you'd be an asset to this school. Go in, he's waiting for you."

With a nervous lick of my lips I pushed open the glass door into a wood panelled office which had all the square footage you'd expect from an impressive, intimidating, no nonsense educational establishment, but wasn't square. In fact, the floor space was roughly twice the size of an average tea towel and I nearly crashed into the headmaster's desk as I walked in since it was situated so near the door. Behind the desk an inordinately tall window stretched between playground and heavens, a golden halo limning the man sitting behind it. He was lean to the point of gaunt, with a hint of skeletal, and his hair was cut short in the military style. It was quite difficult to see what he looked like with the glare behind him and my eyes mostly registered an impression of dark clothing and a serious countenance before I saw him gesture at the single chair in front of him.

I sat, as gracefully as I could possibly manage on a seat which appeared to have been constructed for a five-year-old with height issues and politely waited for him to finish whatever he was writing and actually look up at me. After about a minute I noticed my nerves fading into irritation and two minutes later my irritation began ratcheting upwards into annoyance.

"Name?" he said, still scribbling.

It was only when he spoke that I realised who he was. "Oh, I know you. It is you, isn't it? The one from last night with all the rudeness and the shouting."

His hand paused, and his eyes flicked up, catching my stare and holding it while he threw down his pen, sat back leisurely, steepled his fingers in front of his lips and arched an eyebrow at me. "Name?" he asked again.

It was without question, the same man who had accosted me outside the factory last night. In the light of day, it seemed his most distinguishing feature was not the delicate silver line which rippled down his right cheek, or the rather arrogant sneer on his lips, or even the broad chin or the strong nose, but the pale blue eyes inspecting me across the table, considering, assessing, judging. And because I still hadn't answered he felt the need to say, "Name?" again, this time with more than a hint of impatience.

"Ivy Drummond. I'm right aren't I? You're the one who knew about the air raid."

He leaned forward, and, for some reason that I didn't entirely understand, I leaned back. "Miss Drummond. In the unlikely event that you are successful today in what, may I remind you, is a job interview, you will have the privilege of referring to me as "sir". Until that time, I would prefer not to be called "oi, you from last night."

"I never said 'oi'."

He returned his cold, impassive gaze to his writing. "Age?"

"Eighteen."

"As old as that."

"Excuse me?"

"Given your behaviour, I'd assumed you were much younger. Address?"

"12 South Street. I wrote a letter asking for an interview not two weeks ago, all my details are in that, if you bother to read it. "

"Family circumstances?"

"My dad's a postman. My mother's just got a job in the new sorting office in Regent's Park and I have two older brothers in France. The Somme. At least I think so. We haven't heard from one of them in over a year."

He flickered another glance at me, and dropped it just as quickly. "And your other brother?"

I hadn't mentioned Alfie in my letter, but I assumed Miss Bird had been gossiping. "He's at home."

"Marital status?"

"What's that got to do with anything?"

"I am establishing your character. I assume you are a spinster?"

"Why?"

"Firstly, if you were married you wouldn't be applying for a job and secondly, no ring. Religion?"

"None."

"Why not?"

"God's got a lot to answer for."

"Education and qualifications?"

"South Street Elementary School, Bethnal Green Grammar School. I got a scholarship, and I got my certificate. But for the last few years, since the war started, I've been needed at home. I've kept up with my reading."

"Teaching experience?"

"None, not as such."

He capped his pen abruptly, sat back in his chair and pinned me with those frosty eyes. "No pupil teacher course? No tutoring? Did you at least help out at Sunday school?"

"I don't go to church. And I am teaching Mrs Carmichael's children to read. I'm good with children."

"You're barely more than a child yourself. But assertions aren't a substitute for experience. This reading you've been keeping up with, of what did it consist?"

"The classics."

"Latin? Greek?"

"More like novels, plays and poetry."

"Ah, poetry. Very well. Quote any verse from Paradise Lost. Name the protagonists of Shakespeare's Twelfth Night. In what year did Henry Fielding publish "Tom Jones"?"

I could tell, by the mocking twist in his voice, and the fact that his eyes were now little ice-blue shards, that he was expecting me to fail. I was expecting me to fail. Neither of us was disappointed.

I rushed out, "But you can't teach it like that."

He blinked, slowly. "You can't teach …factually?"

"Not everything. You can't reduce books and writing and poetry to facts and figures, any more than you can tell everything about me from my name and address. Sometimes you have to see a thing, really see and experience it before you can explain it. There's more to English and, and life than just dates and numbers, so much more to feel and wonder at, so much more to understand."

"So I need to read poetry before I can understand life – is that what you're saying?"

There was a very long silence, during which I aimed at and utterly missed meeting the glacial eyes boring into me from across the desk.

Then he said, "Well, thank you for your views on educational philosophy Miss Drummond. That conversation really has been the highlight of my day. Unfortunately, I regret to inform you that on this occasion you have not been successful in obtaining a teaching position at South Street School, but I wish you every success in the future." He picked up his pen and shuffled a fresh piece of paper from the pile. "Good day."

I stood, with as much dignity as possible given that I'd basically been crouching on the floor and fumbled for the door knob. "I expect I won't be seeing you again this time then?"

"Good day Miss Drummond." He repeated, and I took that as my cue to leave, furious to the point of tears at myself, and him and bloody Shakespeare and even Charlotte, whose fault it also was in some small part.

Thankfully, my mother was not at home to gloat when I returned, and I spent some time stomping all over the rag rug in the parlour with my shoes on without beating it out afterwards. Then a noise upstairs distracted me and I realised guiltily that I'd forgotten to take Alfie for breakfast. I clattered up the steps and went left at the top, through my parents" bedroom and into his room. Alfie was sitting on his neatly made bed, clutching his brown collecting bag and staring fixedly at the large pile of branches taking up most of the floor space.

"Oh Alfie," I sighed, sitting down next to him and taking his hand. "Have you been waiting for me all this time? I'm very sorry I'm so late. Let's go then, and don't forget your broom."

Alfie didn't speak, he just listened at me crossly. He didn't have a job as such, but on days when I was busy he liked to go out and sweep the streets, which performed a useful public service as well as enlisting the entire community in keeping an eye on him, whether they wanted to or not.

There was a bakery two streets over and we joined the queue outside it, waiting our turn to gasp at the price they'd be charging for a bread roll and two sticky buns. Food wasn't rationed, but the prices were so high that it might as well have been. I filled Alfie in on my day as we waited, and he listened as patiently and as silently as if he was unconscious, which I usually found quite restful. The peace was short-lived though, because as soon as Mrs Carmichael and her flock of children spied us around half an hour later she promptly pushed into the queue, to a silent chorus of disapproving stares, shaking of heads and frowning. "Ivy, oh Ivy, did you hear? It's Mrs Norton. Poor, poor Mrs Norton. I saw it happen just an hour or so ago. There was a knock on the door and there it was."

"She got a letter?"

"A brown letter from the War Office. Poor Veronica."

"Husband or son?" I had neither so I wasn't sure which it would be worse to lose.

"I don't know. I'll have to go round later and find out. Her sister's with her now."

I bought some extra bread to take round to number fourteen later, not because it would do any good, but because it was so much easier to give and receive baked goods than sympathetic, empty words. I left Alfie munching on his late breakfast and asked Mrs Carmichael to watch out for him before heading round to Charlotte's.

The door to the cottage was open, as always, to let out the steam, and I only recognised Charlotte at floor level by her weathered old boots. There were so many sheets stretched out to dry across the living room that everything at head height was invisible.

"Charlotte," I called.

"Oh, hello Ivy, we're both at the back. How did your interview go?"

That was Mrs Ransome, Charlotte's mother, who would be working the tub while my best friend scrubbed and beat and swung the wet washing that was her only income. Charlotte was tall, and golden haired, with a sweet singing voice and a graceful way of moving that made you think she'd have been a really good dancer. Unfortunately, according to Charlotte's mother, there was no money in dancing, or in singing, or in fact any value in anything that didn't involve scrubbing somebody else's gusset with a bar of carbolic soap. Despite being the best and the brightest in my class, Charlotte had left school at twelve and gone straight to work. She should have got the scholarship that I took, but she'd had the choice between studying and eating, which wasn't really much of a decision.

I answered, "It was dreadful. Can Charlotte have five minutes off so I can tell her all about it?"

"Of course, of course."

"Thanks Ivy. Let's go in the garden shall we?"

I followed Charlotte's boots through the maze of washing into the yard, only to find more flapping sheets, the noise of which usefully camouflaged our conversation. "Well, have you decided?" I began.

"No, don't push me Ivy, I still don't know."

"For goodness sake, Lottie. Did all those books teach you nothing? This isn't a mistake."

"It's only two weeks. It might be nothing. That book said stress, or malnutrition, or chemicals or something can affect it. "

"Yes, I read that too, and I also read the one about the first sign of pregnancy..."

"Ivy," Charlotte snapped, and I lowered my voice again.

"The first sign of "it" was not bleeding and you still haven't, have you?"

"No, but."

"How long now since you did?"

"Six weeks, give or take."

"Give or take? Did you forget how to add up as well? Soapsuds on the brain is it? Don't give me that Charlotte. How long is it since you saw Tom? And I know you know what I mean when I say 'saw'."

"Shut up Ivy. The only things you know come from books. You've never so much as kissed a boy and quite honestly, you've got no idea what you're talking about."

"Lottie, this is really, really important."

"Do you think I don't know that?"

"Are you going to tell him or not?"

"Oh God Ivy, I don't know. Look, I had a letter." She retrieved a damp piece of paper from the pocket of her greying apron and thrust it at me. The date was a week ago.

Dearest Lottie.

It seems like only yesterday that we were saying our goodbyes. Like it's only a single night since I last kissed you. I know it's been weeks. Five weeks, one day, four hours and fifty-six minutes, to be exact but who's counting? The thought of that goodbye is the only thing that's keeping me going in this place. Don't ask me about it, it's not something you need to know. I am just writing to say that I miss you. And that this battle looks like it's nearly over, so I might be able to get some leave and come back to see you really soon. I hope so.

Your loving Tom.

PS Love to Ivy.
PPS Don't show her this, she'll only laugh.
PPPS Hello Ivy, good luck with your interview.

I hissed between my teeth. "Idiots. Both of you. Irresponsible and as bad as each other."

"You sound just like your mother."

"Oh, perfect. Thanks. You need to tell him about the baby, and then he can tell us what he wants us to do. Or you need to not tell him, and we can decide on our own. Either way, somebody needs to do something."

Charlotte sighed, and rubbed her chilblained fingers. "I know. I just wish all of this would go away."

I reached out, squeezed her hand. "So do I." There didn't seem to be much point shouting my frustration at her after that, so I turned back towards the house. "I have to go and pick up Alfie anyway. I'll see you again on Sunday, alright?"

"Mmm. How was your interview anyway?"

"Irrelevant, compared to this. I'll tell you on Sunday."

I let myself out. Mrs Ransome was singing to herself amidst the swish and bang of the paddle and bucket and she didn't hear me leave. Charlotte was the real reason I'd been wandering around in the dark on my own last night, desperately trying to do some last minute revision, because we'd spent hours yesterday sitting in the park where no one could listen in talking about what to do, and then we'd gone to the library to look up anything at all about pregnancy.

It wasn't a subject ever taught in school, girls were expected to discuss sex and babies with their mothers, but given the circumstances, Charlotte couldn't and I wouldn't. Charlotte and my brother Tom had been sweet on each other for years, and although he never said so, I think it was because of her that he hadn't enlisted with Philip at the beginning of the war. Tom had been conscripted, leaving Charlotte in floods of tears, and then he'd gone to do his basic training in Kent, leaving Charlotte in floods of tears, and then six weeks ago she'd borrowed the train fare from me and gone to Folkestone to see him off, leaving her in floods of tears. There was a pattern there, which told me everything about love that I needed to know, outside a book.

Chapter Four

Alfie had made it a couple of doors down from the bakery, sweeping up all the dirt and debris of London with far more efficiency than required. "Are you finished Alfie? Or do you want to stay here for a bit?" I asked.

Alfie carried on sweeping, and was about to say something pertinent I'm sure, when I spotted Mr Andrews and his repellent son marching in our direction. Mr Andrews could pull off a convincing march even in the middle of a busy street.

"Okay, home time then Alfie, off we go, and it's a race, see. First one home gets a bit of bread."

I grabbed his arm and attempted to run home without actually appearing to run, making it back through the gate and inside the kitchen door, turning the key behind me. I pushed a heel of bread into Alfie's hand and bundled him upstairs as quickly as possible, broom and all.

Luckily, my dad had come off duty and was flat out on his bed, shoes off, snoring loudly. I shook him. "Dad, Dad. I think we're about to get a visit. Dad, Mr Andrews is on his way. Get up."

But it was the banging on the kitchen door that woke him, or it might have been the rattle of the handle or maybe the fact that someone was yelling, "Drummond! Drummond!" at the top of their voice right outside.

"Sir, yes sir." Still drowsy, Dad attempted to snap to attention, and there was a nasty crack as something in his back went "pop" and he sat up, trying to rub back and wrist simultaneously. "That bloody, bloody man. Is Alfie in his room?"

"Yes, Dad. I took him out for breakfast. Sort of."

"Make sure he stays there. I'll go and deal with this."

I sat on the top of the stairs as Dad went down them and I could clearly hear the conversation that followed.

"Drummond. Drummond. Open this door at once. Drummond."

"Ah, Andrews. And David. I was expecting you to call round, and let me start by saying quite how sorry I am about last night."

"You'll be more than sorry, Drummond. That boy of yours is out of control. I've said so before. He needs discipline."

"Yes, it was a dreadful accident, I'm afraid. David got in the way of Alfie's fist. Several times. And poor David was just minding his own business weren't you David? Not doing anything wrong. And Alfie's so big and strong and David's...well. You didn't stand a chance did you David?"

"If you can't handle him you need to find someone who can. You can't let that boy wander round the streets beating up civilians. My lad's been assaulted and I'm not going to let you forget it this time. Something needs to be done and if you aren't up to it, then I am."

"I'm quite sure you are Andrews, but I wonder if you know the full circumstances. I'm not sure David was in a position to hear it all."

"Of course I know. Your son smashed up my lad's face. And your daughter, who I caught out on her own again late at night, then threatened him. Your children, Drummond, are a disgrace."

"No, I thought not. Ivy has unmasked a German spy. Living right here among us. That's why she was out so late last night. She was rushing to tell me, so that I could come and report it to you, and she came across Alfie and David near the school. Ivy said to me – Dad, I've seen a German spy. And I really am sorry, but I think Alfie heard that as "David's a German spy". Which is why Alfie punched him in the face. He's very patriotic."

David said, "That's not what happened."

At the same time his father spluttered, "Preposterous. A German spy. Right here under my nose. Preposterous."

My dad carried on smoothly, "Well, of course, that's what I thought. If there was a spy here you'd know about it already wouldn't you, Andrews? This is your patch after all. And then it occurred to me that of course, you do already know about the spy, but you haven't mentioned it to us civilians for fear of causing panic or mass hysteria. Ivy's story is quite convincing, perhaps I can call her down to tell you in person. Ivy dear, could you pop down and talk to Mr Andrews a second?"

I smoothed my hair, adopted the most demure expression I could fake at short notice and pattered, delicate and ladylike, down the stairs. "Yes, Dad? Can I help you? Oh Mr Andrews, sir, I didn't realise you were here. I'm sorry for what happened last night. I'm afraid Alfie just couldn't help himself."

"Ivy Drummond, what is this ridiculous story your father tells me about a spy?"

"Would you care for some tea Mr Andrews, or perhaps a slice of cake? Or won't you even at least sit down before I start?"

My father promptly pulled out a kitchen chair and then sat in the next one along himself, while I glided politely past David, on my way to putting the kettle on the range, accidentally stamping hard on his foot as I did so. Mr Andrews sat automatically, and I began setting out the best tea things while I explained.

"Last night I was on my way back from the library. I'd like to get more involved with the war effort and I hoped they'd have some suggestions. Well, I happened to be walking past Tanners Steel Works when a man came out of nowhere and told me there was going to be an air raid. And then, there was. He knew when and where it was going to happen, which I thought was a bit suspicious and I knew I had to find Dad right away so he could tell you. Alfie got the wrong end of the stick, didn't he, David? In fact, he didn't get the stick at all. He thought David was the spy and punched him. Poor David."

I walked past David with a kettle of boiling water and accidentally splashed some on his trousers. "Was it not you, Mr Andrews, who warned us about the Germans running all the bread shops in the East End, until the shops were looted and they were driven out? I remember you talking to Dad about the landlord of that new pub who had a funny sounding name, Strachan, wasn't it and then all his windows got smashed. And you were right about Mr Swanscombe who owned that dachshund – he was definitely a German. You've a sense for these things Mr Andrews. Don't you think someone knowing about an air raid in advance is suspicious?"

Mr Andrews liberally added our precious milk and sugar to his tea and stirred it thoughtfully. I didn't offer David one. "What did the man look like, Ivy?"

"Tall, black hair, scar on his face. Creepy blue eyes and wearing a black coat."

"Hmm, a black coat…black coat. That sounds familiar. What did his voice sound like?"

"London accent. Very patronising tone. Quite arrogant actually. Rude as well."

Mr Andrews tapped his spoon against the side of his cup. "Hmmmm. D'you know I think I've heard something like this before."

My dad leaned forward, stopped blowing on his tea. "Have you? You mean other people apart from Ivy have seen this man?"

"I didn't make him up Dad, unfortunately. He's alive and well and still busy being rude to people." It was as if I hadn't spoken.

"Yes Jack, I think they have. There have been stories, well rumours, idle gossip mostly, for the last six months or so, about a man in a black coat who's been going around watching air raids. Every time the zeppelins appear this same man is somewhere nearby watching what happens. I thought nothing of it, but all the stories say the same thing. This man is there before the raids. Sometimes days before even, lurking around the streets that end up being bombed."

Dad swigged the rest of his tea and tapped his chin. "Why would this man hang around before a raid?"

"Maybe he's picking the targets, letting the Hun know where to attack."

Dad turned to me, "What do you think Ivy? Does this man in the black coat sound like the man you met?"

"Sounds like the same man to me. I think someone should go and ask him what he's up to. Why don't you pop up the road now and find out? I'm sure that would be the highlight of his day."

"Ivy." My dad was frowning at me, but I couldn't read the message he was trying to telegraph with his eyebrows. "Do you know who this man is?"

I paused, just long enough to remember the tiny chair and the disparaging glances. "He's the headmaster of South Street Elementary."

"What?" barked Mr Andrews.

My dad was more confused than canine. "You didn't know who he was last night."

"I know. But then I had a job interview this morning and I recognised him right away. It's the same man, although he didn't have his coat on."

Mr Andrews came as close to a smile as I think he could manage. "And what is his name, Ivy?" he purred.

"I've no idea. I said he was rude. He didn't bother to introduce himself on either occasion."

Mr Andrews rose from his seat and I stepped backwards hastily, accidentally landing an elbow in David's stomach. "Well, thank you,

Ivy." He raised his hat. "You've been very vigilant. And a great help to the war effort. I think I will go and have a word with this teacher of yours. Out David, out, out. Hurry up boy."

As soon as the latch of the gate clicked behind them I murmured, "Nicely deflected, Dad. One of your best I thought."

"Nonsense Ivy, that was all yours. Are you going to tell me how the interview went?"

"Dreadful, actually, I didn't get the job but if this man gets arrested for spying I can always apply again in a couple of weeks" time when his replacement arrives."

"And did that in any way affect your decision to denounce this chap as a spy?"

"Of course not. But it did make it easier to smile at Mr Andrews."

Later that evening I attempted to cook lamb hot pot, which consisted of vegetables that a sheep might once have walked past in a field served in a very warm dish.

My mother turned up at around eight o'clock, fresh from the afternoon shift at the GPO sorting office at Regent's Park. The post office was delivering something like twelve million letters a year, thanks to the war, and as a result it had built a giant shed five miles across to sort out all the extra post. My mother breezed in through the door with blisters on her feet and gossip on her mind, expansive with new found self-importance. My whole life she'd been telling me that 'a woman's place is in the home' or 'a woman's place is by her man' or 'a woman's place is 'insert something mundane and boring here'. Anything to put me in my place, I suspected. But now she had a new job she was utterly transformed, and I don't mean that she'd become a nicer person overnight. It was more like the wicked queen had learnt to smile like a fairy godmother, but underneath she was still the same old witch.

The four of us sat around the kitchen table, behind the four plates I'd put out, the four glasses, four sets of cutlery and all the while those two empty chairs stared at me silently. Dad said, "Any letters from Tom this morning, Ivy?"

"No, I'm not expecting anything until tomorrow." Tom wrote once a week.

"Anything from Philip, Mother?" Philip didn't write at all. We hadn't heard from him in over sixteen months.

"You'd know, Ivy. You've been in the house all day."

"Actually, she hasn't, Hilda. Ivy's had a busy day. Why don't you tell your mother all about it?"

Dad helped himself to dinner, Alfie had already finished his first bowl and was smearing up the juices with another slice of bread.

"There's not much to tell, Mother. I had a job interview this morning but nothing came of it. I called on Mrs Norton this afternoon."

My mother nodded sagely, but that might have been the stew talking. "She lost her husband. The letters have been piling up in the sorting office for weeks. I'm glad they finally got around to telling her."

The postal service made sure that any letters returned from the front line marked 'killed in action' weren't delivered until the formal letter or telegram was sent out by the War Office. That way you might have to wait a few months but you got to see your notification of death typed out neatly rather than scrawled over the front of the envelope.

"Did you take her anything?"

"Loaf of bread. I thought she might not want to go out of the house for a while."

"Very generous, Ivy. You can pop round the rest of this dinner in a bit, I'm sure I won't eat it."

"Ivy unmasked a German spy, Hilda. Andrews has been round."

"About Alfie? Is Mr Andrews going to do anything?"

"No. Like I said, Ivy's spy rather put him off."

"Who's your spy then, Ivy? Anyone we know or did you pick on a stranger?"

"I didn't pick on anyone, Mother. I just told Mr Andrews about the man I met last night who warned me about the air raid. He's the head teacher up at South Street Elementary."

"Not Mrs Rawling's son? The one with the scar all down his face? He's no more a spy than I am, silly girl."

"Come off it Mother, you don't know any teachers."

"Of course I do. Mrs Rawlings owned the big white house on the corner of Clock Barn Lane, about two miles in that direction." My mother waved vaguely in the direction of the door. "I've known that house since I first moved to London. Mrs Rawlings has been dead for, must be two or three years now. But her son came back from the war not six months ago. He's got some kind of medal for gallantry but he was badly injured getting it and they invalided him out with an honourable discharge. Is that the same man you told Mr Andrews was a spy? I hope not, for your sake. War heroes don't generally like being accused of being on the other side."

"I thought you said you knew the spy, Ivy? You didn't say he was a war hero."

"I do know him, Dad. It was the same man. Maybe Mother's got it wrong."

"Nonsense. I overheard Miss Bird and Mr Murphy the grocer talking about him for at least twenty minutes a couple of weeks ago, and very interesting it was too."

After that conversation I went to sleep with a sense of unease, which made for an uncomfortable bedfellow. The next morning brought two letters for me, and I opened Tom's first. It took only a few days for post to arrive from France and I could get messages from my brother quite quickly.

Dear Ivy,

Thank you for your letter, and for the shoes and for the chocolate. I would like one of those waterproof coats in the advert you sent, but there's no point wasting two months" pay on one. Besides, I might get mistaken for an officer and picked off by our friends over the wire. That happened to a chap here yesterday. I think we'd all got a bit careless, what with the battle finishing and everyone getting ready to ship out. I did well arriving when I did – all that's left to do is the clearing up. I survived the Somme. I might get that tattooed on my arm, what do you think Mum would say?

Don't read her the next bit. It will upset her.

The hunt for Philip Drummond continues. The Rifles fought in the battle of Loos. It was a success, in the way that all battles here are a success. We walked right into the German guns over open fields but we captured the town, achieved our objective, and then ran out of re-enforcements and weaponry, so we fell back. So we won, but we lost again. There's a lot of it around.

Phil isn't listed among the dead, or the missing from that battle, because the War Office would've told us already, it's been about a year, but I thought, what if Phil were injured there, what if he couldn't write because something happened to him? The man I met told me a strange story. Loos was the first time we decided to use chlorine gas – Red Star – against the Germans, but it didn't go according to plan. There's a lot of that around as well. All these cylinders of Red Star were sent up to the front line and set up ready to let off at the Germans. But someone had sent the wrong keys with the cylinders and a lot of them couldn't be opened. They just sat there in no man's land until the

Germans exploded them and the gas blew backwards into our own lines.

We gassed our own men. And I thought - what if one of them was Phil – maybe he was injured and he's stuck in a field hospital somewhere, unable to see, to hold a pen, or remember his own name. I'm going to try to check the hospital records to see if I can find out.

Let me know how your interview goes. I reckon you'll make a terrible teacher. You'll just sit there telling children stories stolen from all the books you've ever read with that dreamy look in your eyes like you used to do with Alfie. There won't be any writing lines or hitting people with a stick or making them stand in the corner when they get a question wrong.

Thinking of you and Charlotte.

Love Tom.

The other letter was written in an unfamiliar hand and dated yesterday. The paper was thick, the handwriting accomplished and the message entirely unexpected.

Dear Miss Drummond,

I am writing in relation to the appointment at South Street Elementary School you kindly attended some short while ago. While I was not able to offer you a teaching position, I am pleased to say that a vacancy has become available as an assistant to our first year teacher, Miss Redpath.

Your duties will be to assist our youngest pupils in mastering the basics of reading, primarily through example. I believe that your skills and experience are suited to this task, which will also expose you to the basic tenets of pedagogy, should you one day decide to pursue formal training.

You will understand that the remuneration for this post will be nominal, given your qualifications. If you decide to accept this offer, kindly confirm in writing, and I will expect to see you on Monday next.

Yours sincerely,

W. Rawlings. Headmaster

The subtext of that was, come and read to the children because you aren't fit to do anything else and, by the way, I'm not paying you. And also, I know a lot of long words.

I'd have been annoyed if I wasn't so unreasonably excited. I'd just got my first proper job. Well, my first job. Well, my first excuse to get out of the house on my own on a regular basis without having to look after Alfie, go shopping, run errands or be nice to my mother's friends. And I was going to be earning my own money to spend on whatever I wanted, because even a nominal sum earned yourself feels better than whatever your dad chooses to give you on the odd occasion he remembers.

It was perfect. Nothing could go wrong. Except of course, I remembered, crumpling the letter in my hand and flopping down onto the parlour chair, that I'd just had my new employer arrested as a German spy. Not the most promising course of action on your first day. Never having been employed as anything other than 'skivvy' before I tried to imagine what a patriotic, yet loyal employee would do and that's how I came to be dressed in my Sunday best on a Saturday, clutching an acceptance letter written on my mother's best paper, halfway to the big white house on the corner of Clock Barn Lane. I could at least give him the chance to explain himself, then warn him about Mr Andrews, or not, depending on the explanation.

Chapter Five

The house was large, but tall, in the annoying way of buildings in London where there wasn't quite enough land to make up a proper house and most of the internal space consisted of stairs. There were four storeys and a basement, but the house was grey rather than white, coal fires having put paid to the impractical colour of the render some time ago. Nubs of iron like baby teeth left in the mouth too long poked out of the wall in front, from where the railings had been removed and melted down into guns.

I raised the knocker on the faded black door, some mythical beast worn into smooth tameness by the touch of too many hands. The sound echoed loudly though hidden spaces but nobody came, so I cracked it again. At length there was a shuffling and the door opened to its tall, spare owner, dressed in dark trousers, a shirt that was none too well pressed and a dark waistcoat, half unbuttoned.

He looked haggard, with black smears under his eyes and enough stubble on his cheeks to make me think he hadn't shaved. Seeing me, he rubbed his face roughly, folded his arms, propped himself against the door frame, and said, "Miss Drummond. I don't recall giving you my home address."

I was conscious of a fluttering in my stomach at the thought of swallowing another dose of humiliation, but I was determined to find out what was going on. I tapped the letter I was holding against my other palm. "No need. My mother knows everything, and besides, you said to write."

"Indeed, but we have a system in England where you pay a penny, you get a little piece of paper to stick to your envelope and you put it in a metal box and someone brings it straight to my door. Ask your father, he'll know." He held out his hand for the letter.

I said, "That's not why I came."

His hand dropped away. "No, I thought not."

"Do you want to talk about it right here in the street?"

"I don't want to talk about it at all."

"I do. You'd better invite me in."

He swung the door wide with a sigh and stepped back to let me pass. "The word "invite" rather suggests I have a choice doesn't it?"

Inside, the house was cool, dark and smelling faintly of old lavender. My heels clicked loudly across the tiled floor. Mr Rawlings gestured me into the first room on the right while he retreated towards the back of the house. "You'll want some kind of refreshment. I assume we are observing the social niceties?"

"Yes, please. Tea, please," I called after his back and stepped into the parlour.

The furniture was stately, but threadbare, all curlicued and swagged in a grey and mauve palette that was fashionable fifty years ago. There was a large mirror over the mantelpiece entirely covered with black cloth, and all the photographs standing on the piano had been turned face down. There were no pictures on the wall, and no ornamentation of any kind, even the glass shades that should have covered the gas lamps on the wall were missing.

I'm not a fanciful person, but I had the distinct impression that no one living had walked these carpets for a very long time. Shivering slightly, I turned on my heel and followed the scream of the kettle into the kitchen, passing several closed doors on the way. The kitchen housed an enormous black range pumping out heat like there was no limit on coal, a dresser stacked full of crockery, a spotless white sink, several cupboards and a pine table twice the size of ours. The table was piled high with books and pieces of paper covered with more of that cursive script, but there was a pair of discarded shoes under the nearest seat, and the writing nearby was smudged with what looked remarkably like dribble.

I placed my letter on top and arranged myself carefully on the next chair while he clattered around the kitchen, muttering and making a very poor job of the tea. The leaves and the water were dumped into the pot without even warming it, two cups had a cursory wipe and he carried the whole lot, chinking, to the table.

"I hope you don't want sugar." He dumped a cup in front of me and sniffed the jug he was about to place next to it. "Or milk either."

"I'm sorry for your loss," I inclined my head carefully in the direction of the parlour.

"I'm not that worried about the sugar." He shrugged, and blew on his tea.

"No, I mean your mother."

"Oh. Thank you. She's been dead three years though; you're quite tardy with your condolences. Did you know her?"

"No, but you're still in mourning. The mirror is covered and you're wearing black." I remembered when my Nanna Kate died my mother had gone through a similar period of last century grief, when she'd kitted out the whole house in black and stopped the clocks from chiming until Dad was late for work one day and insisted that enough was enough.

He flicked his eyes over me once. "That's not why the mirror is covered. So what can I do for you, Miss Drummond?"

"And you are?" I wasn't meeting him for a third time without a formal introduction.

He sat back and poked my letter with a finger, regarding me coolly. "Does this say yes?"

"Yes. Probably."

"Then you can call me sir."

"I'm not calling you sir."

"Headmaster?"

"Not when we're in your kitchen."

"Mr Rawlings?"

"The first time we met you pulled me under a bridge in the dark and held my hand, and we're not even courting. The least you can do is tell me your first name." For the first time since I'd known him he wasn't quite able to meet my gaze and I actually grinned.

"Will."

I held out my hand for him to shake, which he did, reluctantly. "Pleased to meet you, Mr Rawlings."

He pushed his chair further back and rested his elbows on his knees. He was one of those people who just couldn't keep still, constantly fiddling with something or changing position. The only thing about him that seemed steady was his eyes, and when he fixed me with his pale glare I felt like the chloroform and the pin weren't too far behind.

He said, "And the purpose of your visit here today is?"

"Two days ago, on the night of the - "I was about to say "air raid" but switched it to "hand-holding" and watched his eyes wince away from me again. "Two days ago I found you standing outside Tanners Steel Works, so convinced it was going to be bombed that you'd broken into the building to check there was no one left inside. I will repeat the question I asked you then. How did you know there was going to be an air raid?"

"I guessed."

"No. Not the exact time and place."

"I overheard a man in a pub."

"No. Imaginary man. Imaginary pub. I bet you've never been inside a pub in your life."

"I," he said, "I." He looked at his socks, pursed his lips a few times, screwed up his chin, shook his head and finally made a decision. "No. Now it comes to it, I'm not going to tell you."

"Fine. I told Mr Andrews you're a German spy."

He hauled himself upright again. "That seems a bit drastic don't you think? Who's this "Mr Andrews"?"

"He's in charge of civil defence in our area, or he thinks he is."

"A little man with a big moustache? He came to school. Marched right into my office and demanded to see me."

"What did you do?"

"Threw him out. Told him to make an appointment and come back on Monday."

"Did you shout at him?"

"I may have been a little…authoritative."

"Were you rude?"

"I'm never rude."

I nearly reached out to pat his knee, then thought better of it and just said, "You're a lovely, shouty, rude German spy."

"I'm not a German spy."

"You are. So I'm not coming to work for you."

"I can live with that."

"Instead, my big brother Alfie and I, since neither of us will have anything better to do, will stand outside your house all day and every night."

"I can live with that too, as long as you don't stand where I can see you. Why is Alfie still at home, Ivy? What's wrong with him?"

I was surprised as much by his change of subject as by his sudden use of my first name. "He was just born different. I don't think anybody knows why, although my mother strongly believes God gave him to us for a reason. He's too...literal. He understands the world through objects like - that tree relates to that stick or that lunch relates to my stomach. But he doesn't understand people at all, like you can say one thing and mean something else, or what to do if someone's crying, or anything about how relationships work. It makes life very hard for him."

"And you have to look after him?"

"I don't have to. I choose to. I keep him out of trouble."

"That must be very restrictive for a girl like you."

"You mean the sort of girl who's always out gallivanting and talking to boys? I'm not like that."

"Then what were you doing out on your own at night? But I interrupted you mid-threat. You were busy standing outside my house. Do carry on."

"Yes. Alfie and I will be waiting outside your house and when you go out we'll follow you, because I'm going to bet that's what you do. You put on one of those black coats you've got hanging in the hall and you go out at night and lurk around in the dark waiting for an air raid. And then, when you come back, you're so tired you fall asleep at this table. That probably explains why you're in such a foul temper all the time."

"What good would following me around do? Apart from making you ridiculous and me irritated?"

"That all depends on what I really came here to ask."

"Oh, there's a reason you're here? I thought it was just for casual accusations and random insults."

"Do you help?" He seemed to fall in on himself, arms and legs crossing, chin tucking in, shoulders hunching against an attack I wasn't aware I was about to deliver. "Leaving aside the issue of how you know in advance about air raids, which you've basically admitted but won't tell me. Leaving that aside, because I expect Mr Andrews will drag it out of you on Monday however much you shout. Leaving that aside and, just so you know, I'm not going to, not long term – do you help? If you know a house is going to be bombed do you warn the people who live there? Do you go in before it happens and get them out or do you just stand around and watch them die?"

He looked up at me the long way round, his gaze travelling slowly over the floor, up over my shoes, my long black skirt, my starched blouse with the flowers on and up to my face, like he was having to force it inch by painful inch. "I can't help anyone," he murmured.

"I'd worked that out for myself, thanks. You see I've heard lots and lots of stories about people being killed in air raids, but almost none where they get miraculously saved. You say you're not a spy, but I don't think you're on our side either. That's where Alfie comes in. He's six foot four, built like a boxer and he carries his own broom. He doesn't do inconspicuous. If people start seeing Alfie and shortly afterwards there's a big boom, they're going to put the two together like Mrs Carmichael does already. Alfie and I are going to follow you around like your own personal warning system and we're going to tell everyone we meet about the strange, scary man who can predict air raids. From now on, Mr Rawlings, headmaster, sir, or whoever the hell you are, you won't be alone." I threw myself back into my chair, unsure when I'd stood up, or for quite how long I'd been shouting.

His gaze hardened, tempered and reforged itself into steel, a muscle in his cheek flexed, flexed and flexed again but his words were clipped and measured. "What a shame. I was quite enjoying having you here. It was entertaining in an annoying sort of a way. But I will not be harangued by an ignorant child who has no idea what she's talking about. Miss Drummond, would you kindly just get out."

There was so much anger in the last two words they felt like a slap in the face, and possibly a push downstairs and a good kicking at the end. There was no point in saying anything further. I stood to leave and he didn't bother to show me to the door, but as I walked down the hall, I heard him say softly, "I'm always alone."

It took until I was sitting at home in the kitchen on my second cup of tea for my legs to stop shaking. I had no intention of pursuing the matter any further; Mr Andrews could deal with it. Mr Rawlings was right, threatening anyone with Alfie was simply childish and in actual fact, I did have far better things to do than chase him around the streets of London. I threw the letter from the school into the fire and gave up on education as a career.

Then I spent two hours helping Alfie read a page of the newspaper and we went out for a long walk, meeting my mother on the way home so we could carry her shopping. I cleaned out all the fireplaces, beat the rugs, swept the floors, blacked the range, stripped and made the beds in preparation for taking the sheets to Charlotte in the morning and made a meat pie for dinner (heavy on the pie, light on the meat). I set the table, served the food, cleared the table, darned four pairs of socks, started knitting a new shawl and fell into bed without having let a meaningful thought cross my brain since being thrown out of the white house. I had horrible, horrible dreams and woke up crying for Tom.

Sunday was a day of rest, because my mother went to church and I could lie in as long as I wanted. I hauled all our dirty sheets round to Charlotte's house to be washed at about midday. It was a strange arrangement, my mother paid for the washing to be done so she could feel like she was doing Charlotte's mother a favour, and Charlotte's mother took in our washing at a special rate for exactly the same reason. It meant that we slept in not entirely clean sheets, but with a feeling of self-righteousness.

"Hey Ivy," said Charlotte, opening the door with a grin. "I've got an apple and I'm not afraid to use it."

I returned the smile and the slightly wizened fruit she handed me. "Courtesy of Mr Murphy, I assume. Did you flash him your shoulder again?"

"For shame, Ivy Drummond. It was only my ankle."

"I'll be reporting you to my brother, you shameless hussy."

She threw the sheets into the house and closed the door behind her. "It's your brother's fault that I am a shameless hussy. Churchyard or park?" she asked.

"Churchyard. You're unusually happy this morning. Has something happened that I should know about?"

We walked away from the house, Charlotte carrying the oilcloth and me with my picnic basket, going out for lunch as we did every Sunday. "Nearly, I was in a terrible mood yesterday and today my stomach is enormous, my bosom is practically bursting out of this dress and I'm sure I'll be bleeding by nightfall. I feel great. You know, rubbish, but great."

"Oh, thank heavens for that. Not that I don't want a niece or nephew eventually, but I'm too young for wrinkles. No one will marry me if I have wrinkles."

"No one will marry you anyway, wrinkles or not."

There was a spot in the graveyard where you could watch the worshippers come out of church without being seen, so we set up the oilcloth there and sat down to swap a week's worth of gossip, and almost the same amount of leftovers.

"I'm not sure I like this vegetable pie, Ivy. Look, there's David Andrews. Did you hear he got beaten up by a Hun? Quite nasty, his father said. It might scar, that'd be a shame wouldn't it?"

"It's a meat pie. Although the butcher wasn't specific about the type of meat. He's got those really pointy teeth and every time he smiles at me I forget what I'm saying. It was Alfie that hit David. The Hun was someone else entirely." I gave her a potted history of my dealings with Mr Rawlings.

"I don't understand why you'd go round to his house in the first place, Ivy. What did you think he'd do – say yes, you caught me, I'll come quietly. You're lucky he only threw you out."

"I really want a job, Lottie, I'm so bored with my life. I feel like I'm standing on the side of the road and watching all the traffic go by, when what I really want to do is jump on a bus and go with it."

"There's plenty of jobs. I'm going up to the munitions factory in Bow next week, they're looking. And I heard about a new shirt factory that needs girls. Don't tell Mum though."

"Are you going to tell Tom?"

"About the job?"

"About the baby. Or lack thereof."

"Of course. When I'm about forty and we've got four children already. That'd be a good time to mention it. I can see Mrs Norton. Did you hear she lost her husband?"

"I can hear her crying through the walls."

"What would you do if your husband died?" she asked.

"The one I won't ever get because of the wrinkles? Survive, I guess. Carry on. What would you do?"

"Exactly what Mrs Norton's doing I expect. Break my heart."

On Monday there were no letters to be read, no gossip to be shared, no news to be pored over. Life carried on in that irritating way it has when you're waiting, when the hours seem to lengthen and the space between one tick of the clock and the next can be forever. I had nothing to do but wait – for Tom and Philip to come home, for the end of the war, for my life to start. And then just before eleven the front door knocker sounded and the contents of my stomach made a desperate break for freedom through my mouth. The only people who ever came through our actual front foot were either religious or dead, and neither was welcome. A front door knock at this time of day could only mean a letter from the War Office.

I ran to open it nevertheless, hoping to be wrong, and this time, there was no dour faced postman but a small boy holding out a single sheet of paper. He was no more than ten, kitted out in trousers an inch too short and a home-made jumper he'd probably never be big enough to fill.

He said, "Are you Miss Ivy?"

"I am, I think. Who are you?"

"Billy, Miss." His sparkling black eyes darted here, there and everywhere as he bobbed and shifted on my front step, like a robin in boy form. "I'm to give you this."

I accepted the letter and found a few pennies in the pocket of my apron to put in his hand in exchange. "Are you from the school, Billy?"

"Yes Miss. You're pretty Miss." He bolted back up the road, his boots too big, one lace trailing, coins securely held in one fist.

I opened the paper, which contained only two words in swirling calligraphy.

You're late.

I wasn't sure quite what to make of that. I turned the paper over a few times hoping for something more but finding no inspiration. Clearly my presence was still expected at the job I'd accepted and then turned down and the man who had thrown me out of his house still wanted me in his school. Alfie was out sweeping, we'd finished reading for the day; both my parents had already left for work and I only had a day of chores to look forward to. I swept my hair up into a fairly tidy bun, folded my apron, put on my coat and closed the door on a cold and silent house.

Chapter Six

South Street School had so many pupils it had been built with three entrances, one for boys, one for girls and one for everyone else. Up the steps from the front door was a long echoing corridor, with a waxed parquet floor and children's artwork plastered all over the walls. This floor housed the youngest children, the assembly hall and the administrative offices, as well as the girls" toilets, which were permanently occupied, and the boys" toilets, which permanently stank of urine. Up a flight of stairs was the second floor where all the older girls were taught, and where the staffroom, storerooms and head teacher's office could be found. The top floor contained the older boys' classroom, mostly to keep the noise from distracting everyone else, as well as the specialist teaching areas - needlework, sewing and cooking for the girls, woodwork, metalwork and anything else that might possibly explode or cause an injury for the boys. Lessons were underway and the halls reflected back the sound of chanted times tables, the halting stop-start of a struggling reader and from the top floor, a dull roar.

I paused outside the headmaster's office, watching a dark shadow pacing behind the glass. Miss Bird found me before I could muster enough courage to knock. "Ivy, love, first day is it? I'm so pleased you've come to join us, we really need the help. You know your way around already of course, so let's introduce you to Joyce and we'll get you started straight away."

She bundled me back down the stairs and rapped on the door of the reception classroom. More than fifty small faces turned my way - boys and girls, all under six, sitting on long benches behind equally long wooden desks facing the blackboard. Miss Redpath strode smartly across the floor to shake my hand. She was ten or so years older than me, all shiny boots, swishing skirts and big blue eyes, full of laughter.

"God, am I glad to see you," she whispered. "Watch out for Danny at the back with the blonde hair, he's a menace." Then she turned to the children. "Class. This is Miss Ivy. What do you say?"

"Good morning Miss Ivy," they chorused.

"Miss Ivy is your new reading teacher. Miss Ivy?"

I had no idea what I was doing, no experience of teaching and I'd never been on the wrong end of a classroom in my life. However, I knew enough about children not to show it. "Good morning class. I'd like the back row to come over with me in this corner and sit down. Nice and quietly please, and don't bring anything."

I walked confidently to the back of the room where I'd spied a new looking stack of Ladybird books and selected one at random. Then, I voluntarily chose one of those awful tiny chairs to sit on and fixed my new students with an authoritative eye. I tried to anyway; possibly it came over as myopic. I opened the book and said, "I'd like each of you to read a sentence so I can find out what level you're at. If you don't know a word, try to spell it out. We'll start with you – what's your name?" And I was off on a desperate race to memorise fifty children's names, faces and abilities faster than they could come up with a plan to confuse me.

I didn't notice the time pass until halfway through lunch when I was in the classroom with the children I'd kept behind, Danny – less of a menace when he wasn't showing off to his friends, Marigold – who could read anything I put in front of her and might be a child prodigy and Eric – who I suspected of a hearing problem because nobody could wilfully ignore that much shouting. The classroom door opened behind me but nobody came in and then, just as quietly, it closed again. I was reading with the front row by a quarter to three when there was a loud tap on the door and a policeman entered. There was a collective intake of breath and some admiring sighs from the boys.

"Miss Drummond is wanted in the office ma'am," he said, tapped his heels together and saluted entirely unnecessarily, to some scattered applause.

"Settle down children," Miss Redpath called.

I gave her a shrug. "Go and sit back in your places children." I sent my charges to their desks and then followed the officer from the room. "Can I ask what this is about?" I trailed him slowly up the stairs, convinced I already knew.

"I'm taking the headmaster into custody. Defence of the Realm

Act offences, you don't need to know the details. Andrews says you can identify the chap. Here we are."

He preceded me into the same wood panelled office I'd visited before which, with the presence of four people and a desk, was now standing room only. I said "Sir," to the room at large, because that was probably how I was supposed to address all of them, and caught the arch of an eyebrow from the owner of the office as I dropped my gaze to the floor and clasped my hands behind my back.

Mr Andrews started, "Ivy Drummond, can you identify this man as the individual you encountered on the night of November 28th 1916 outside Tanner's Steel Factory?"

"Works. Tanners Steel Works. Or so I am reliably informed."

"Was this the man Ivy?"

"Sir."

"You'd better look at him to make sure."

So I did. Despite the enclosed space Mr Rawlings was positively lounging behind his desk, a complete contrast with the policeman standing to attention behind him and Mr Andrews ramrod straight, front and centre. He looked better, less tired, more ironed and his sharp blue stare seemed to thaw slightly as I caught his eye. He gave me an almost imperceptible nod, like he was giving permission, although I wasn't waiting for it. I was acutely aware I was about to send him to prison, or worse, given that Mr Andrews would probably spend several hours interrogating him first.

But I didn't know him, I didn't trust him and I didn't have any choice so I said, "Yes, Mr Andrews. That's the man I met."

I stepped out of the office but I only went next door to Miss Bird while they took him away. She kept saying "Oh my goodness, oh my goodness," and wringing her hands on her apron, skirt and anything else within wringing distance.

"Do you think he's coming back, Miss Bird?"

"Of course he's coming back, there's been a mistake. The headmaster's a war hero, he's been injured, he's not on their side. How am I going to manage without him?"

"I'll help you."

It was a foolish offer. I was no teacher and the most I knew about the inner workings of a school was where to buy more chalk, but that was how I came to spend the rest of the week reading with the younger children in the mornings, and the afternoons sitting behind the headmaster's desk, sorting out the paperwork. I didn't have to sit at the desk of course, I could have moved everything into Miss Bird's office while she was off teaching thrift, cookery and sewing, but I found the smell of old lavender and soap that persisted around his chair quite comforting, and also, let's face it, I really enjoyed the feeling of power.

He made notes about everything, and had a wide ranging and varied correspondence, which I tried to deal with, as best I could. He'd written a long and detailed treatise about school dinners, so I wrote to Mr Murphy to order some vegetables to go with all the dripping and suet, and adjusted the menus for next week with instructions to the kitchens. He'd written to several local employers – including Mr Tanner interestingly – trying to find work for some of the twelve-year-old boys due to leave school in the summer. I followed up the responses, and wrote to the munitions factory, the shirt factory, the post office and a couple of other places I could think of along the same lines asking them to consider some of our girls. There were some letters from local neighbours complaining about stones through their windows and kicking of balls against their front doors after school, and for them, I asked the kitchen to make a few cakes and sent Billy round with a note of apology.

By Wednesday, I'd drafted in Alfie as a cleaner come crane. The classrooms and the playground were soon swept clean and after sharing a lesson with Miss Grafton, who also taught woodwork, Alfie spent several happy afternoons with the older boys lifting benches for the children to fix, mending broken desks, putting up shelves and generally messing around with wood. On Friday I started organising the school nativity play because it was early December after all and nothing should be allowed to come between children and Christmas, not even war. I kept copies of all the letters I sent and noted down every action I took and I made plans to have a look at the school's finances to see if we couldn't afford some new library books. I had a new key cut for the headmaster's office.

Tom's letter surprised me when it came, because the hardest, busiest and most exciting week of my life had rushed past me at a brisk jog, and I hadn't even noticed it go.

Tom had written,

Dear Ivy,

Do you remember that time we went to Nanna Kate's in Kent, and Alfie got lost in that wood? Me, you and Philip were looking for him for hours and Phil was shouting and losing his temper, and then Alfie just looked down from that tree he'd climbed and jumped straight onto Phil's head. You laughed so hard you wet yourself. Anyway, I was thinking about that the other day because I went back down the lines carrying a message. There's a lot of messages going back and forward now that the fighting's stopped and I volunteered to take one back to Captain Someone or other and I got a bit lost in a forest along the way. It was just a hill really, with a couple of trees and pine needles on the ground to cover the mud, but it was so quiet, no guns or shouting or anything and when I looked up between the trees the sky was still blue. It reminded me of that time in the woods when we were children, that's all.

Reassure Mum that I'm fine, and that I'm thinking of everyone back home.

I'm thinking more about the people here, to be honest. I'm getting closer to finding our darling brother - I think Philip might have been injured at Loos. That chaplain I mentioned has been really helpful. There's a doctor in one of the hospitals behind the lines I need to speak to, he treated gas casualties last year. There were a few from the Rifles who weren't too badly off, and were sent away to convalesce. Phil might be in England right now, sitting in a cosy ward somewhere in the country, maybe with damage to his chest or lungs that means he can't speak. I'll ask this doctor when I find him.

I'm clutching at straws here, I know, but I don't want to believe he wouldn't write to us if he could. I don't want to think he'd let Mum worry all this time. She always loved him best of all and he certainly wasn't bothered about the rest of us. What could possibly have happened to him that was so bad he wouldn't write?

I'm sorry you didn't get the job, the man sounds like a complete idiot.

Love to Charlotte when you see her.

Tom.

I made fish sausages for dinner (sausage in shape only, there was zero percent pork content but probably fifty percent mouldy old loaf) and the four of us were attempting to eat them when the gate banged open and there was a knock on the kitchen door.

Dad opened it saying, "Ah, Andrews, do come in, would you care for a fish sausage?"

Mr Andrews sat in Philip's chair and consequently the table was the subject of one of Alfie's hardest stares for the next twenty minutes. "Fish? No, thank you. I don't think so. I come with news of your spy."

"Well," my dad leaned forward. "Is he in prison?"

"No. He isn't a spy. He's something much worse than that."

"Like?" I leaned forward too.

"Well. It's the strangest thing. Young Davies arrested him. Good chap, Davies, his father was in my regiment in 99, Davies took him down to the station and put him in the cells, but the man wouldn't say anything. Just sat there and stared at me. It quite put the wind up young Davies, I tell you. So I thought, we'll leave him there, soften him up a bit. And Tuesday comes and he's still sitting there in the cell against the wall, hasn't slept, hasn't moved, just sits and stares. All day Tuesday he won't speak, and by Wednesday morning, well, Davies is convinced there's something wrong with him because he's still not slept. So I start asking around. I know his name and that wound on his face says he's been injured, so I talk to a few people and they talk to a few people and I manage to find, not his commanding officer, because he's dead, but a chap who served with him in Mons in 1914, first battle of the war. Turns out Mr Rawlings – age thirty-one, married, of The Grange, Amesbury Road, Hertfordshire – goes over to Belgium with the British Expeditionary Force, distinguishes himself in battle, gets injured and then…....."

"Then?" Dad and I spoke at the same time.

"He's captured by the Germans," wondered my dad.

"He becomes a spy and turns up later in London," I continued.

"No," said Mr Andrews. "He goes mad."

"What? He doesn't seem very mad to me," I protested.

"He gets taken to a field hospital where they patch up his head. He's been hit by some kind of heavy artillery, and when he wakes up he starts shouting the place down. I spoke to one of the doctors there, a good man, works on the Military Medical Board now, expert in mental cases and he remembers William Rawlings quite well. Can't stand to look in a mirror, can't sleep or screams and cries his way through the night, hallucinates during the day – when he's on the ward every time another solider comes in your chap will start yelling his head off in the corner. They had to sedate him and keep him in solitary confinement in the end, and he got shipped off back home as fast as possible."

"What's the matter with him then?" I asked.

"Shellshock."

"I didn't think anyone talked about shellshock anymore. Aren't there two kinds now, Andrews?" asked my dad.

"Oh yes – made up and even more made up. There's shellshock where you get wounded, and you can get honourably discharged for that, and then there's shellshock when you haven't been wounded, when you get a weekend off, told to pull yourself together, and sent back to fight. It's just a coward's way out if you ask me. Shellshock doesn't really exist."

"I don't understand. Is he ill or not? How does he know about the air raids?" I was finding it hard to equate sarcastic, scary Mr Rawlings with screaming-in-the-corner Mr Rawlings.

"He doesn't know about the air raids Ivy, he's hallucinating, like as not. He's been shot in the head, he probably sees ghosts."

"Or flying monkeys." I was remembering what I'd thought the first time I met him.

"Or angels," chipped in my mother. "It wouldn't be the first time men in that battle have seen things." She was handing round the fish sausages.

My dad said, "That was just a story Hilda, the angel of Mons. It was made up. It was in the papers last year."

"That doesn't mean it was made up."

"Don't you remember back in the summer all the papers were saying that the war in France was going well, and we had thousands and thousands of letters coming back 'killed in action'. The papers weren't right then, were they?"

I butted in, "Anyway – so he's not a spy, and he can't predict air raids?"

Mr Andrews said, "It's co-incidence Ivy. He was on the wrong street at the wrong time and you put two and two together and came up with fourteen. Rawlings might be completely insane but I'll say this for him – he knows how to keep his mouth shut. Not a word out of him in five days and he hasn't slept because Davies has been checking on him every ten minutes to make sure. We let him out about an hour ago. There's nothing to charge him with, unfortunately."

I sat back, considering. "So if he hasn't said anything and you've found all this out by asking around, couldn't you have done that before you sent him to prison? What did you have to arrest him for?"

"Discipline, Miss Drummond." Mr Andrews stood up to leave. "I know you don't see much of it round here, but there must be respect for the natural order of things. Your Mr Rawlings was bloody rude."

I opened the kitchen door to show him out. "I did warn you, Mr Andrews. Good night."

I swung the gate to let him out, with every intention of bolting it behind him, but there was a sort of rustling noise, and as Mr Andrews cleared the alley and turned in the direction of the White Star I stepped out into the darkness and peered around the door. There was definitely something there; the hairs on the back of my neck rose and I fumbled for the lock.

Then a hand shot out of the darkness and latched onto my upper arm. I was yanked forwards, colliding with a hard chest, a man's body. His other arm came round my waist, his face pressed into my hair and his lips breathed, "Ivy."

I stood rigid in his embrace. "Mr Rawlings, this hobby you've got of jumping out at me from the shadows is quite concerning. You might want to reconsider it."

He stepped away immediately, instantly invisible in the darkness. "I'm sorry."

"That makes one of us. If you've come here for an apology you're not going to get one. You wouldn't tell me what was going on, and you left me no choice."

"What is it you're not apologising for?" His voice was soft, barely above a whisper and he was only a few feet away, slightly closer to the wall.

"For putting you in prison for five days."

"Yes. I deserved that. I won't keep you long. I just came here to explain."

"There's no need. Mr Andrews has explained already."

"Explained what, exactly? I think I'm going to need to sit down, sorry." There was a dull scraping sound as wool encountered brick and came off worst, and his voice now floated up from significantly closer to the ground. "Sit with me." It came out more as a plea than a command.

"I'm not sitting on the floor in this weather, thank you. Come inside."

"Another time, perhaps. What did he tell you?"

"More than you did. He said you were hit on the head. That you've got shellshock. That you hallucinate, and you can't predict air raids."

"The facts then. And wasn't it you who told me that there's more to life than facts and figures? More to see. That was the only reason I gave you a job in the first place you know, because you said that. Although the bit about poetry was rubbish."

"Look," I reached out for the wall with my fingertips, put my back to it and stood next to where he was resting. "You're tired. You're rambling.

You're sitting next to the rubbish and I'm sure you'll be embarrassed by this conversation on Monday, so why don't you just go home and we can both forget we ever met. You can be the headmaster and I'll just be a teacher. Assistant teacher, or whatever it is I am. I might even call you sir."

"It's not just air raids."

"Excuse me?"

"You know, it really is so much easier to talk to you when I can't see your face."

"What do you mean "it's not just air raids"?"

"Won't you sit down, please, just for a minute? I won't take long, I promise."

"Oh, for goodness sake." I sank to the ground next to him, the chill seeping instantly through my skirts. At least, I hoped it was the chill and not yesterday's omelette.

His left hand encountered my leg, drifted upwards until it found my right hand and laced our fingers together. He squeezed tightly. "Ivy," he said, and drew a deep breath. "I can see the future."

I exhaled. "Alright, what am I going to do next?" Poor, sad, deluded man, I thought. I am going to get up and go inside the first chance I get.

His thumb snaked between our intertwined fingers and ghosted across my palm. "You're going to get up and leave me the first chance you get."

He swept a gentle arc across my skin, tracing creases and indentations, learning the patterns of my hand. My heart rattled my rib cage so hard I thought it was about to escape. "Good guess," I said, although I wasn't quite so sure I was leaving any more.

"It doesn't work like that. I don't know what's going to happen, not all the time, but sometimes I see things. Fire mostly. And Ivy, I know what it sounds like. It sounds like that to me too. I'm not mad. I wanted to explain it to someone."

"I recommend someone with medical qualifications."

"No, someone specific. I wanted to explain it to you. You looked so guilty standing there in my office and I wanted to tell you that it's not your fault. I can't help anyone, I'll make it worse. That's it. Now you can forget we ever met." His fingers sagged, released mine and he tried twice to heave himself upright before he finally succeeded. "I'm going home now."

But I followed him down the alley and watched while he staggered down South Street, stumbling into Mrs Carmichael's door, weaving too close to lampposts, tripping over the kerb and I sighed. I went back into the house, to fetch my coat and my brother.

"Mother, Alfie and I are just going out for a walk. We'll be an hour or so." I called in the direction of the sitting room. Luckily, Alfie was still at the kitchen table. "Come on, brother dear, we've got a secret mission to go on. Remember the sick man that Mr Andrews was talking about? He needs our help." A brisk trot and we caught up. "Walk on that side of him, Alfie and I'll walk on this side. When he falls over, pick him up. Mr Rawlings, this is my brother Alfie. Alfie, this is Mr Rawlings. We're going to walk him home."

"Hello, Alfie. Why don't you call me Will?"

Alfie didn't answer, carried on walking, but Mr Rawlings either didn't notice or didn't care.

"Pleased to meet you, Alfie. I live in a big white house at the end of a road. Can you watch out for it and tell me when we get there? Where do you live?"

Alfie wasn't about to answer that one either, because it was clearly such a stupid question. I answered for him. "You know where he lives. 12 South Street."

"An excellent address. Do you have your own room Alfie?"

I waited, and then answered anyway. "Yes, he has his own room."

"Can you describe it to me Alfie?"

"Oh for goodness sake, I'm not describing it. If you want to tell Mr Rawlings about your bedroom Alfie, then you're going to have to do it yourself."

But Alfie shuffled his feet along the pavement and carried on listening, which reminded me how long it was since anyone else had actually attempted to have a conversation with him. I was so accustomed to seeing him as my brother I rarely remembered to think of him as a person at all.

"Alfie's room has a bed, and a chair, and in the corner of his room is a big pile of sticks."

"Do you collect sticks Alfie, or are you making something out of them?"

"Your guess is as good as mine, Mr Rawlings."

Will Rawlings managed to sustain this one-sided conversation for an entire two mile walk, blithely asking Alfie questions to which I supplied answers, although I could see the hand that Alfie kept having to use to prop him up and how his footsteps began to slow and drag the further he walked.

At the front door in Clock Barn Lane Mr Rawlings retrieved a key from under a loose piece of railing. "Goodnight, Alfie. Goodbye, Ivy."

"Goodbye, headmaster." But I spent most of Saturday in the library reading about shellshock and trying to forget the sensation of him holding my hand.

Chapter Seven

Charlotte opened the door to me on Sunday lunchtime with a pale face and a look of barely suppressed panic.

"Churchyard or park?" I asked.

"Park. It's closer."

I had to wait until we were out of earshot to confirm my worst fears. "Lottie? You are bleeding aren't you?"

"Eight weeks and two days and no sign. I worked it out. I'm pregnant, Ivy."

"Any other symptoms?"

"I'm getting sick in the mornings. I'm pregnant." Her voice was flat, and when we sat down on a bench in the park she wouldn't look at me, picking at her fingernails instead.

"Have you told Tom?"

"Written the letter. Haven't posted it yet."

"Alright then. Alright." There was a long silence, during which I tried to resolve the mixed feelings I had about my potential nephew or niece, whose arrival would now need to be camouflaged rather than celebrated. I reached over and squeezed her hand. "It will be alright."

She shook me off and with a sidelong look replied. "Do you know what happens to unmarried mothers, Ivy? Do you know what my options are?"

"Whatever they are we can manage it between us."

"I doubt it. If I can't work, I can't afford to feed a baby, and if I have a baby, I won't be able to work. So Option One, the workhouse. Eat porridge, make rope, have the baby and then both die of consumption."

"Nobody goes to workhouses anymore, unless they're really poor."

"Which I will be if I can't work. Option Two – I go to the Salvation Army's mothers" hospital in Hackney and have the baby there, because no ordinary hospital is going to let me in if I'm not married. Then the sisters try to find a nice foster family to give the baby to. Option Three – I go to a refuge house, have the baby there and then some horrible baby farmer sells it to a not so nice foster family and it works from the time it can stand. There is an Option Four, but you're not the right person to be talking to about it."

"You mean that woman over in Marchmount Square don't you? What about Option Five, where Tom gets leave, comes home and marries you and you move in with us until the war is over?"

"That's a good option, Ivy. I like that option. How likely do you think it is to happen?"

"I don't know. Shall we wait and see what Tom says?"

"All I can do is wait and see, but as soon as I start to show my mother's going to throw me out. "

"You can come and live with us. Don't forget that. You've got other options."

"God Ivy, how did this happen to me?"

"I hope that's a rhetorical question although I can tell you exactly how, if you like. I read it in a book. Fish sausage?"

"Actually, yes. That sounds delicious."

"At least the baby appreciates my cooking. No one else does."

"So tell me about your week, Ivy. Tell me something that'll make me laugh."

I told her, but she didn't laugh. I think both of us were still thinking about Option Four.

My second week at work opened in thunderous showers and a wind so cold my skirts were beginning to freeze by the time I reached school. The fire in the reception classroom had only recently been lit and there was frost on the inside of the window panes. South Street Elementary didn't require children to wear uniforms because most couldn't afford it but this was a day on which I wished someone had made long trousers and coats compulsory. The children were huddled tightly together in their rows and more than one set of teeth was chattering, and in a different way than usual.

Joyce Redpath and I exchanged a glance. "How do you think the headmaster feels about noise?" I asked her.

"Disapproving? Let's find out. Younger children with me, that's it, up you get, come and sit round the stove."

"Older children," I called. "You are now all enrolled in my new speed reading class. You read a sentence, you run round the classroom. Everybody not running will be jogging on the spot and reciting the alphabet backwards. Let's go."

There was quite a lot of shouting after that, some running, many red faces and shortly afterwards, a loud tapping at the door. The headmaster sailed in wearing some kind of voluminous black gown made only of sleeves and raised his voice to be heard. "Miss Redpath, your class is somewhat riotous today."

I advanced on him from the other side of the room before he could criticise any more. "Headmaster, this fire needs to be lit an hour before the children come into school, the window coverings in this room can't keep out the chill and the majority of these children don't have adequate clothing. We're trying to keep them warm."

He frowned at me, and then relaxed it slightly, which I suspected was his approximation of a smile. "Pleased to meet you Miss Drummond. Welcome to South Street. You are welcome in my office at three o'clock to present your solutions to the issues you raise. Miss Redpath, may I take my class, unless you have something else planned?"

"By all means headmaster. Danny, Marigold, Eric, Heather, Stephen, Annabelle, Richard, Oliver, Victoria, Jane, Gabriel, Tobias. Go with the headmaster please."

He waited until the children had assembled and then led them out of the classroom without another word.

"What did they do wrong?" I asked Joyce.

"Nothing, as far as I know. Quite the opposite in fact. He takes them out for special lessons once or twice a week, but I don't think they do much learning. It mostly seems to be reading stories, playing games and eating lots of sweets. They come back happy. The same children, every time mind, it makes some of the others jealous. Are you really going to see him after school then?"

"Absolutely. I'm not sure what to do about the windows but I think I've got an idea for the clothes."

She shook her head. "Rather you than me. I'd rather teach a class full of Dannys than get called to his office."

It had warmed up slightly by home time, and the children ran off happily enough. I tapped on the office door and went in, this time disregarding the dwarf chairs in front of the desk and electing to stand. He put his pen down. I crossed my arms. He pinioned me with his very best, most intimidating stare. I stared right back, until my palm tingled and my stupid stomach went butterfly soft at the remembrance of his touch.

"I have a proposition for you, Miss Drummond," he said coldly and I stopped reminiscing and concentrated. "I notice that in my absence you've spent quite some time involving yourself in the affairs of the school."

"I wasn't sure if you were coming back," I snapped. "And Miss Bird asked for help."

He raised a finger, possibly to let me know he was about to be patronising. "Let me finish. Aside from the standard of your handwriting, which is barely legible, you seem to have quite a talent for organisation. Would you be interested in spending say, an extra hour a day after your teaching duties are complete managing some of the school administration?"

"Do I get to sit in your chair?"

"Have you been sitting in my chair?"

"Yes."

"Then no. No chair."

"Will you be here?"

"No. You'll be quite safe." He picked up his pen and drew the stack of paper forward, dropping his gaze to it again. "And Miss Drummond, would you bring your brother into school with you tomorrow please? I wish to see him."

"What do you want with Alfie? What's he done?" There was that same familiar touch of panic at the thought of my brother and authority coming into contact.

Mr Rawlings was practising his calligraphy again. "Nothing. I just want to talk to him."

I waited a few moments, to make sure that actually was the end of the conversation and then stepped towards the door.

"And Ivy," he said, when it was half closed behind me. "How is this "pretending we never met" going for you? I think I'm doing quite a convincing job."

"Keep trying." I may have shut the door harder than I intended.

At nine o'clock the next day Alfie came into school with me and at three o'clock, bizarrely, he was still there, but now with a large bunch of keys on a string tied to his trousers. I caught him outside the headmaster's office, which was dark and locked. "Alfie, what are you still doing in school? Why haven't you gone home?"

He smiled at the floor and brandished a bit of paper. I snatched it off him as he practically ran down the second floor corridor. Clear, simple instructions were written in large print across it.

8am Unlock doors. 8.15am Light fires. 8.30am Sweep floors. 12pm Lunch. 3pm Lock doors. 3.15 pm Put out fires. 4pm Walk Ivy home.

My mouth fell open and I followed Alfie down the corridor to where he had opened a small cupboard. It was full of brooms.

I unlocked the headmaster's office with my new key, sat behind the desk and carried on where I'd left off on Friday, but the sound of Alfie sweeping up and down outside and periodically stopping to polish things was quite distracting. Eventually, I wrote a note on a piece of paper and left it on the desk where Mr Rawlings would be sure to see it in the morning.

Mr Rawlings. Thank you for giving Alfie a job. That was kind and I am grateful. By the way, you might want to check the figures in the first, second and fifteenth columns on the ledger. I've marked the place. I don't think your tallies are quite right.

I didn't see the headmaster for the whole of the next day, although I did run into Alfie quite a lot, busying himself around the school buildings or sitting in his storeroom admiring his new collection. There was a note on the headmaster's desk that night. It read:

Miss Drummond, Are you implying that I can't add up? This from the girl whose writing looks like someone has thrown the alphabet at a wall and hoped for it to stick. I didn't give him a job to be kind. I needed a caretaker. What are your plans for the classroom?

The next day I wrote, as neatly as I could possibly manage.

Mr Rawlings, I'm not sure about the windows, but I'm going to advertise in all the shops I can think of this weekend to see if anyone has any old clothes they want to donate to the school. There is nothing wrong with my handwriting. See?

On Friday he'd left another note, on top of a stack of papers.

Miss Drummond, I took the liberty of preparing these posters. I wanted people to know that the school needs donations - not that we've lost a dog or sell an excellent brand of shaving soap, which I thought was a risk if you wrote the advertisements, given the standard of your handwriting. You were correct about the figures; we do indeed have enough funds to procure some additional library books.

At home, Alfie was happy because he had a job and Dad was happy because Alfie had a job and Mother was probably happy but couldn't bring herself to show it. "I just don't understand who would trust Alfie enough to give him a job?" she kept saying. "What use can he possibly be?"

Even Tom, miles away in France sounded happy on the Christmas postcard he sent, but then, he clearly hadn't yet received Charlotte's letter.

Dear Ivy,

Happy Christmas to Mum, Dad and Alfie. God bless us every one etc. My present to you is this. I found that doctor. Philip wasn't injured. The Post Office Rifles came to the Somme back in October, which means Phil's battalion is somewhere here, very close by. I might be able to find someone who actually knew him, or knows where he's gone. Or better yet, Phil might be here himself. I keep walking down the trenches expecting every tin helmet to turn around and have my brother underneath. That's the best present I can think of.

Love to Charlotte, as always.

Tom.

Charlotte was the only one not happy, and the one with every right to be. When I met up with her on Sunday she drifted around the park aimlessly, ranting about anything but what I most wanted to discuss. She hadn't heard back from Tom, and she was waiting, stuck in limbo like the rest of us.

My weeks passed in busy days of teaching, followed by afternoons spent answering letters, organising events, arranging timetables and mulling over what notes to leave on the headmaster's desk. I wrote,

Thank you for the posters. I gave one to Mr Murphy, the grocer, one to the butcher with the pointy teeth, one to the bakery that does the best sticky buns and there's another in the library and a few in the GPO. Alfie picked up two bags of old clothes off the doorstep when he opened up this morning. Were you an artist before you became a teacher?

It was the only contact I had with him, apart from one Tuesday afternoon when I happened to be passing the woodwork room on the top floor and caught Mr Rawlings in there, stripped down to his shirtsleeves teaching Alfie how to hold a plane. Neither of them saw me, but I watched Alfie smiling for at least ten minutes and it made me smile myself. Shortly afterwards tall shutters began to appear over the classroom windows, home-made affairs which looked like they'd been ripped out of a grand house somewhere and hastily, and rather messily, reassembled.

The notes went on.

Miss Drummond, I'm a product of the best education money can buy. Boarding school (it's everything you can imagine), Oxford (see boarding school), and then I was a lecturer (which is a teacher for grown-ups). With all this education, I hope I'm still capable of writing "wanted" on a couple of bits of paper.

I wrote,

Mr Rawlings, lecturing people is one of your many talents. Where does the army fit in to all that education?

He replied,

My mother was very keen that I enlisted.

It didn't look like that was a subject he really wanted to discuss. But that afternoon, as I was standing at the back of the hall watching the school play with Alfie nodding by my side I heard footsteps behind me. The children were busy parading round dressed as donkeys or forgetting their lines and looking embarrassed or staring at each other while a packed crowd of cramped mothers smiled and applauded and wiped away surreptitious tears. I looked up over my shoulder to see the headmaster standing there, a softer expression in those pale blue eyes than I was used to seeing. I smiled at him, and for the first time since I'd known him, he smiled back. And even though there was a war on, even though both my brothers were lost in it somewhere, even with Alfie and the burdens he brought at my right hand, I still felt happy.

That night I left a note on the desk, asking the question that had been niggling at me for a couple of weeks. The question that would explain why his shirts weren't properly ironed and why he was sleeping in his kitchen.

Where's your wife?

On Saturday morning when I came downstairs there was already a hand addressed envelope in the hall.

She left me. Don't ask me about her again.

Then finally, a proper letter from Tom.

Dear Ivy,

I just got a letter from Charlotte. I'm going to assume you know already, but if you don't, stop reading right now and go and see her, she needs help. I've got Charlotte into trouble, Ivy, and I don't know how to get her out. She didn't say much but it sounds like she's sure. What a Christmas present. My hands are shaking as I write this, and it isn't just because of the cold.

I've applied for leave on compassionate grounds. I went to see the Captain and came clean but he's not much older than I am, straight out of some posh school somewhere and I can tell he's not going to say yes. He thinks I'm to blame, which I am, of course. I should've married Charlotte when I got the call up papers, but I was so focused on the chance to go and look for Philip that I didn't even think about it.

Ivy, I want you to tell Mum about Charlotte. I know you two don't get on, but she's my mother and she'll help, I know she will. Go and tell her right now, she'll be in the kitchen, go and tell her. And then go and see Charlotte.

I'm sorry Ivy.

Tom

I didn't, of course. Tom didn't know my mother as well as I did, he loved her as a son loves his mother - unconditionally, and blithely accepting that her word is law. Mothers and daughters are different; daughters know nothing is ever that straightforward.

So I went to see Charlotte instead, craved another ten-minute break from her mother and stood outside in the flapping garden. "I heard from Tom," I said. "He wants me to tell my mother about the baby. What did he say to you?"

"That he wants you to tell your mother about the baby. When are you going to tell her?"

"I'm not."

"But you said we should wait for Tom to decide what to do. He's decided. Why are we not going to do it?" she asked.

"My mother will never take you in."

"I'm carrying her grandchild. She can't be as bad as all that."

"She's not bad. In fact, she's very, very good. Holier than thou, and anyone else you can think of. That's exactly the problem. Do you know why I do all the cooking and cleaning? Because the minute she comes in the door she's straight out again to see Father Moran or go to a prayer meeting or polish the church or whatever excuse she's using today. Never once in my entire life has she been there when I needed her."

"It's not your decision though is it? Tom trusts her, I think you should."

"I'm not telling her."

"I think you should respect Tom's decision."

"Tom isn't here." I objected.

"I am. Respect mine."

The wet sheets swirled around her, the wind tossed her hair and there was a determination in her face I hadn't seen since she told me she was going to run away from home at the age of eight. She had as well, but she'd only got as far as Mr Murphy's.

I sighed. "Fine. I'll tell her. But you won't like the answer."

I caught my mother in the early afternoon of the following day, Christmas Eve. Nanna Kate's decorations had come out of their box and Dad had set up a purloined tree in the back room. The fire was crackling in the range and my mother was plucking the small, scrawny duck we'd be having for Christmas dinner along with a few potatoes, turnips and carrots from the raised beds we'd put in the backyard. I was attempting to make mince pies from potato flour and honey, but I wasn't holding out much hope. Dad had taken Alfie fishing.

I hadn't thought of a good way to approach my mother, but then, I'd been trying to come up with one for the last six years and Christmas Eve was about as good as it was going to get. "I had a letter from Tom, Mother. He's asked me to pass on a message."

"Why didn't he just write to me himself then?"

"You'll have to ask him that. He wants me to tell you that Charlotte is pregnant."

"Irene's daughter?"

"She's pregnant, Mother."

"She's no better than her mother then. Why did Tom want you to tell me that?"

"He's the father of the baby."

"No, he isn't."

"He says he is, Mother."

"I'm sorry Ivy, did my youngest son get married without me noticing? No, I didn't think so. He's not the father of anyone's baby and it has nothing to do with me. Honestly, Ivy. You should know better than to pass on idle gossip."

"Didn't you hear me Mother? Tom and Charlotte are having a child together – your grandchild."

"I have no grandchildren, and I don't expect any either. Now pass me the big knife so I can get the head off this duck."

"But Mother, I can show you the letters."

"Not another word, Ivy. I won't hear a word on this subject again."

The kitchen table rang with the sound of hard, heavy bangs as my mother inexpertly decapitated the bird, bone shearing with a cracking protest, flesh tearing, slapping meaty gristle on the wood. Calmly, I folded my apron, calmly washed my hands, put on my coat and calmly left the house. There was snow in the north, but in London we just had the cold and the biting wind, which wasn't quite so picturesque. I wandered the streets, seething and crying by turns. I hadn't really expected any other reaction from my mother but to know that she had cast off a baby quite so easily was more than I could live with.

So I walked and I thought about Charlotte's options. If Tom didn't come back and marry her, she would be forced out of home, by poverty if not by her mother, if he didn't then there weren't any options left I wanted to consider.

What I needed was someone to give me some advice, someone with an insight into whether Tom was coming home or not, someone who could see the future....

Chapter Eight

I looked up to find the front door of the white house on Clock Barn Lane already open and Mr Rawlings standing on his threshold watching me pace up and down across the street. He nodded once in acknowledgement, then went back inside, leaving the door open. I wasn't sure that asking him for help was a good idea, but the chance that he might be able to took me up the steps. I hung up my coat and scarf in the hall and went down the passageway to the kitchen, to find tea already steeping, next to a jug of milk and the biggest bag of sugar I'd seen in two years.

"Miss Drummond," he said with a sweeping gesture towards the table. "This hobby you've got of coming round unannounced is quite concerning. It might be misconstrued."

"Misconstrued how?"

"I might get the impression you actually like talking to me." He was teasing me, but in that odd, utterly serious way he had. "What can I do for you this time? Have you thought up some more fabulously awkward questions to ask me? I enjoyed your last note."

I sat forward, clasped my hands together and met his gaze quite easily for a change. "I have a problem and I need some help. Your help, specifically. "

He raised his eyebrows at me to continue over the rim of his teacup.

He looked better, I noted, collecting my thoughts, less tired, less pale, less gaunt and a lot more approachable, although that might have been wishful thinking. "I have a friend who is in trouble."

"Is this the sort of friend who will turn out to be you in half an hours" time?"

"No. It's a real friend. Those of us who don't spend all our time hiding in our office instead of going to the staffroom have them."

"And is this trouble just trouble, or the sort of trouble that young ladies can get into when it's a euphemism for things that can happen between men and women?"

"The euphemism kind."

"I see. And are you definitely sure it's not you?"

"Definitely. I'd never get into that sort of trouble with men. I've never so much as..." I thought better of that sentence, although I did blush slightly when I realised where it was going.

He cleared his throat. "What can I do about it?"

It seemed such a stupid thing for me to ask, especially of a man who had been so injured and was still suffering from that injury, like I was trying to use the damage done to him for my own ends. "I just wondered if... that is you said that you...." The blush spread its rosy wings and flew across my face.

"I, what?"

I had to look away then, examined the floor tiles in minute detail. "You said you could see the future and I want to know if my brother Tom is coming back from the war."

By the time I looked up he was across the other side of the room stoking the range. "I pass the test then?"

"What test?"

"The Ivy Drummond I'm-not-going-to talk-to-you-in-person-for-weeks-while-I-work-out-if-you"re-mad-or-not test."

"What are you talking about? You're the one who doesn't want to talk to me. Last time I came here you told me to get out."

"And you told me to pretend we'd never met." He turned back to face me, leaned against the chimney breast. "Do you think I'm mad then, or not?"

"Can you see the future?"

He shrugged. "Can I do my job?"

"Yes."

"Am I kind to small children and animals? Do I behave appropriately in the company of adults?"

"Sort of. You prefer to write to people than see them face to face and when you do condescend to speak you're so rude you get yourself arrested."

"You got me arrested."

"I thought you said that wasn't my fault."

"I thought you said I was rambling."

"And sitting in egg."

"Apart from the egg then, do I appear to you to be insane?"

"I read up on shellshock in the library. Do you see things that aren't there? Do you relive what happened to you in the war? Do you have great difficulty talking about it?" I could see his shoulders tensing up as I spoke. "That doesn't make you mad – it makes you ill. Which answers your question, and mine too, actually. I'm sorry I came; I shouldn't have bothered you with my problems when you're dealing with enough of your own already. This was a bad idea." I was suddenly ashamed of myself, and embarrassed, to have come barging into his house and asked such a foolish thing. Only the very ill would imagine they could see the future, and only the very selfish would try to use that illness for their own ends.

I turned to leave and he sighed. "Thank you for coming anyway. That's the closest anyone's ever come to believing me."

I paused with my hand on the back of the chair, tapping my fingernails against the carved wood, caught by the brave, lost tone of his voice. I didn't really believe him, not deep down, but I wanted to. I pivoted slowly, folded my arms, and because I didn't want to go home, and because he looked almost vulnerable standing there, and because I didn't have anything to lose I said, "Prove it."

A smile broke across his face, washed through his eyes and left them shining. "Thanks goodness for that. I thought you were actually going to leave for a minute."

He almost ran across to the kitchen table and began scrabbling amongst the stacks of paper, discarding stray books. I picked up some of them and read the spines. "Atlas of London." "London streets – a complete guide." "Anatomy of the mind." "Trauma injuries – treatment and cure." In this last I noticed a folded piece of paper tucked in the flyleaf. It was a page torn out of a newspaper advertising the benefits of electric shock treatment for ex-soldiers afflicted by nervous conditions. I put it back where it belonged without comment.

"Exhibit A, your honour," he said finally, pushed a paper into my hands. "And B, C and D." All had dates and a similar combination of words:

26th August. Tanners Steel Factory, Fire.
2nd September. Tanners Steel Factory? Works. Fire. Explosion.
October 17th. Tanners Steel. Bomb.
November 1st. Tanners Steel Works. Fire.

"I record everything I see," he said. "It's all here somewhere."

I pointed at the page. "So this is the date you had the dream presumably, and this is the place and this is what you dreamed."

"I see it Ivy, I don't dream it. Nobody dreams of air raids."

"What do you dream of?"

"Nothing. I have nightmares. Now come on. I want to show you something else." He strode out of the room and I heard his footsteps receding down the hall and then clumping up the stairs, two at a time.

"Where are you going?"

"Bedroom," he called down. "Come on."

"Call me naïve," I said, following rather more slowly. "But shouldn't we be married before you show me your bedroom?"

He popped his head over the bannister. "You're very keen to rush into marriage. Why don't we start with you using my first name? Or you're very welcome to call me "sir" in the bedroom. Whichever you prefer." And he grinned.

I hadn't thought his face was even capable of a grin but it disappeared with him back into a room just as quickly.

There was probably a bed in there somewhere I thought, but it was currently covered with paper, as were both the bedside tables, the desk, and chair, the bookcase and shelves and there was more paper strewn in heaps all over the floor. It was like someone had dismembered a library. "Promise me you'll be careful with the matches in here," I said.

And then I saw the map. It took up most of one wall, the different panels arranged to form a picture of most of London, the river circling through the middle, crosshatched in a faint blue. Clusters of green and red pins blotched the face of the city, obscuring some streets entirely while others were unscathed. And although I looked at it hard, I couldn't discern a pattern.

"Where did you get that?" I asked in awe.

"I made it." He sounded proud, balancing on the balls of his feet, tipping back on his heels, bouncing around with enthusiasm and generally unable to stand still. "That's what I do. What I did, before the army. I was a lecturer in geography, but in my spare time, I made maps. I joined the British Expeditionary Force as a cartographer primarily, but after... afterwards, when I moved back to London I needed a map and I drew this."

I was squinting at a tiny St Pauls Cathedral, an intricately rendered Houses of Parliament. "It's beautiful, Will."

"It is, isn't it? I think this is the most accurate piece I've ever made."

"Did you have one of these of Hertfordshire too?" I asked innocently, while he was still admiring his creation.

"Yes, but it wasn't nearly so challenging. Too many fields."

"And did your wife mind having it in your bedroom?"

"Of course she did. It was in the study, she'd never have let me..." Then he pulled himself up short and turned on me with narrowed eyes. "I thought I told you never to ask me about my wife again?"

"Sorry, sir. What do the pins mean?" That explained why his wife had left him then, I thought. I didn't think I'd want one of these in my bedroom either, and, given the sheer investment of time and effort it must have taken him to draw it, he probably hadn't been doing much else in his bedroom for some time.

"The green pins are individual locations, places I've seen things, the red pins show the sites of air raids that have already happened, as closely as I can tell and the grey pins are called nails and they're how the whole thing stays on the wall. Don't read too much into those."

I stood back, considering. Much of the map was wreathed in green. "But Will, there must be thousands of them. How can each one be something you've seen? If you only moved back to London six months ago that would mean you've been seeing whatever it is you see hundreds of times a day."

"I do. It's all around me, every time I step out of the house. It never stops."

"What if you don't look around you? What if you just go to work and come home again and look at the pavement all the way?"

"Then I have nightmares."

"Well, that sounds better than seeing—what is it, fire?—everywhere you look."

"Not these nightmares, Ivy." He was looking fixedly at the map but I had the distinct impression he was trembling. "These are violent. These are nightmares where I wake up in the morning and find I've hurt myself. And other people too, sometimes."

I suspected his wife hadn't taken too kindly to that either. "Was that why you made yourself stay awake all the time you were in prison? So you wouldn't have nightmares?"

He nodded grimly. "I didn't want to give them the satisfaction of watching."

"I don't expect you'd have done much damage, a skinny thing like you. You should see Alfie when he gets going. He once pushed my brother Philip so hard there's still a dent in the wall where his head hit it. Alfie doesn't mean it though. He lashes out sometimes without even thinking about it. You just have to accept it and move on."

Will was looking at me wide eyed. "Skinny thing?" he asked eventually.

"Tell me about the red ones then."

"The red ones are actual air raids, as closely as I can plot them." He stepped further and further away taking me back with him until my calves were against the bed. "Now look from here. There's far more green than red, yes? But there's a whole area of red over there and no green at all. I've never seen any air raids in that area but they've happened. In fact, the correlation between the green and the red isn't that strong overall. There are places like Tanners, and may be eight or nine more where I've got it right but statistically, that could be a co-incidence couldn't it? I was trying to work out the probability of being right the other day, I've got the calculations here somewhere."

He wandered off towards the desk and rummaged in the chaos.

I did some quick counting. "Will, there's too much green."

"I know," he muttered. "I can't make it stop. I've tried everything I can think of, but it never stops."

"No – come back over here and look at this properly. Look at the facts and figures, you like those. The zeppelins have been bombing us say, twice a month for the last two years, but you've got thousands of buildings destroyed on your map. It looks like Westminster gets off unscathed but there's great sections of the East End that have been wiped out, whole blocks of the city gone. At the current rate there just aren't that many bombers. The war would have to go on for..." I did some quick mental arithmetic. "Two hundred years?"

He was shaking his head. "Three years' tops. We've already lost too many men. Win or lose it has to end soon." He gazed at the map with something like wonder on his face. "Do you think I'm wrong then? Do you think it's all in my head?"

"I don't think you're very well, no. But maybe the Germans invent a better way to drop bombs, and you'll end up being right in the end. You said it wasn't just air raids you saw though. That was the reason I came."

He was at the end of the bed, eyes round and glassy and without looking, scooped up a sheaf of papers and thrust them into my hand. "Read for yourself."

Billy Bonner. Uniform, navy. Carrying something in a bag. Early morning sunshine. Postman?

Nathaniel Carver. Sound of crying. Smell of cut grass. Sadness.

Emily Cox. Carries a baby but with white hair and wrinkles. Will make a fantastic grandmother.

I picked up a stack of papers, put them down and picked up another handful, and then another, searching for one name and not finding it. His hand closed around my wrist.

"You won't find it, Ivy. I didn't write down what I saw about you."

I shook him off, carried on pawing through the names. "I don't care what you saw about me, it's Tom I came here for."

He reached out, seized my wrist again and forced me back onto the bed next to him, enclosing my hand in both of his. His eyes searched mine and I saw sympathy in them. "That's not how it works. When I look at people sometimes I can see things about them. Odd images. Smells. Impressions of where they've come from and where they're going. But I have to see them for myself, Ivy. I can't tell anything about your brother if I've never met him."

"You've met me though; you can see things about me. What do you see?"

His eyes slid away from mine, down to where we were holding hands, and his thumb crept into the curve of my palm again, in a tentative caress. "Ivy, you've just demonstrated, quite brilliantly, that the things I see might be absolute nonsense, and that's air raids, when I can at least try to prove the visions are accurate by looking at the numbers. I can't do that with people. I've no way of proving any of it at all, and I don't want to hurt you with something that might end up being completely wrong."

"What do you see about me?" I removed my hand from his and stretched it wide in front of his face. "Go on, take a closer look."

He frowned at me, sat back a little. "I don't need to see your hand."

I frowned back at him. "Don't think I haven't noticed. Almost every time we meet you take my hand. You're feeling the lines on it aren't you - lifeline and heart line and whatever the others are supposed to be. Like palm reading. You're telling my fortune. What do you see?"

He closed my hand back into a fist and replaced it in my lap. "That's not how it works."

"Then why do you keep holding my hand?"

"And another awkward question. You really are excellent at them. Do you practise? Now get your coat and let's go out. I keep saying "it doesn't work like that". I want to show you how it does work."

"Then will you tell me what you see?"

"Perhaps. If you still want to hear it."

When we left the house the sky had taken on that dull, metallic sheen that means imminent snow, and I bundled my coat around me, securing my hat and scarf tightly. Will donned his long black greatcoat which, viewed in the half light, was patched and faded and smelled quite strongly of damp. "It was my father's," he shrugged when I eyed it disapprovingly. "And now, Miss Drummond, I am going to escort you on a sightseeing tour of the East End of London, the like of which you have never before, and may never again experience."

"Will it take all day?"

"Oh. No, sorry, I can be done in five minutes if you like. It's Christmas Eve isn't it? You must want to get back to your family."

I tapped his arm. "I want it to take all day."

A smile flashed and faded. "Now, miss, if you will accompany me across the street, I will show you what I mean." He didn't touch me, but he kept a hand hovering just under my elbow as we went down one kerb, and up the other, as if I was so unsteady on my feet that I was liable to fall into the road at any time. It was both chivalrous and ridiculous. "I draw your attention to number one Clock Barn Lane, a house which is old, grey and very tall, and resembles my late mother in many respects."

"It also smells."

"Does it? Well then, a house that is old, grey and in need of airing. Nothing terrible is ever going to happen to it, but I think at some point there will be children living there."

"And you know this because?"

"I hear them laughing sometimes in the rooms late at night."

"A house that is tall, old and creepy then, like its current owner."

"Thank you kindly. But that's not the point. Which is, of course, that I can't see anything bad happening to it. Next, numbers three, five, seven, nine, eleven and so on. All entirely unremarkable." We began walking down the road. "And then we get to number forty-one. I look at this house and I see fire. And for forty-three, and forty-five."

"A little more detail, if you please. What exactly do you see, step by step?"

"I look across the road, and my sight goes out of focus, blurry, and then I can see fire."

"So the houses are destroyed?"

"No, they're still there. The fronts are anyway. The fire is behind the windows."

"Is it coming out of the windows? Is it burning the houses down?"

"No, it's just there behind the glass."

"Why do the windows still have glass in them if the house is on fire? Does the fire not get worse?"

"No, it's exactly the same. Nothing ever changes, and I walk past these houses every day on the way to work."

"And are there people in these houses when they're on fire?"

"Yes."

"Alright, let's knock on the doors and warn them. When is this going to happen?"

"I don't know."

"You don't know?"

"I can't tell when it's going to happen, only that it is."

"But you knew about Tanners – you were waiting for the bombers."

"I'd been there every night for a month Ivy, before they actually came."

I rocked back on my heels, considering. "There must have been something specific about the factory that made you keep going back."

"It just seemed important to me to be there when the bombers came, that's all. I'm not so sure now."

"Does it seem so important that you go to forty-one, three and five?"

"No. Do you still want to go and warn the people who live there? You can try, if you like."

"I understand the point now, thank you. The warning would be too vague to be of any use. Let's carry on then, next street."

We turned the corner into the next road. "This is an interesting one. Numbers one hundred and twenty-two and one hundred and twenty-six, but not one hundred and twenty-four."

I stood and looked at the three houses together, struggling to see what would make the house in the middle bombproof. It had a red front door, but other than that it was very similar to the houses on either side, except with an extra window. As we walked up the next street, I memorised the numbers of the houses with red front doors and waited to see if he if he would point them out.

"Seventy-eight. Sixty-three and the one called "The Cottage.""

Not red front doors then – he didn't list any of those. In the next street I picked double fronted houses with Georgian symmetry and perfectly matched windows. He didn't. In the next road I chose single storey tenements, ill-kempt and neglected. He didn't choose those either. After two hours the snow came, and my feet were starting to tire, and I began to miss the odd kerb and need the support of that outstretched hand. The daylight was fading fast, sucking his eyes into pools of darkness.

Half an hour later, "Enough?" he asked. "Shall we go home?" I could hear the strain in his voice.

"How many nights a week do you do this?" I responded.

He shrugged. "Most?"

"For how long?"

"Can be six or seven hours. Until I'm asleep on my feet. Then I don't dream."

"And it's six or seven hours of seeing houses on fire, with people trapped inside?"

"It's a sightseeing trip you'll never forget. I wish I could."

"Well, we'd better stop it then, hadn't we?"

"That's fine. You've been remarkably patient. I'll walk you home, and then I'll carry on."

"No. I mean we'd better stop you seeing these horrible things. I'm going down the next street, and its…" I squinted at the sign. "Chicheley Street, I know that one. I'll go down it on my own, you come next, meet me at the end and – this is very important – don't say anything." I left him standing there and strode off down the pavement looking for the pattern I thought I'd spotted in the dwellings on either side. When I reached the junction with Marchmount Square I stopped and waited until the boots tramping a couple of feet behind halted. "Thirty-five, seventy-five, ninety-seven and ninety-eight," I sang out.

"Thirty-five, seventy-five, ninety-seven, ninety-eight and a hundred and five," he repeated in disbelief.

"One hundred and five – are you sure?"

"One hundred and five – how did you do that?" He came right up close, put his hands on my shoulders and stooped slightly so his eyes were on a level with mine. "Ivy, how did you do that?"

I stood steady under the pressure of his hands, bore the discomfort as his fingers tightened. "There's a pattern."

He took half a step back, released me so I went on. "It's not infallible. Sometimes you do pick properties that don't fit, like one hundred and five and I don't really see how you ended up at Tanners, but for the last four or five streets you've been consistently choosing the same type of house."

"I'm choosing?"

"I think so, yes. Didn't you realise?"

"I'm choosing?"

"I can see a pattern."

"Which is?"

"The mind is its own place, and in itself, can make a Heaven of Hell, a Hell of Heaven."

"Poetry. Well that explains everything quite nicely. All my questions are answered, let's go home."

"It's Milton, Paradise Lost. You wanted me to quote a verse, that's your verse."

"Consider me duly impressed. Now explain what you mean."

"You show me yours and I'll show you mine."

"If that's an explanation, I think I preferred the poetry. Alright, we need somewhere with people. What's open at six o'clock on Sunday on Christmas Eve?"

"I know a place, two streets up and three across."

"I don't understand how you ended up at Tanners either. Are you ever lost?"

"Not as such, I'm a postman's daughter and Dad used to take me out on duty as often as he could. I was thinking about my friend the night I got lost – the one in trouble. The one you're about to help me with. Here."

I tapped on the locked side door of the White Star, which was, for all the outside world would ever discern, closed and barred for the night. But my dad spent as much time in the pub as my mother did in church – beer was his religion.

"Hello, Mr Reckitt." I said into the crack of the door. "It's Ivy, may I come in? I brought a friend."

"Quickly then." Inside, the bar was lit by candles and firelight, although the blackout blinds were down as well, to prevent any stray spark of light escaping. There were no more than ten or twelve people huddled in groups on the stiff chairs. Mrs Carmichael waved at me from one corner and I could hear Mr Andrews" booming laugh from somewhere near the fire. Will loomed, tall, dark and awkward behind me so I sent him to sit on a bench by the window while I added more expense to my father's already extensive account.

After Mr Reckitt served me, I placed a glass on the table and decided Will might need an explanation. "This is a public house. It's Mr Reckitt's house – he's the one over there behind the bar memorising what you look like so he can tell my dad later. People come to pubs to drink and talk to each other. That's where the first person says something, and then the second person says something back, and then they both laugh or possibly punch each other. That happens quite a lot here too. No one makes anyone else sit on tiny, tiny chairs, or stares at them so hard their eyes break, or asks them to list publication dates for books they've never read. This is what it's like to have friends."

He shuffled towards me on the bench until his leg was pushed up tight against mine and he leaned close enough to whisper in my ear. I shivered a little, and hoped he didn't notice. "I'm going to have to be very quiet so nobody hears. Who do you want to know about?"

"Start with Mr Reckitt behind the bar."

Under the cover of drinking Will raised his eyes from the table and glanced across the room. "He's fallen out with his wife, he feels very guilty about something and I can see a cold, dark room with lots of bottles."

I thought hard. "His wife was supposed to have gone to stay with her daughter in Folkestone six months ago. Has he murdered her and buried her in the cellar?"

Will's breath was warm in my ear. "That's quite a vivid imagination you have there. I think he's just been watering down the beer. Tastes like it anyway. Next?"

I tried to speak without actually moving my lips. "The man over by the fire with the pointy teeth. He's the butcher."

"He's a vampire." Will murmured, bending even closer.

I wasn't quite so circumspect. "A vampire? Really?" I spoke too loudly, turned my head too quickly and nearly collided with his nose.

His eyes were laughing at me and they'd turned a shade darker in the candlelight. "Of course not, I made it up. I don't get anything from him at all apart from the fact that he works with meat."

I was having some difficulty in looking anywhere but into his eyes so I gestured with my chin. "Mrs Carmichael, over in the corner."

He twisted slightly, and then paused while he took a much longer look and drank most of his pint. When he turned back his cheeks held a touch of pink. "Well, that explains all the children."

"What does that mean? What do you see?"

"There are some things, Ivy Drummond, which can happen between a man and a woman that you're too young and innocent to be told about."

I reached under the table and pinched his leg. "I'm not that innocent. Tell me."

The corner of his mouth quirked upwards as he said. "Yes you are, little miss never been kissed."

"I never said that. I said "I'd never get into that sort of trouble with men. I've never so much as" and then I drew a polite veil across the whole subject."

"Which is what I'm doing now. And, by the way, if you don't want me holding your hand I suggest you remove it from my leg."

I snatched it back, flaming scarlet, and I think he'd started to laugh when Mr Andrews banged his empty glass down on the table in front of me. "Poor choice of company to keep, Ivy. Very poor. I'll make sure your father is informed, for all the good it will do."

Will didn't move, but he carried on whispering into my ear. "He becomes some kind of judge, very well respected and dies, old and happy in his bed. I'll wait for you outside."

Then, without so much as a look at the other man, he drained his glass, replaced it on the table and stalked out.

"Yes, of course Mr Andrews, sir. I don't know what I was thinking." I dodged around him and was almost outside by the time I'd finished speaking. Will was waiting on the corner, shoulders hunched against the starlight, giving every impression that he'd forgotten how to laugh once more.

"I've shown you how it works," he said. "Explain the pattern."

I searched South Street until I found the house I was looking for. "That one over there, one hundred and seventy-eight. Am I right?"

He squinted at it, nodded.

"All the houses you choose look the same. Single storey, front door to the left, two windows to the right, quite a high roof. I'd say they were cottages, especially the one you pointed out two hours ago called "The Cottage." That was a bit of a clue. Would you like to tell me what a cottage on fire means to you?"

He recoiled as if I'd slapped him.

"Will?"

"Yes, I remember what you want. I see two things when I look at you. One I can't tell you, only show you, and the other won't make you happy."

"I don't want you to make me happy, I want you to tell me what you see."

"Alright. I see you alone. You're an only child."

He walked away so quickly I couldn't think of a word to say.

Chapter Nine

Christmas passed through my life trailing a slight sense of disappointment. The hand-made gifts that hadn't quite turned out as expected, the stubborn lack of sugar which destroyed cakes and puddings, the two empty chairs that everyone saw and nobody mentioned. I had a letter from Tom.

Dear Ivy,

There were no Christmas truces this year, no jolly games of football and carol singing over the wire. Christmas was cold and miserable and a long way from home. I got a soldier's box, but I ate the chocolate and smoked the cigarettes and it didn't make up for not seeing you, and Charlotte.

I can't help thinking that you could have tried harder with Mum.

Go and see Father Moran. I'm sure there's some speck of Christian charity in him somewhere. Mum believes anything he says and if he says "help your almost daughter in law", then she will. He blessed me before I went away, you know. There were tears in his eyes. He can't be all bad.

Charlotte hasn't written to me this week – is she alright? I'm worried.

I haven't found Philip yet either, but I did hear that the Rifles were based about two miles further down the lines than us, so I'm going to volunteer as an errand boy again and see if anyone knows where they are. Maybe I can get Phil to write to Mum, maybe she'd take Charlotte in if she thought the baby was Phil's (I know, I know, but it's probably true.)

I don't know much about Mons, I'm afraid. All I've heard is that it was an open battle over fields, and we were outnumbered two to one. I think that was the one where they all started seeing angels or archers or something halfway through – sounds a bit mad to me too.

Love Tom

PS Love to Mum (can't hurt).

I went to see Charlotte. Stupidly, I was expecting her to be wielding an enormous belly, but I guess pregnancy is a much slower process than you think it will be from the outside and she looked the same as ever. We were back in the churchyard, sheltering under a dripping yew, chewing soft apples from Mr Murphy and trying to pretend that nothing had changed.

"I don't understand what you're saying, Ivy. Do you think he can see the future or not – I'm confused?"

I threw the core of my apple as far as I could, splattering it all over a gravestone by mistake. "I did at first, when he saved me from that air raid, but the more I've got to know him, the less sure I am. Half of what he sees is shellshock and the other half is probably co-incidence. The best he could come up with in the pub was that Mr Reckitt waters the beer, Mr Andrews is going to die in his bed and Mrs Carmichael likes men, which I could have guessed myself."

"He's wrong about Philip, Alfie and Tom – you aren't an only child and you aren't going to be one either. I can only see one thing he's right about – you are innocent. You can't follow men around like that, Ivy. You shouldn't have gone to his house."

"Says the woman who followed my brother all the way to Folkestone and then innocently lifted her skirts and hoped nothing bad would happen."

"If you think that me and Tom were together just that one time you're more innocent than I thought."

"Remind me why you're my best friend again?"

"Because I can stop you being as stupid as I am."

"I don't think Will minds me going round to see him anyway. He just doesn't like to show it."

"Will, is it now? Next thing you know you'll be lifting your skirts and hoping nothing bad happens."

"Why didn't you write to Tom this week?"

"I did. I gave the letter to my mother to post. I was too busy throwing up at the time. She probably forgot to put it in the post-box."

We were both silent for a moment considering that one. "What if she didn't?" I asked.

Term started again and January's weather was the same as December's, just with less tinsel. Joyce Redpath and I sat in the staffroom at lunchtimes and compared chilblains while Alfie slowly and methodically made every single teacher a cup of tea. I saw the headmaster once that week when he came in to take his special class, and although I continued to storm through the paperwork every afternoon there were no more notes. I refused point blank to believe what he'd told me about my brothers and I had no desire to ask any more about it.

On Friday I came home to find my mother engaged in a furious, if extremely quiet argument with Mrs Ransome in the back yard.

"It's your son that did it, it's you that'll be paying for this baby, not me."

My mother hissed, "Your harlot daughter is nothing to do with my Tom. I hear she lies down with any man that'll give her tuppence, same as you."

"Same as you, more like. I know you Hilda Campion, and what's more I can count. How many months was it after you were married that your Alfie was born? Did you make it to four, or was it three? I remember letting out your wedding dress time and time again and then you sailing down the aisle looking like you'd swallowed a football. Why is Alfie like he is, if not that his mother couldn't keep her legs together until she was lawfully wed?"

"My James stuck by me. Whereas Michael's still living with that girl in Bow, isn't he? They've got two boys now, and a lovely shop while you're doing my laundry and your daughter's pregnant by whoever happened to be walking past last Tuesday."

"I'll go to Father Moran, you see if I don't. You'd better come up with some way out of this or everyone in Poplar's going to know what a fine young man your son Tom is. And if you don't pay up, I'll tell them all about you as well."

"My son Tom's a fine young man fighting in France, no one's going to blame him. Whereas everyone will know your daughter is a slut."

"You've got a week Hilda, or everyone will know what I know, and think how angry Father Moran's going to be then."

Charlotte's mother banged out of the yard with such violence that the rebound of the gate against the wall broke the bolt clean away. I hid in the engulfing darkness of the alley for a good twenty minutes before I ventured inside. Even then I couldn't work out why my mother had referred to my dad as "James".

I didn't get to see Charlotte that Sunday. Her mother waited for me at the front door with a forbidding look and a sharpened tongue and like a coward, I pretended I hadn't seen her and crossed the road.

The knock of the front door on Monday at half past seven precisely caught me unawares. Dad had already left for work, and Alfie and I were getting ready to go to school, my boots laced and my shawl on, and I opened the door fully expecting to see Father Moran's pasty, unsympathetic face. Only religion and death ever came through that door.

There were four postmen standing there, which I thought was an unusual number to deliver one small, thin, brown envelope. I took it when it was handed to me. The four postmen had shined their shoes, and their navy uniforms were brushed free of dirt, the brass buttons polished, blood-red braid a vivid twist of contrast. The letter was addressed to my mother, typewritten. There were four postmen at the front door.

I had a letter. A brown envelope.

I remembered that I hadn't had a letter from Tom last Friday and I hadn't even noticed. The hand holding the letter started to shake. A voice said, "Do you think you could please find my father?"

But I was far, far away and long ago, scampering after three brothers as they chased each other through a forest streaked with sunshine.

One of the four honour guard handed me a box wrapped in brown paper which I set on the parlour table. "Miss Drummond," he said, and nodded once.

There was only me in that room, only me in the whole world who knew that this was the last moment we would ever be a family. I tore the top of the form in opening it.

Dear Madam,

It is my painful duty to inform you that a report has this day been received from the War Office notifying the death of:

(No) 17343 Rank: Private

Name: Thomas Drummond

Regiment: 1/17th County of London Battalion Poplar and Stepney Rifles

Which occurred at: place not specified

On: 3rd January 1917

I am to express to you the sympathy and regret of the Army Council at your loss.

The cause of death was: killed in action.

I couldn't read the signature.

I swallowed several times and asked Alfie to go and sweep the yard as I walked upstairs to find my mother. My parent's bedroom was to the left at the top of the stairs, and the door was closed because my mother was still pretending to be asleep. She wasn't actually asleep, because Alfie had to walk through her bedroom to get downstairs and no one could sleep through that. She was propped upright in bed, her head lolled unconvincingly to the side, the shape of an open book outlined under the covers. I shook her shoulder and dropped the letter into her lap, letting her feign rousing before she read it for herself. I stood straight-backed and still, on parade and awaited instructions. My mother did not shriek, or faint, but soft tears began a slow drip-drip from her eyes.

"Fetch Father Moran, Ivy," she ordered, and her voice was a rasp.

I clattered back down the stairs, went through the front door and began the long climb to St Marys. My mother's church was the opposite way to South Street School, up Holloway Hill and through the churchyard where Charlotte and I went on Sundays. The church was a jaundiced yellow stone, splotched with lichen like it had caught some terrible pox. I had not crossed the threshold in six years.

Father Moran was inside, fiddling with the cloth on the altar and although he must have heard my footsteps he still made me walk all the way up the aisle before turning. His round, white moon face bobbed towards me.

"It's a pleasure to welcome you back, Ivy Drummond. You always have a place in this church."

I said, "My mother needs to see you urgently, Father. Will you come?"

"Is there news, Ivy?"

"Yes, Father." My eyes were fixed to a point beyond his left shoulder and I didn't flinch as he came closer and made the sign of the cross.

"Then I will come."

I didn't wait. I walked back home. I may have fallen a few times. I went into the kitchen and set a tray with tea things and put the kettle on the range to boil. Then I went into the yard to find Alfie.

"I have something to tell you Alfie." I said. This wouldn't be the first time I'd have to tell him either. When Nanna Kate died I'd had to explain it to Alfie on seventeen different occasions, I counted. Alfie didn't pause in his sweeping, but he was listening.

"Tom is not coming back from the war, Alfie. Tom is dead."

Alfie continued sweeping the yard, back wall to front wall, around the vegetable beds, front wall to back wall and repeat. I went inside, poured water into the pot and carried the tray into the parlour.

My father slammed the back door open, red in the face and panting.

"Ivy? Ivy! Which one, Ivy? Which one?"

I stood in the kitchen doorway, my back straight, my feet firmly on the floor, my arms by my sides. "Tom, Dad."

A dreadful wail ripped from my father's throat and his legs buckled under him. He went down on the kitchen floor in a heap, great, heaving sobs wrenching out of his chest. I stepped over him and set out another cup, reboiled the kettle and made more tea. The front door knocker sounded so I opened it to let Father Moran in, ushered him into the parlour and offered him refreshments. My mother came downstairs, pale faced, in a black dress I hadn't seen since Nanna Kate's funeral, fingers white as she clutched her rosary.

I went back upstairs to the bedroom, picked up the death notification from the bed and carried it round to Charlotte's house. Her mother was clearly going to shout at me before she noticed what I was carrying and then her hand went to her mouth and she let me in. Charlotte, at the back with her hands in the tub didn't see me coming. I stood behind her, shoulders back, chin high, steady and still until her mother said, "Charlotte."

I gave her the letter. She read it. She reached for me, thrust out both her arms and reached out to me for support, distress mangling her pretty face, her mouth shaping a soundless, half formed "O". Head back, shoulders straight, my heels clicked across the flagstone floor as I walked away.

I passed Alfie on my way back into the kitchen, still sweeping the yard. "Do you remember what I told you earlier, Alfie? About Tom being dead?"

Alfie said nothing, but carried on sweeping. My father was no longer in the kitchen and the front door was thundering with a demand to open. Most of my mother's Bible reading group came through when I unlatched it and seated themselves in the parlour so I made more tea, and served the last of the Christmas cake. The front door called me again, and this time Mrs Norton was standing there with a loaf of bread. I took it, nodding my thanks. She didn't bother trying to say anything and neither did I, we both knew how futile that conversation was. I spread the bread with butter and left it out for Alfie's lunch with some cheese and an apple. Then I took some money from the housekeeping pot on the shelf and went to buy eggs and flour, because there was no more cake in the house.

Mrs Carmichael joined me in the queue. "Ivy? I saw the postmen at the door, Ivy. Is it Tom or Philip? I'm so sorry, Ivy. It's not both of them is it? Ivy? Are you alright Ivy? You look strange."

"It's Tom, Mrs Carmichael."

She left me alone then, standing in a line with my basket and my shillings.

When I was younger I never understood my brother Philip. He was second eldest, after Alfie, but he treated the rest of us like we were his own personal household staff, forever issuing demands and shouting orders. That time in the forest it was Philip who had run off first, telling the rest of us not to follow him. Alfie did, because he'd follow anything that moved, and Tom and I – so alike in age, looks and temperament, chased after Philip because we knew it would annoy him. We spent a lot of time at our Nanna's in Kent when we were children, just running through the woods. After Nanna Kate died we never went there again.

I shopped, I paid, I walked calmly home, one foot following the other in a pattern it took some concentration to achieve. Alfie was still in the kitchen when I got home. He'd finished his lunch so I put his plate in the sink, cleared the tea things from the parlour, which was now empty, and then washed up, dried and stacked everything away.

Alfie sat at the table the entire time. I went over and patted his shoulder. "Tom is dead, Alfie. Did you hear?"

Alfie said nothing, but after another hour he left the kitchen and went out of the back gate still without saying a word. I made two cakes and started on dinner – boiled potatoes, cabbage and corned beef (there was no actual corn in it, or beef). Then my mother and Father Moran came home and there was another round of drinks to be served. I stood straight, I was polite, I did my duty. I laid the table, set out dinner and sat there by myself while nobody came back to eat.

My father stumbled in around seven, reeking of alcohol, wolfed down his congealed dinner without comment, went into the back room and fell asleep. I started on more pastry.

Alfie got lost first, of course, even though he was following Phil and it made Phil even more angry that he had to stop running away from all of us and try to find his brother instead. Alfie couldn't help being the centre of attention, he was too different to be anything else, but Philip spent much of his time like a child in a classroom with his hand in the air, desperately hoping to be noticed. Then Alfie jumped out of a tree and landed on Philip's head and I honestly don't think I've ever laughed so hard in my life, before or since. That was the last time I could remember all four of us together, happy. It was the last time I could remember feeling truly safe.

The back gate banged open, I hadn't got round to asking Dad to mend it, and then Will Rawlings let himself into our kitchen, with Alfie in tow.

Alfie's face was bleeding, one eye shut in an enormous bruise, a front tooth missing, cuts all along his jaw.

Will said, "Help me with him Ivy, someone's beaten him up. That's it Alfie, just sit down there. Fetch something to wash his face with, Ivy. I found him in the caretaker's cupboard in school. I saw a light on and I went back in to check. He won't tell me who did it and I don't know how long he's been there."

I fetched a clean tea towel, rinsed it under the tap and then dabbed at Alfie's face, cleaning away the blood and grime.

I said, "Tom is dead Alfie. You do know that don't you? Tom is never coming back. Never."

"Ivy!" Will sounded horrified. "Leave it, I'll do it."

The tea towel was yanked out of my hands. I went back to kneading dough. "That's better Alfie. All done. All clean. I think you should have a bit of a lie down now though. It's been a busy day hasn't it? Can you show me your room, Alfie? I only came round to see it. Would you show it to me? No, leave your sister, I don't think she's feeling very well. Let's get you upstairs for a bit of a rest shall we? Alright then."

Philip and Alfie never got on. I think Philip resented him, I remember Phil would never stand with me and Tom in the playground, defending Alfie against the bullies like David Andrews and his friends. Phil always tried to pretend he wasn't actually related to the rest of us when we were in public, and in private for that matter. The only person Philip ever seemed to care about was my mother, and the feeling was entirely mutual.

I cut out pastry circles, destroyed them, re-rolled the dough, and did it again. I stood straight, I stood tall, I rolled and cut, rolled and cut.

Will's hands on my shoulders span me round. "Ivy, are you alright? Ivy? Ivy. Can you even hear me?"

I stared at him but I didn't really see him. I saw the forest, and I remembered how cross Mother was with Alfie when she noticed the bruise on Philip's head. Tom said he'd accidentally hit Philip with a stick but Mother always believed Philip above any of the rest of us and Alfie was punished anyway.

"Go and sit at the table, Ivy. Do you remember eating anything today? Or having anything to drink? Ivy?"

He pulled out a chair, and I sat at the table, because it was expected of me, and that was all I had left.

"Alright. Good. Where do you keep the tea? Somewhere over here maybe? Yes, in the tin, and then cups. That's a lot of cups. Why does anyone need so many cups? And the kettle is on the range of course, and there's the strainer, and then sugar. There's honey in the sugar bowl. I'm not putting honey in tea, that's just wrong. So tea and bread. Not long now. Just missing a plate."

A plate and a cup appeared next to my right hand.

"Eat, Ivy. Drink the tea. It's hot and well, hot. That's what you have for shock. Hot sweet tea and lots of blankets, as I recall."

I ate and drank because he told me to.

"This is the shawl you wear to work isn't it? I wonder why you have it on in the house. You take it off in the classroom. Let's take it off. And then boots off too, I think. We won't be needing those."

He knelt at my feet and unlaced my shoes, setting them neatly beside the kitchen door. "Are you finished? Right, off we go to bed then. And be quiet. Your dad's asleep and I think your mother's praying, and while I'm big enough and old enough not to care what they think, I really can't be bothered with a long explanation."

He took my hand and guided me silently though the house, sneaked upstairs into my bedroom and barricaded the door with a chair under the handle, leaving the lights out and the blackout curtains open. Then he pushed both beds together against the wall and stripped the room of spare sheets and blankets, piling them all into the middle of the mattress.

"Now we need some kind of nightdress, nightgown, something like this maybe. This will do." He passed me something of Tom's he'd found in one of the cabinets. "Put that on Ivy, and don't worry. I can't see a damn thing."

I could hear the thud as he took his boots off, the rustle of his clothing. I stripped down to my vest, put on the nightshirt and climbed into bed. Starlight crept timidly through the windows, danced a square pattern across the floor. Will slid into the cold bed next to me, put his arm around me, and rolled me over so I was lying with my cheek on his chest, curled tight into his side. His fingers sought my other hand.

"Let it out, Ivy," he said.

There was a thing inside me, a great murderous monster in my heart that had been straining to get out all day and was only held back by the straightest of straight backs, by shoulders that were set and locked and by dry eyes and duty.

"Let it out, Ivy," he said again, squeezing my hand tight. "Cry, yell, hit me if you want to. I don't know who the hell is supposed to be looking after you but they're doing an appalling job. Your brother died today. You need to let it out."

The first tear stung my eye, hot and harsh and what one had started, another continued, until I was crying freely, soaking his shirt while he held my hand and whispered my name. I cried until my stomach clenched and my eyes were too sore to bleed any more tears. I know it was hours before I slept.

I was woken in the night by an elbow to the stomach and a sharp stab of pain. My eyes were raw, my throat still hoarse from sobbing and Will had thrown me off, along with all the blankets and was thrashing about in the middle of Philip's bed, his hands clenched into fists, and all the muscles in his shoulders standing out as he strained against something I couldn't see. From between his teeth he grated, "No, no, not in there." Then his fists came up and he flailed around, accidentally catching me in the side.

I reacted without thinking, throwing my leg over both of his, clambering on top of him, clutching his hands and pinning his arms to his chest with my body weight. I used the same tone of voice I had practised on Alfie. "Will, don't look at the cottage. Don't go near it. Can you see the field to the left of the cottage Will? Look at the field to the left. It's a big field, Will, its August and the field is full of long grass and the bees are buzzing around the flowers. Walk into the field, Will. We need to map it. Can you map the field Will? How big is it? Walk it with me and count. Are you ready? Count the paces and map it out. Are you ready? One, two, three. Off we go - count and walk."

Almost immediately his body relaxed undermine, the tension ebbed away and his breathing deepened as I slumped against his side.

I woke to the thrum of rain against the windows and January's grey, disappointing dawn. Will was still sleeping, his breathing rumbling deep in his chest, my arm around his body, my head on his shoulder. I felt safe, under the covers, warm and secure and protected although I remembered little of yesterday, and had no idea what horrors the day would bring. I knew I was never going to see my brother again. He was out there somewhere in the rain and the wind, and he wouldn't ever be coming back. As soon as I got up I was going to have to face that.

I burrowed more closely against Will and he awoke with a start. "Ivy? Ivy, you're crying again. Did I hurt you? What did I do?"

I hugged him. "There isn't anything you could do to hurt me. I hurt enough already."

He raised himself enough to look down at me, "I wasn't out last night. I must have had nightmares. If I hurt you, I want to know."

I sighed, closed my eyes and tried to go back to sleep. "You had a bad dream. I talked you through it. There was hand holding. You'd have enjoyed it."

He was silent for a while and then he found the hand I had splayed across his chest, brought it to his lips and kissed the back of it.

"I never want to get up," I said.

"I've had whole days where I felt like that." His hand strayed over my waist to my hips and urged me closer with a gentle pressure.

"Did you ever just stay in bed?"

"At first. And I stayed in my room a lot even when I wasn't in bed. Eventually I realised it was better to get up, get dressed, go to work, come home. Put one foot in front of the other. You just have to carry on."

"So this... how I feel now. This will get easier?"

"I didn't say it would get easier. I think you get used to it after a while. There are some days, just recently, when I actually want to get out of bed in the morning."

"Do you want to get out of bed now?" I glanced upwards to see him rolling his eyes at me.

His hand stroked up and over my waist again. "Stupid question."

"Good. I want five more minutes."

"Have you seen what Alfie is building in his bedroom? It's incredible."

"It's just a lot of sticks. Will, do you really think I'm going to be an only child?"

"I regret ever telling you that. I should have kept my mouth shut. It was thoughtless and selfish and I'm sorry."

"Yes, yes, but were you right?"

"I hope not. I shouldn't think too much about it. It's a distraction. I'm a distraction. What matters is you and Alfie and your parents coming to terms with what's happened. I need to go."

I clutched at him. "No, you said you didn't want to get up."

"I don't want to, I have to. I'm due at school in two hours and I should probably change."

He pulled away from me, sat up on the edge of the bed, still fully dressed in the clothes he was wearing yesterday, which were now rumpled and tear-stained.

"I can't do this on my own," I cried, feeling that warmth and protection draining away and the cold dark flooding back in.

He looked down at me, the intensity of his gaze searing. "That's the only way you can do it. But if you need me, just hold out this hand," he reached under the covers and extracted my right hand, uncurling the palm and touching his lips to the centre of it. "And I'll be there."

I folded back in on myself, hugging my chest to keep back the tears while he picked up his boots and jacket and shifted the chair wedging the door. "On a slightly more practical note, I'll also be on the corner of South Street every night at eight o'clock in case you need to talk."

I didn't speak to him again for three weeks.

Chapter Ten

I got up. I went to work, I came home again. I lived. I existed. Alfie wouldn't go anywhere without me, although he wouldn't tell me who had hurt him.

That first Friday, I still expected to receive a letter from Tom in the post and I must have checked the doormat thirty times, although by the following week it was down to fifteen.

In the evenings we sat down to family meals where I couldn't even remember what I'd made, and the silence of the empty chairs was an undertone to every attempt at conversation. Alfie and I went for long walks in the forest on Saturdays and his collection of sticks grew to prodigious proportions. I stayed in bed on Sundays – I had no words for Charlotte. I didn't meet Will, I had nothing I wanted to say to him either.

And then in early February another letter arrived, this time from the chaplain of the Poplar and Stepney Rifles, a letter of such stunning stupidity that it quite took my breath away.

My dear Miss Drummond,

Firstly, let me extend my sincere apologies for intruding on your grief, so soon after the loss of your dear brother, I realise what a difficult time this must be for you and your family.

Secondly, I realise that receiving a letter from your brother's chaplain may be distressing for you – not least because Thomas did acquaint me with the somewhat fractious relationship you have with the Lord – have no fear, you will read nothing in this letter which assails your conscience in any way. I merely wish to furnish you with some additional details surrounding the circumstances of your brother's death, which may provide you with some comfort in your tragic loss.

I should explain that I came to know Thomas early on during his short period with the Rifles. He was a most assiduous young man, and questioned me frequently as part of his diligent search for his brother. I believe he questioned most of the battalion in the same fashion and I'm sure his comrades have equally fond memories of this bright eyed young man, and his kind and engaging manner.

I have this account on good authority from one of my colleagues who was present on the occasion of your brother's demise, and whose hand it was that collected the letters in your brother's possession for delivery back to you. I trust those letters arrived safely, your brother carried them to the last.

On the third of January Thomas had volunteered to take a message further down the line and it was in the course of this activity that he became involved in an advance already underway. You will be aware that Thomas had not experienced many active engagements, due to the stage of the battle at which he joined, and it is my belief that his youthful enthusiasm and courage prompted him to take risks which more seasoned soldiers might not have considered.

A number of our troops had gone over the top and were advancing against a German position when one became injured, trapped in the wire between the lines. It is my understanding that this poor, wounded soldier was calling out for help, and your brother Thomas, motivated by these cries, voluntarily scaled the ladders and went out to assist his endangered comrade.

In the course of this rescue mission your brother was shot, and he expired only shortly after reaching the man he had gone out to save. Sadly, that soldier was also lost, but I have ensured that both men have been laid to rest together, in the sight of the Lord. Your brother died in an act of valour and heroism which does him credit.

I trust this knowledge may go some way to temper your loss.

I remain, your obedient servant.

Oliver Groat.

I read the letter and I was angry. Not so much angry at the wordy chaplain, who thought he was doing the right thing, but at my dead brother Tom who had also been trying to do the right thing and was consequently dead because of it. I couldn't understand why he'd risk his life for a complete stranger, when he had Charlotte and a baby to think of at home, when the most important thing he had to do was stay alive.

Before the war, Tom had always been brave, in the sense that he wasn't afraid of public speaking, or he'd hit a man who insulted his brother, but it was civilian brave. I never thought he was the sort who'd sacrifice himself in a grand gesture. I didn't have the luxury of grand gestures, it would take enough courage just to get up in the morning and struggle through the next fifty years. And I didn't have to do it with a fatherless baby.

I folded the letter into my pocket where it smouldered on my conscience until Sunday when I went to see Charlotte. There was no answer at the front door so I went in through the back. Charlotte was in the kitchen looking as wretched as I'd ever seen her. Her hair was greasy and tangled, her face dirty, all her clothes were grey and stained and she registered my arrival with barely a flicker of recognition.

"Breaking your heart are you?" I put a hand on her shoulder. "Is it doing any good?" She hung her head. "No, I didn't think so. Come on then."

She didn't protest when I led her back to South Street. I heated the water for a bath, sat with her while she washed, lent her new clothes and washed the old ones and then force fed her everything I could find in the pantry. In the bath she resembled a child's drawing, all big round body and sticks for arms and legs. After a while the colour returned to her face though and she began to talk.

"The Marchmount Square lady came round, Ivy. My mother sent for her. She said she could get rid of the baby but I wouldn't let her. I screamed and screamed until she went away. I can stay as long as I can work, my mother said, after that I'm on my own."

"I like your mother nearly as much as I like mine," I told her. "But she is wrong in one tremendous respect. You are not on your own."

"Tom is dead. How am I not?"

Tears began leaking from the corners of her eyes again. I folded her hand into mine. "Because I am here. And soon your baby will be here too, to love, and hold, and care for, and we can bring him up to know who his father was. Both of us. Think how many thousands and thousands of young men have been killed in the war. You won't be the only one left with a baby. Think how many thousands of young women won't ever get married now either. I'm probably one of them, like you said. I can help you. We can get through this together - without our mothers."

She squeezed my hand back, smiled wanly. "Thank you, Ivy. But I think it's a girl."

"Then she can be called Ivy, after her spinster maiden aunt. I think it's the least you can do."

"She can be called Thomasina, after her father."

"You'd curse a daughter of yours with 'Thomasina' for a name?

You're even more like your mother than I thought."

She smiled a bit more brightly. "So where will we live Ivy, and what will we do for money?"

"I haven't worked out all the details yet, but we've got a while. The most important thing is that you start looking after yourself. Go home, and eat as much as you can, sleep as much as you can, don't scrub the sheets as well as you did, what's your mother going to do - throw you out? She's doing that already. Just get through the next few months until I can sort the rest of it out. Everything will be fine, I promise."

I walked her home and thought about courage. Charlotte had found some, and I was angry enough at Tom to discover my own, so I went to church.

The service had already finished by the time I arrived at the lych-gate. I left it long enough to be sure my mother had actually left this time before I cracked the heavy oak door and slipped inside. I tracked the priest to his cosy vestry, where he was busily employed in the service of our Lord by drinking a glass of wine by the fire. He set it aside when I knocked once and came in without waiting for a reply, but he didn't get up. I imagine he'd been waiting for this conversation for quite some time.

"Father Moran," I began, not entirely sure how to approach the subject when it came to it. "I want to talk to you about my mother."

He watched me carefully. "Go on."

"I'm aware you have a certain... influence over her."

"Only as her spiritual counsellor and guide Ivy, your mother makes her own decisions."

I struggled with a desire to shout at him, but long years of conditioning had crept over me like moss on stone and I couldn't raise my voice to a priest in his own church, however much I wanted to. "You are more to her than that, Father. I know it as well as you do."

"She makes her own decisions," he repeated. "Did you really come here to ask me about your mother, Ivy? After all this time? Is there nothing else you want to ask?"

"I want you to make my mother do something for me. She won't listen to me, but you're her... I know what you are. You can ask her to do anything you like and she'll do it."

"I doubt I have quite that much influence. I can think of a number of occasions where she hasn't done as I've asked. What is it you'd like her to do?"

"My brother Tom has fathered a child. He wasn't married to its mother, but it is his baby, my mother's grandchild. I want you to get my mother to take it in."

"And if I refuse? I assume you are planning to start threatening me?"

"Do I need to? You know what'll happen if you don't do it."

He picked up his glass again and swirled the scarlet liquid inside. "Ah, Ivy. Eighteen years old and still such a child. Your mother is quite worried about you, you know. She talks about you so much I find it's become quite – what's the best word – boring."

"Will you speak to her or not?" I snapped, quite sure that my mother had never once mentioned my name to this man.

"I know all about you, Ivy Drummond. I know about everyone. I saw the illicit liaisons enjoyed by Charlotte Ransome and your brother Tom among the gravestones outside when they thought the church was closed and no one was watching. I've been watching your brothers for some time. I know that Alfie is violent, and it's only a matter of time before he hurts someone properly and gets put away. There's nothing that I, or anyone else can do about that. I know about your brother Philip, the first to enlist, the bravest of the three. I know your father is an alcoholic and I've been told about you, wandering around alone in the dark, drinking in pubs with unsavoury men. There is nothing about you that I don't know Ivy, and the only thing that surprises me, the only thing – is that you waited six years to come and talk to me about your mother. I thought at least we might have an honest conversation, after all this time. But I see you prefer childish threats."

"I will tell my father."

"I'm sure he already knows."

"I'll tell everyone else then."

He took a delicate sip from his glass, leant his head back against the seat and closed his eyes. "No one will listen to you. I might have helped your brother Tom, had he asked, but I shan't help you. Don't approach me about your mother again."

I went home hating God, and hating my mother even more. I tried to give her some indication of this over the dinner table, but she simply complained about the food and bullied Alfie, as usual. At eight o'clock I left my family behind and went in search of someone who would listen to me.

Will was leaning against the wall at the corner of South Street, but he kicked off it, with an exclamation of "Finally," as he caught sight of me.

"Have you really been here every night?"

He shrugged and offered me the crook of his elbow to slip my hand through. "The people in the house opposite keep watching me through the curtains. They think I'm a German spy or something. So how are you?"

I struggled to keep up with his loping strides as he tugged me off down the road. "I've been better. I've also been worse."

"You've lost weight. And you're too pale. Are you sleeping?"

"I could ask you the same question."

"I asked first."

"A little. I wanted to say thank you for coming round that night. It helped. I'd have told you at the time but you were too busy running away so my dad didn't catch you in my bedroom."

"It wasn't your father I was running away from, Ivy – it was the really bad breath, and the terrible hair you have in the mornings, and the deafening snoring, and the fact that you dribbled on me in your sleep."

"I don't have bad breath, do I?"

"Was that what you came to talk to me about?"

"No. I wanted to talk about my friend with the baby."

"Ah. I understand. You're not going to ask me about her future are you?"

"No. Not unless you're offering to tell me."

"I've never met her; I can't tell you anything that you don't already know. Do you want me to give her a job then? Or recommend a good hospital? Or marry her myself and raise the child as my own?"

I pulled my hand out of his elbow and stepped away from his side. "None of those things. I wasn't going to ask you to do anything. I just wanted to talk to someone, as a friend."

"Good. Only, you usually need a reason, however spurious, for coming to see me. I was just checking we'd got beyond that. I can do friends."

I eyed him suspiciously. "We'll see. Why are we going to school?"

He was busy unlocking the back gate, fiddling with an extensive array of keys in the pitch dark. "It's closer than my house, and frankly, I'm sick of standing around in the cold." He stuck out his hand for me to take. "Watch your step."

"Yes, thank you. I do work here. I'm sure I know where I'm going."

But I took his hand anyway and let him lead me up the steps and through the adult entrance.

Inside, moonlight walked the corridors, slanting in through the tall windows in sheets of pale radiance, but the contrast with the usually bustling thoroughfares was eerie, and I clung a little closer. "Are we going to the staffroom?" I whispered, although there was no one else around to hear.

"I'm not staff."

I trailed him up the stairs to the first floor. "Alfie's cupboard then, it's bigger than your office?"

"That's not my office, it's just where I keep my desk. This is my office."

He inserted a key into a doorway I'd never paid much attention to, a wooden entrance immediately before the glass door with "headmaster" etched across it. He hurried me inside and then turned the key behind us. A fire was already lit in the stove in the opposite corner, but the room was so large I could barely see half of it. Will fumbled with candles and gas lamps and slowly shadows hardened, reformed, coalesced into furniture.

Two large windows were cut into the back wall, covered with long fingers of blackout blinds, shuddering and shaking as a draft touched them. There were bookshelves ranged against the walls and I toured them, straining my eyes in the gloom. One held a selection of board games, decks of cards, spare dice; one held art materials, paints and rolled up paper, another contained jars of sweets, mostly empty, mugs, cups and glasses. One even had some books. In front of the fire were two large, squashy sofas, heaped in blankets and cushions and surrounded by side tables rammed with assorted knickknacks, a globe, an old hurricane lamp, a few fossils. In front of them a large, metal trunk acted as a table for stray cups, coasters, broken toys. One wall was almost completely covered with a map of the world, blessedly free of pins. The whole room smelled of old leather, dust and wood smoke and Will stood in the middle of it, watching me almost shyly as I explored.

"This is your office?" I asked after a while.

"My study. I bring my classes here as well."

"Remind me to ask you about your classes. But first you can tell me if that's a door over there. It is, isn't it? That's a door that leads into your proper office on the other side where I sit every night after work and sort out your post." I gave him a hard look. "You're not in here, by any chance are you? While I'm in there working?"

He opened a cupboard. "Would you like a drink? There's brandy, whiskey, sherry too, I think and probably port somewhere in the back."

"Will?"

He sighed, poured something into a square, heavy glass and handed it to me. "Yes, I'm in here. Maybe on Monday we can have that door open for a change. Although it's quite endearing listening to you talking to yourself. Particularly when you're trying to decide what note to leave me."

I sniffed whatever alcohol it was, set it down on the coffee table and chose a seat on the settee closest to the fire, piling up the blankets and covers into a comfortable nest around me. There was a brief pause, a hesitation, and then Will sat on the chair opposite, where the shadows promptly swallowed half his face and left the other bathed in soft orange. I started, "Do you think anyone listens to me, Will?"

"I do."

"You don't count. I don't think you ever speak to anyone else. Do you think anyone out there listens to me?"

"That depends on what you have to say."

"Which is a polite way of saying no. That's fine. You're probably right. My friend Charlotte is having a baby – my niece or nephew – and I've promised to help her raise it, because Tom isn't here, and I'm probably never having children of my own."

"Do you want children of your own?"

"I do. But I don't think I'll ever get married so it's not very likely."

He sipped his drink, swallowed. "Is that a statement you're expecting me to challenge? As a friend?"

I picked up my own drink, which was brandy, I think, finished it and made a face. "I'm not expecting you to have a view on my marriage one way or the other. The point is that I've promised her I'll look after her and I don't know where to start. I can't get my mother to even acknowledge the baby exists."

"I don't see where your mother comes in, strictly speaking. You're an adult. You're working. If you aren't waiting to get married why not leave home and set up on your own? Then you could look after as many babies as you like."

"Not on your nominal sum I couldn't."

"You're good with numbers. On Monday you can work out if I can afford to pay you what you're worth."

"I can't leave home. Ever."

There was a silence. The fire popped. Will drained his glass. "This is the part where you tell me whatever it is you so clearly wanted to talk to me about this evening. Not that you need a reason for coming to see me, obviously. Or have anything specific you want to discuss with a friend."

"Can I have another drink please?"

He retrieved the bottle, handed me a refilled glass and then sat at the other end of the couch I was on, becoming so much at one with the darkness that I only caught occasional flashes of his profile when the fire flared or the candles guttered.

"When I was twelve," I began, stopped, drank some more, started again. "When I was twelve I still went to church. My mother and I, every Sunday, dressed in our best. I'd go to Sunday school, sing in the choir, pray, believe in God, all of that. No, no. I can pour it myself, you just sit there and don't say anything. You're right, it really is a lot easier to talk when I can't see your face. So I'm twelve and I'm innocent. You've teased me about that before, but back then, I really was. I was in the churchyard after the service one day and everyone else had gone home, but my mother had to stay behind and arrange some flowers or something, she said, so she was still inside with the priest, Father Moran. There are big yew trees in the graveyard, and I was climbing one and I fell, and hurt my arm, so I went inside to find my mother so she could make it better. But I was too quiet. I should have been crying. I found her in the vestry and I swear, I didn't understand what was going on, so I watched for such a long time. My mother was... She was..."

It was stupid really, I couldn't get the words to come out properly and my hand shook as I raised my glass for another slug of courage.

"My mother was on her hands and knees on the carpet. Her skirts were tossed over her head. Father Moran was kneeling behind her. His trousers were down and he was doing something to her that I didn't really understand except that she was making these noises and I could tell he wasn't hurting her, so I just watched. And he looked at me, looking at him through the crack in the door, and he smiled, and he carried on pushing himself into my mother until he shouted out and she fell over and I went and waited outside the church for her to come out."

My left hand was clenched around the glass, but my right took matters into its own hand(s) and fumbled along the settee. Will moved in one smooth motion, seizing my groping fingers and stationing himself under the blankets next to me.

"It's funny. I know. Stupid Ivy, she's so naïve. But your mother is supposed to tell you about things like that. Sex and things. It's different for boys I expect. My mother and I never had that conversation. She showed me instead. So I waited for her outside the church and when she came out I told her I'd seen her naked with the priest and I called her a filthy whore and said I was going to tell my father."

I concentrated on trying to scar Will's palm with my fingernails, while the memory burned into me.

"She hit me. Slapped me round the face as hard as she could and she said I had no idea what I was talking about. That I had no idea what sort of pressure she was under having to look after Alfie all the time, as well as the other boys, while Dad wasted all his time in the pub. She said if I told my dad then she'd have to leave us all, and she'd be glad to go because then she wouldn't have to cope with Alfie any more. She hated her life, you see. She wanted a way out. And I was naïve, like I said. I was also only twelve. And I didn't really want her to go, I just wanted her to stop sleeping with the priest. So I offered to look after Alfie for her. I said I'd care for him and do the cooking and the cleaning and the housework as long as she didn't leave us and as long as she didn't see Father Moran. I actually thought that would be better than being without my mother, at the time. Stupid Ivy, right? I was only twelve. The next day I took over.

You asked me once why I look after Alfie. The answer is because no one else will. I can't leave him. My mother doesn't love him, she does the bare minimum for him that she can get away with. I never told my dad about her, I've shielded her secret all these years and I've kept everything going so we can all pretend to be one big happy family. I can't ever leave home, because there's no one to protect Alfie. But that means I can't help Charlotte either, and with Tom dead then what's the point in me trying to hold it all together anyway? If I'm going to be an only child I may as well go home right now and tell Dad his wife is probably still a filthy whore and that nothing I've done for the past six years has been worth a damn thing."

I slammed the glass down hard enough to crack it.

"I have a question," said Will, in a voice so neutral I could tell how much effort he was putting into it. "And it's a good one, so listen carefully. Do you help?"

"Excuse me?" I glared at him, but his eyes were soft with dancing firelight and the glare didn't take.

"Do you think that looking after Alfie for the last six years has helped him?"

"Obviously. Better than no one doing it."

"And what about looking after your father, running the house, has that helped?"

"Only my mother."

"What about what you're trying to do for your friend and her baby—that's helping isn't it? And you've even been trying to help me, although I don't deserve it."

"Your point being?"

"I've never seen anyone try to do so much for other people and expect so little in return. What happened with your mother sounds awful. I've no idea if you should tell your father or not, really I haven't, and I don't have any suggestions on the baby problem either, but I do know that whatever you decide to do, you'll do it for the right reasons. It will help. You'll help. That's who you are."

I had been stared at many times in my life, but the quality of this stare, the way that all the ice it had once held had melted into a liquid fire required a response. I put my hand up quickly, without thought, and ran the pad of one finger over the line of scar tissue that whipped across his skin. It was smooth and cool to the touch, and it led over his cheekbone above his ear into his hair, until my palm was cupping his face. His whole body stilled under my hand. He didn't blink. I wasn't sure he was still breathing.

"How did this happen?" I asked, sounding the depths of his eyes.

"Flying glass. A window broke. I was on the wrong side."

I felt the bunch and release of the muscles in his jaw as he formed the words, a light susurration against my palm. "Did it hurt?"

"Yes."

"Does it still?"

"No," he said, and his voice was ever so slightly too loud in that quiet, tender moment. "Ivy, would you consider doing that again when you haven't drunk three brandies in half an hour?" Every line of his body was straining towards me, but his voice was steady and calm, and entirely under control. It was something of a mixed message.

"Don't you want me to touch you?" I asked.

He exhaled loudly, half a sigh and half a groan and he pulled my hand off his cheek roughly. "You could win awards with that question. Well done. Now sit there, keep your fingers to yourself and let's talk about something else." He let me go and shifted around under the blankets until a little distance had opened between us.

I curled my legs up onto the settee, rested my chin on my fist and addressed his folded arms, crossed legs and stubborn chin. "What happened to you during the war?"

"No."

"Why did your wife leave you?"

"No. Try again."

"What else do you see when you look at me? What's the thing you can't tell me only show me?"

"I see someone who's gone from precious to annoying in twenty seconds flat."

"Alright then. Why haven't there been any air raids since November? In your professional opinion as oracle, fortune teller and reader of tea leaves."

"Thanks. The raids haven't stopped. Maybe that plane was the start of something new and it's taking time to get it ready. I'm still seeing the fires, although following the advice of my amateur psychoanalyst, I'm trying not to look so hard at a certain type of house."

"Does that work?"

"Seems to. I think it helps to know what triggers the memories. At least if I'm aware of what I'm doing I can start to control it."

"Do you think there'll be another air raid soon then?"

"I don't know. They're coming. And I met a man in Mr Murphy's shop the other day, a Canadian, who had a rosy future involving a barracks, a bomb and the seaside. Sometime soon."

"Did you warn him? No – no. Sorry, no need to look like that. Far be it from me to ask you any questions that make you feel awkward. Although I can think of one or two I'd like to know the answers to. Why don't I go through them and you can stop me if I accidentally land on a conversation you might want to engage in?"

"You can ask me anything you like, Ivy."

"I can ask. You never answer. Here goes then – stop me at any time.

Do you believe in God? Were you close to your mother? What's wrong with poetry anyway? Where is Hertfordshire? Is geography the most boring subject known to man – ooh look a glacier just moved or bit or ooh, if we stand here for a couple of million years that tectonic plate might wobble. How do you afford so much sugar? When was the last time you washed these blankets, they smell of lavender and mothballs? Where can I get Marigold extra tuition, she's reading books for a twelve-year-old at the age of six? When did you forget how to laugh?"

He relaxed against the settee, put his feet on the battered metal trunk and his hands behind his head and favoured me with a small smile. "There are many fascinating facts you need to know when embarking on a study in the field of geography. Let me elucidate some of them."

"Oh dear God," I prayed. "I promise to start believing in you again if you make him answer a different question."

So we talked until the fire held no more than embers and I knew a lot more about tectonic plates than I had before. There were a few fascinating facts in there about Will too. He could still paralyse me just by looking in my direction for more than a couple of seconds, which was beginning to become embarrassing, but it was quite easy to distract him out of it, simply by edging slightly closer, or licking my lips or brushing his hand accidentally on purpose. A couple of times I caught myself watching his mouth, not because I was paying careful attention to what he was saying but because I was imagining kissing it.

Chapter Eleven

The next day I awoke early, despite a late night, and I got out of bed before it was strictly necessary, for the first time in weeks. There was a sense of anticipation about the morning that hadn't been there yesterday and it lingered into the afternoon, until the bell rang at precisely three o'clock and I unlocked the headmaster's office at five past.

A door to the left of the desk camouflaged by a bookcase now stood open and from inside a kettle was whistling and a spoon chinked loudly against porcelain. I took up my accustomed seat at the desk, noting the neat stack of paper in front of me, the freshly sharpened pencils, the fact that someone had reordered the piles of correspondence rather than simply throwing them into a heap. I felt lopsided, off balance. I was still dragging around the stone of Tom's loss inside me, but a couple of times today just remembering something Will had said, or the way he'd said it had made my lips twitch into a smile and my steps as light as air. I was simultaneously looking forward to seeing him, and overcome with shyness at the thought of it, which was a bizarre reaction to someone I'd already technically spent the night with.

A cup of tea appeared near my right hand. "Since when did we have coasters?" I squinted up, eyes narrowed, to find him leaning over my shoulder, immaculately presented in a crisp white shirt, brown worsted waistcoat and trousers and a red cravat tucked under his starched collar. At such close range there was still a hint of soap in the air when he moved.

"What does it say on that door?" he frowned.

"RETSAMDAEH?"

"Precisely. I own the coasters."

I sampled the tea. "That's as may be, but I'm sitting in the chair and there's not enough sugar in that. Take it away and try again."

He was back a few minutes later, reading over my shoulder as I wrote. "Ivy," he said, and his breath against my neck made me shiver. "You have a problem with commitment."

I didn't stop writing. "I've just never met the right person. I wouldn't consider it a problem."

He stabbed at the page. "It's two Ms and one T."

I continued scribbling. "You have more of a problem with commitment than I do, Will. That says commencement. Now run along, I'm working." I let him get through the door before I called. "How do you spell "pedantic" again?"

He came back after a few minutes though, this time flicking through a book and perching on the desk so that my hand inched closer and closer towards his left leg as I wrote. I tried to think of shorter sentences.

"Right. I'm up to page two of Paradise Lost and so far, it's overly complex, full of arcane language and quite dull."

He held the book open directly above where I was attempting to write so that I had to push it out of the way. "Now you know how I feel about geography."

"Come and explain it to me then. Or read it out loud. Or choose a different book." He yanked the pen from my hand. "You don't need to work now. Come and sit with me next door and let's do something else."

I pushed the chair back slightly and folded my arms in exasperation. "What is the matter with you today?"

He was bouncing around on the spot like a small child offered a present, enthusiasm radiating off him. "I think," he confided, leaning forward conspiratorially. "That I'm happy."

The boyish grin and the laughter dancing in this blue eyes soothed my nerves and I smiled back wholeheartedly. I pushed back the chair, stood, "Yes sir," I said.

"I love it when you call me that. Come on, I have an idea."

He tugged me into the study next door, positioned me carefully in the centre, and then pushed the collection of settees and side tables back against the walls, although the old metal trunk was too heavy to move and stayed where it was. Then he approached one of the bookcases and fiddled with something, until with two sharp smacks of his hand and a muttered curse "Alexander's Ragtime Band" came swinging out of the hidden gramophone.

"Do you know how to dance?" He put a hand on my waist and wrapped his other hand around my fingers. "It doesn't matter if you don't. Just hang on."

He whirled me round the room in some kind of ungainly waltz while

I clutched at his shoulders and tried to avoid stamping on his toes. But when the record wound down, his steps slowed and lengthened until the two of us were standing pressed together, swaying slightly.

I leaned against him, caught in the bright beam of his stare. "It's nearly time," he murmured. "Do you feel it?"

But there was something niggling at the outer edges of my consciousness, back in the place where I hadn't lost all reason, and it distracted me. "I feel," I said, trying to put my finger on the unease creeping down my spine. "I feel hot."

His brow creased, but he said, "That's alright. I also own windows."

There was a long stick propped in the corner of the room and it was the work of a few minutes for him to reach up and hook open the top panes to let in a bitter breeze, accompanied by an unusual, repetitive sound. At first, I thought it was just the crack of a wet sheet, or the slap of a wind caught skirt, but as I listened more carefully, I discerned the whistle that came before the solid, meaty whack, the odd, animal grunt that followed it.

I picked up my skirts. "I don't like that noise, Will. What's that noise?"

Premonition lent haste to my strides as I flew from the room, down one flight of stairs and out of the front door, following the whoosh and thwack round to the side alley, and the school's back gate.

Alfie stood over something dark, lying puddled in a heap on the ground. In his hands was the wrong end of a broom handle which he slowly extended behind him, and then brought down in a dreadful, smashing arc onto the thing lying on the cobbles in front of him. I ran towards him without pausing, encountering the back swing of the broom which cracked me on the side of the skull and brought the taste of fresh blood into my mouth.

"No, Alfie," I shouted, pushing past him to stand over the body on the ground. "Stop."

But Alfie didn't stop. I wasn't sure he even recognised me at all, and the broom, interrupted in its backwards journey now came hurtling down towards my head, picking up speed.

From behind Alfie, Will barked "Alfred Drummond. Stop now," in a tone of absolute command and with an unquestioned authority I'd never heard him use before.

Alfie stopped, his lips peeled back from his newly gapped teeth.

"Oh Alfie," I moaned, stooping to check the silent form spread at my feet. "What have you done?" It was David Andrews, as I fully expected it to be, still breathing, but broken and bleeding. "What did you do, Alfie? What did you do?"

I was aware of Will extricating the broom from Alfie's grasp and leading him further away. "Shall I fetch a doctor, Ivy?" He didn't look away from Alfie, putting himself squarely between my brother and me.

"Take him home, Will. Then go and find my dad, he'll be in the pub. And fetch Mr Andrews as well as the doctor. This is beyond anything I can mend."

"Come on then Alfie. Your sister says it's time for tea. Shall we go home and see what there is to eat?"

Will led Alfie away and I tried to make David more comfortable, or at least, I tried to stop him choking to death on his own blood, since comfort was out of the question. This was my fault. All my fault because I had been concentrating far too hard on myself over the last month or so, and hadn't been thinking enough about Alfie. I hadn't pursued the broken tooth, and the beating someone had given him on the night of Tom's death. I hadn't questioned who had made Alfie so afraid that he'd had to follow me round for weeks. I'd been thinking about Tom, but more about Will, and Alfie hadn't come into the equation at all. I didn't need to be able to see the future to understand what had happened.

Somehow, David had caught Alfie unawares on that dreadful day in January, and had attacked him in retaliation for the bloody nose he'd received a couple of months before. Today, Alfie, afraid, unable to understand his own strength or grasp anything but the most rudimentary consequences, had defended himself long after the fact with a broom handle and nineteen stone of muscle. And I'd been dancing while he did it.

My dad arrived at a run, jacket askew, reeking of strong liquor. He saw David, and stopped short, raking a hand through his hair. "Alfie did that? Christ, what can we do? What can we do?"

"I don't know, Dad. There's a doctor coming. We can stand by Alfie; I don't think anyone else will now."

Mr Andrews barrelled into the alley, shoving my dad back against the wall and bending down to shake his son. "David? David? Can you hear me lad? David? Drummond, your boy is going to pay for this. Alfie is going to pay for what he's done this time. I'll have him for this. David? Can you open your eyes, son? It's your dad. David?"

Two men and a stretcher rounded the corner of the alley and Dad and I took the opportunity to slip away, our presence no longer necessary or welcome.

We walked home step by slow step, stunned into fragmentary conversation. "Is that prison then, do you think, Dad?"

"Ah God Ivy, how do I break it to him? He won't understand."

"I'll tell Alfie, Dad. This is my fault. I think David was the one who hit Alfie on the night that we heard about Tom, but I didn't do anything about it."

"I wish you'd told me, Ivy. I wish I'd known."

"Alfie's been missing a tooth since January Dad, you could have asked."

"You could have told me."

We walked a few steps further and I made a decision. "I need to tell you something else then, Dad. Do you remember my friend Charlotte? The pretty one with the blonde hair? She used to come round a lot. She and Tom were close. More than that actually, Tom wanted to marry her but decided to get himself killed instead. They were so close that she's having his baby. She's nearly five months gone and she's about to get thrown out of home because her mother's a horrible, evil, twisted old hag. Can Charlotte come and live with us?"

"What does your mother say?"

"My mother resembles Charlotte's mother in many respects. She won't hear a word about it. I even asked Father Moran if he could have a word with her since they're so close but he wouldn't."

"Father Moran is no friend to our family, Ivy. Don't involve him. I'll speak to your mother."

He didn't though, because when we got home she was in the kitchen shouting at Alfie and there wasn't enough oxygen left for the rest of us to get a word in.

"Alfie Drummond, you'll be the death of me. I didn't spend all these years looking after you, working my fingers to the bone for you to go attacking people in the streets. They'll put you in prison, Alfie. They'll lock you up and throw away the key. And as for you Ivy, what were you doing when Alfie was out fighting? Why weren't you looking after him? I said this job was a bad idea. You should be at home, both of you, where you belong."

Dad slumped into a chair, I leant on another for support. "It was

David Andrews Alfie hit, Mother. He probably deserved it, some of it, but he was quite badly hurt. Alfie hit him with a broom handle."

Although he was looking at the floor, Alfie smiled that innocent, gap toothed grin which, by the sheer power of enamel and dentine, managed to prove my guilt.

"It was David that did that to you Alfie, wasn't it? I'm sure it was. But you weren't supposed to hit him back, Alfie. Never hit them back."

"This is down to you, Ivy. Are you happy? Are you proud? Your brother is going to prison."

"Hilda," my father snapped. "You aren't helping. Now Alfie, this is what will happen. A man will come and ask you if you're sorry that you hurt David and you're going to say that you are. And then he's going to take you to your own little room where you don't have to worry about anything apart from doing what they tell you. Just like you do with us. Do exactly what you're told and then they'll let you come home to live with us again. But if anyone tries to hurt you when you're in your room Alfie, you can hit them back. It doesn't matter what Ivy just said. If someone hurts you, you can hurt them back."

"I don't think that's going to help either, Dad."

"What else can I do Ivy? I don't know how to help him."

Alfie shifted from foot to foot awkwardly until I made him a sandwich through the tears queuing patiently in my eyes. Sooner than I expected the gate opened and there was a smart rap on the back door.

I opened it to Officer Davies of the unnecessary salutes and tapping heels. "Alfred Drummond?"

I nodded. "In here."

I let him in and watched as Alfie calmly and contentedly chewed his dinner, listening while the officer said, "Alfred Drummond. You will need to come with me to the station to answer questions about the attack on David Andrews earlier today."

Alfie simply swallowed.

"Do you understand what I'm saying?" He turned to me. "Is he deaf? Captain Andrews said he was slow but I didn't know he was deaf as well."

I leaned over the table and spoke to my brother. "Come on then, Alfie. I'll make a packed lunch for you shall I? This is the man Dad was talking about, the one who's going to take you to your own room. We'll go for a walk with him now, won't we?"

"Not you miss. A police station is no place for a young lady."

"I'll go, Ivy. You stay with your mother," my dad volunteered.

I'd rather have gone to the station, but I put the rest of Alfie's meal in his favourite bag and followed the three of them out of the door, out of the gate, and then out of the alley and halfway down the road until Dad started shaking his head at me. Alfie was a good little soldier, and did exactly as he was told.

Then I went back inside and sat with my mother in the kitchen. The clock ticked. The kettle tinked as it cooled down. The tap set up a drip-drip-dripping rhythm into the sink. I had nothing I wanted to say to her, nothing civil anyway, so I picked splinters out of the table, polished the surface with a spit moistened finger.

At length, she brought me a wet rag. "No, not for the table," she said. "There's blood on your face."

I dabbed at my cheek, finding a swelling bruise and dried blood in my hair where Alfie had walloped me with the broom. Then my mother tutted, seized the cloth from my hand and roughly swiped at the scratch herself. "You missed it."

I batted her hand away and she sat down.

The silence clotted, congealed, formed a thick crust over all the old wounds that lay between us.

"I told Dad about Charlotte," I admitted after a while, still without looking her way, engrossed in wiping the same stain over and over.

"And you went to see Father Moran. He told me."

I sighed, "I'm not sure how much longer I can keep doing this, Mother." I went to bed without another word.

But it was a bad night. I kept reliving all the many varied situations that Alfie had got stuck in that Tom, Dad and I had pulled him out of. The tiny girl with the broken nose who'd been knocked off the end of the slide when Alfie came flying down, so focused on his turn he'd not even seen her – that Dad had smoothed over with profuse apologies. The pocket money I'd given to Mr Murphy to make up for Alfie repeatedly taking and eating apples in the shop without paying. The man outside the White Star, who'd pushed my brother, and had got a push back in return so hard he'd come back the next night with all his friends and had only been stopped by Tom's best right hook to the jaw. I didn't see how Alfie could possibly slide out of this one.

And then the next day a letter arrived that meant he wouldn't have to.

Chapter Twelve

It lay there on the mat by the front door all day while I went to work, taught children whose faces I barely saw, exchanged words with colleagues I forgot immediately afterwards, until the bell rang and I went to the police station to try to see my brother.

"He's been charged with assault and battery," the officer behind the desk told me. "You can't come in."

The letter waited for me patiently all that time, making itself comfortable in my house, settling in. I've no idea why my mother didn't open it, it was addressed to Alfie, and he had no secrets from the rest of us. Maybe she knew what it was. I did too, as soon as I saw the envelope. I'd seen one before. I opened it, read it, and then I walked without stopping all the way down South Street and into the White Star, where I laid it on the table in front of Mr Andrews, ignoring his spluttering protests and the insults he tried to fling my way.

"It's your choice," I said.

He read the letter and nodded.

Then I carried it to the white house on Clock Barn Lane, which was shuttered and dark so I found the key hidden under the loose railing and let myself in anyway. I sat on the bottom of the stairs while the house complained and groaned around me, floorboards creaked under the pressure of weightless footsteps and the smell of old lavender came and went. Will arrived eventually, wiping his feet on the doormat, hanging up his coat on a hook, his hat on a peg above, before closing the door and plunging the house into utter black.

Then he turned and spoke into the darkness. "I waited for you after school."

"You have very good eyesight," I remarked absently.

"I spend a lot of time in the dark. I'll draw the curtains. Don't go anywhere."

It was some time before he returned, time I spent recalling the exact wording of the Military Service Act poster. The Act applied to unmarried men who, on August 15th 1915, were 18 years of age or over and who would not be 41 years of age on March 2nd 1916. All men who were unmarried or widowers without any dependent children on Thursday March 2nd 1916 would be deemed to be enlisted for the period of the war. They would be placed in the reserve until called up in their class. Men exempted were those discharged from the army or navy, those disabled or ill or time expired men, men rejected, clergymen, priests and ministers of religion. Men who might be exempted by local tribunals included men more useful to the nation in their present employment, men for whom military service would cause serious hardship owing to exceptional financial or business obligations or domestic position, men who were ill or infirm and the conscientious objectors.

I remembered going through all this with Tom when he'd got his call up notice, but stupidly, I'd never expected it for Alfie.

Will returned, having switched on the electricity in the kitchen, but carrying a gas lamp into the hall, which he placed on the floor at the foot of the stairs and sat down next to me on the third step up.

I handed him the notice without comment.

Notice paper to be sent to men who belong to the Army Reserve under the provisions of the Military Service Act 1916.

It stated Alfie's name and address and gave his class number and number in the military register, and then it officially warned him that he was required to report for service on 1st March 1917 and no later than 9am on that date to the recruiting office in Bow, bringing the paper with him. A railway warrant was enclosed.

"But he'll get an exemption, surely. Alfie is ill. We can apply to the tribunal."

"He's not ill. He isn't sick. There's no diagnosis for what he is. There isn't going to be an exemption."

Will folded the paper, put it behind him in the dark. "Yes, there is. We will write an appeal. Alfie will not go to war. He won't Ivy, I promise. He won't go. Is he out of the cells yet?"

I shrugged, "Soon, probably. I showed the notice to Mr Andrews. I'm pretty sure he'd rather Alfie went off to fight as soon as possible than press charges and see him in prison for the rest of the war."

There was a silence. "Are you in shock again? Do you need blankets, or anything else?" he asked after a while.

"Possibly." I said slowly. "I'm numb. I can't feel anything about this. I still have to remind myself that Tom isn't coming back. Not having Alfie around either is too much. I can't make it mean anything."

"What can I do to help?"

"You can tell me what you see when you look at my brother."

He got up and walked away, headed to the far end of the hall and stood with his back against the front door. When he finally replied, his voice was rough. "Don't ask me that, Ivy. I don't want to hurt you again."

"That's what I thought. It's not good news is it? I'm alone. I'm an only child. All my brothers are going to die. And there's that other thing you wouldn't tell me. The mysterious I-can't-tell-you-only-show-you thing. That's worse isn't it? Am I going to die too? Am I going to burn? Am I in one of the houses you see on fire?"

I heard his footsteps hurtling towards me, a burst of speed that ended in him flinging himself to his knees on the step below, sinking his fingers into my hair and tilting my face up. I was so surprised I forgot I was supposed to close my eyes, and just watched as his flicked shut and the warm, gentle pressure of his lips met mine. It was over in an instant, and he was back on his feet at the bottom of the stairs, watching me intently with a familiar frown on his forehead.

"That's what I see," he shrugged. "More or less."

I felt a sharp moment of relief, an indrawn breath I didn't know I'd been holding. "That wasn't so terrible."

"Not so terrible. Not so great either. Was that what you were expecting?"

"I was expecting you to say something awful, not try to kiss me."

"I know. That's why I tried." He paused. "Tried? Really? You're counting that as a try, not an actual kiss?"

"I'm not in much of a position to judge, Will. That's the first time anyone's either tried or succeeded. Now tell me what you see when you look at Alfie."

He held out his hand. "Lots of sticks and some dust. It's alright to cry."

I took his hand and let him pull me to my feet and enfold me in a tight hug. I said into his shoulder. "I'm not crying. I don't understand what that means."

His hands dropped to my waist as he stepped back. "Nor do I, I thought you would. Are you not upset then?"

"I'm not upset." In fact, I could feel that unbidden smile troubling my lips again. "Is everything you see always right, Will?"

With his left hand, he picked up my right, and placed it securely on his chest, leaving it pressed there while he splayed his fingers over my back. His right hand found my left, repositioned it somewhat higher up near his neck, before settling itself at the base of my spine.

"Not necessarily. There are a lot of things I want to be wrong about. Occasionally there are things that I really, really want to be right." He stared at me for a long moment, long enough that I forgot about everything but the feeling of his arms around me and the way his body was pressed against mine. "The night we first met, the first time I saw you properly, under that bridge with not much more light than this, that very first time I looked at you, I saw us standing, right here, at the bottom of these stairs. I was kissing you, but the bit I really remember, the bit that's kept me going for months now, is that you were kissing me back."

His mouth descended towards mine and this time my eyes closed in anticipation. His lips were warm but light as he pressed a series of quick staccato kisses onto my mouth, kisses that slowed and lengthened as I began to relax into the sensation, kisses that deepened when I opened my mouth, even a little against his. He paused, then came back with a smooth, gentle rhythm that taught me when his lips would open, when they would close, and what I was supposed to be doing to match them when they did. I was hesitant, at first, too shy to do more than acquiesce, but when he tested my mouth with his tongue, the unexpected pleasure of it sent a shiver down my back, and my arms came up around his neck. I kissed him back then, and I kissed him properly, mimicking the hot, hard drive of his lips against mine, the sweeping explorations of my mouth with a foray into his. The shudder that ran through him encouraged me to do it again, and again, until I left my uncertainty behind and concentrated on the thrilling rush of mouth against mouth, of the tight embrace of his arms, the way every flicker and tremble of the enjoyment I felt spilled out of me and found a reflection in him.

It was some time before he withdrew from that kiss, disengaged himself and regarded me solemnly, one eyebrow raised. I grinned at him like an idiot, and he smiled slowly. "Yes, me too."

I sat on the bottom step, while my breathing returned to normal, my lips tender and swollen. Will took a seat next to me.

"You knew that was going to happen from the first time we met?"

"I didn't know. I hoped."

I reached over, squeezed his hand. "And that's why you kept holding my hand isn't it? Because you knew we'd be doing that eventually."

He squeezed back, but let go quickly. "No, I kept holding your hand because I wanted to. You try seeing the things I see sometimes. You're lucky it was just holding hands."

"What does that mean?"

"The first time I saw you was under a bridge, in the dark. The second time – when you came to my office for that interview – it was broad daylight. What I saw was a lot more detailed."

"Detailed, how?"

He leaned back on one elbow, stretched out his legs and looked me right in the eye. "It can't possibly help you to know exactly what's in my head. Most of it is just wishful thinking. Let's leave it at that."

"Let's not. If you ever want to kiss me again, tell me."

"If I tell you, you might never want to kiss me again."

"That's a risk you'll just have to take."

"I liked you better when you were sweet and innocent." He sighed, and then unleashed one of those ice-blue freezing looks on me. "I saw you up these stairs, in my bedroom, in my bed, with me. Any more details you'd like to know? We weren't sleeping."

I think even my toenails managed to blush. "Oh, I, oh."

"I expect you need to go home now, don't you?"

"Um. Yes, I think I should."

"I think you should too." He preceded me down the hall, opened the door and waited politely, although I was now acutely sensitive to how close I was to him, my skin tingling with the proximity. "Goodnight Ivy," he said, shutting the door.

I walked all the way home trying my very best not to think about Will's bed, and consequently I ended up imagining a hundred different things he might have seen us doing in it, in a fair amount of detail. It was only in the pitch black alley beside my house, with my hand about to release the broken latch that I thought of a sensible question. "What happens if I decide I don't want to go up the stairs, Will?" I asked the darkness.

His voice came floating out of the shadow. "Then I'll spend the rest of my life just holding your hand."

The noiseless footsteps I hadn't been paying attention to and the silent presence warding me home disappeared. I went into the kitchen to find my mother and father in their accustomed seats around the table and the atmosphere so charged you could have sold it to power half the street.

"Is Alfie home yet?" I asked, dropping the call up notice onto the table in front of my mother.

"He's in his room," said Dad. "He's very tired, but he's here. Andrews told Davies to drop the charges. He didn't stay long enough for me to ask him why. I was sitting outside that cell most of the day."

My mother finished reading and pushed away the letter with a fingernail, looking quite a lot like she was going to be sick. I forwarded the letter down the table. "Alfie's been called up, Dad. He has to report to the recruiting officer in two weeks. I showed the letter to Mr Andrews when I got back from work. I expect that's why he let Alfie out".

Dad scanned the letter but his reaction was angry rather than ill. "Do you think Andrews put in a word somewhere to make sure Alfie got this? I wouldn't put it past him."

"I doubt it Dad, David only got injured yesterday."

"Yes, but I wonder if this hasn't been coming since Alfie punched him in November. We'll appeal of course. I've heard of other boys who've not had to go if their brothers are already fighting. And Alfie is obviously unfit. You only have to look at him. We can deal with this Ivy. He won't go, I promise."

That was the second promise I'd been made on the same subject that evening – I hoped the tribunal was listening. "Shall I go and tell him, Dad?"

"Yes, but gently. Before you go though, Ivy, your mother and I have been discussing the subject of our future grandchild."

My mother shifted in her chair and shot my father glances capable of matching the German artillery for sheer firepower and destructive potential.

"We've decided, and this letter of Alfie's just strengthens that decision, that we should help Charlotte and Tom's baby. Your mother is adamant that she doesn't want the child in the house—she is still harbouring a grudge against its other grandmother, it appears—but I think there's something we can do by way of financial support. And I for one would like someone to call me Grandad. Maybe you could speak to Charlotte on our behalf?"

"Thank you Dad." I went over and kissed him, because today suddenly seemed like a good day for kissing. My dad spent far too much time down the pub and not enough with his family, but at least his heart was always in the right place.

I ran up the stairs as happy as when I'd been standing at the bottom of a similar flight not two hours ago. Alfie was lying on his bed staring at the ceiling, which was just as well, because most of the rest of the room was covered in wood.

"My goodness, Alfie, what are you making?" I asked after opening the door.

The pile of sticks was taller than me and looked much like a giant conical basket, branches and twigs carefully interwoven to form the sides with a gap at the top, and another at the front, which would allow Alfie to enter his creation by the simple method of wiggling on his belly along the floor.

There were large grey circles under my brother's eyes and deep lines around his mouth. I lay down on the bed next to him and he shuffled over against the wall, like we were both children again, and I was about to read him stories by candlelight. "It's good to have you here Alfie. I missed you. Dad said you were very good and did exactly what the policemen said. You don't have to go back there again either. That's good, isn't it?" He didn't respond, but then, I knew he was listening so I carried on regardless. "There's a letter downstairs asking if you want to go off where Tom and Philip went, to France, but I think we're going to say no, if that's alright with you. I'm going to write back and let them know we need you here at home and that you won't be going. It's back to work for you tomorrow as well Alfie, and that school is in a mess at the moment, I can tell you. It really needs a good clean. Can you help me with that Alfie? Alfie?"

He was already asleep.

I threw a blanket over him and went to bed myself, although I spent most of the night dreaming about another bed entirely.

The following morning, I beat Dad to the bathroom and went to see Charlotte, who looked singularly unimpressed to see my smiling face at the door so early in the morning. "What's the matter, Ivy? Are you in trouble?"

"No. And nor are you. I just came round to say that Dad wants to help you bring up the baby and he's going to support it financially. I'm going out today to see if I can find you somewhere else to live and a job that doesn't involve buckets."

"That's fantastic Ivy. Better than fantastic. Is that why you can't stop smiling?"

"Yes. Probably. I'll see you on Sunday, now go before your mother realises I'm here and tries to put me in the mangle."

My second stop was at Mrs Carmichael's but by the look of her crisply curled hair and her fully dressed, caterwauling children, they'd all been up for hours. She opened the door, "Ivy," and then hissed in a whisper that would have woken up the whole street. "It's six in the morning. Are you in trouble?"

"Yes. Can I come in?"

"Oh goodness dear, it's not your young man is it? Not that he's all that young, mind you. Old enough to be more careful I should think."

"I need to talk to you about babies Mrs C. Can I come in?"

She swung the door wide, nudging a crawling infant out of the way with her foot. "There's a very capable woman over in Marchmount Square, or so I hear. I don't recommend that sort of thing myself, but I know people who've used her. She's very discrete. Shouldn't your mother have spoken to you about this beforehand?"

I picked up the baby and was promptly jumped on by the rest of the children, who hunted as a pack and were always in search of fresh meat.

"Ivy, read us a story."

"Ivy, can you do my hair?"

"Ivy, play jumping jacks."

"Ivy, listen to my spelling c-a-t "cat"."

I attempted to satisfy their many requirements while simultaneously holding an adult conversation. "It's not for me, it's for my friend."

"I've heard that before, there's never a friend. It's quite common, Ivy. A few years ago there were lots of girls chasing after the soldiers, khaki fever, it was called, and I've heard of girls becoming pen pals with men on the front line and marrying them the first time they get leave. Or not even bothering with marriage. It's quite hard to say "no" to someone if you think you might not see him again. Believe me, I know."

"Do you remember my friend Charlotte? Her mother takes in washing. Charlotte's expecting my nephew or niece in about four months" time and she needs somewhere to rent and a new job while she waits for the baby to come. Between me and Dad I think we can cover the rent but I need to find somewhere that won't mind taking in an unmarried mother, and someone prepared to let her work until the baby comes. I thought you might have some ideas."

Mrs Carmichael prevented the baby from eating my blouse, threw a hand of jacks, tied a plait, opened a book and feigned interest in basic spelling, all while maintaining eye contact with me and holding up her end of the conversation. "This is your friend with the blonde hair, the pretty one? I know her, I take it Irene Ransome won't let her stay, Irene always was a hard faced, unfeeling girl. She's a distant relation of mine, you know. I've got a feeling she was your mother's bridesmaid once. Does Charlotte want to keep the baby after it's born or give it up?"

"Keep it."

"There's not many people would take on an unmarried, pregnant woman Ivy, war or no war. I'll give it some thought. Now, is there anything you want to ask me for yourself? Maybe how you can avoid getting caught like Charlotte?"

I blushed uncomfortably. "No, Mrs C. Nothing like that."

She beamed a red cheeked, wholesome and hearty grin at me. "Don't believe him if he says he'll pull out, Ivy. I did, and I've got this one here to show for it." She hefted the baby and I made a break for the door.

Chapter Thirteen

Alfie and I made our way to school at eight, and he went about his morning routine as if assaults and cells and call ups had never happened, or were utterly meaningless, which was a blessing. I taught children whose faces I knew as well as my own, pursued long and detailed conversations with my colleagues in which I was genuinely interested and ended up at three o'clock standing outside the headmaster's office while Miss Bird rang the bell.

I was still there fifteen minutes later when it was yanked open. "If you're going to loiter in the corridor I suggest you do it outside the wooden door over there, rather than outside the glass door here, where I can see you. Have you decided whether you're coming in or do you need another fifteen minutes?"

I looked at his shoes, because I found I'd spent rather too long imagining all the other parts of him. With an exasperated sigh, he reached out for my wrist and pulled me bodily into the room.

Then his shoes leant against his desk. "Can you talk to me?"

I shook my head.

"Look at me?"

I shook my head again, a bit more forcefully.

"Touch me?"

I shook my head so vehemently some of my hair pins fell out.

"And this is all because I mentioned you and I going to bed together."

I put my hands over my face and nodded hard.

"For goodness sake, Ivy, you're a grown woman." Then he stepped behind me, put his arms around my waist and pulled me back against him, breathing in my ear so gently it made me shiver. "Just so you know." Whisper soft kisses followed the curve of my ear and his teeth nibbled my earlobe. Then he blew the hair away from my neck and kissed his way down it, punctuating every word with a touch of lips on skin. "You will come to my bed willingly or not at all. I will never do anything..." At that point he stopped, because he'd encountered the neckline of the high collared blouse I was wearing and he couldn't get any further without taking it off. After a silence, in which he made it clear he was simply going to wait for me to make my mind up, I reached up a trembling hand and undid the top few buttons at my throat so that he could carry on.

"I will never do anything that you don't want me to do."

I sagged against him, rolled my head back on his shoulder and released a few more buttons. Electricity jolted through me at every touch of his lips on my body, his arms tight about my waist, holding me close. His lips met the join of neck and shoulder, his mouth opened, his tongue soothed my skin in preparation, and he began to suck. I put my hand up and backwards, searching for his cheek, holding him in place for a few minutes before he shifted position slightly and possessed my mouth instead. He plunged inside me, a deep and lingering kiss, but quite an awkward one and I thrust against the pressure of his embrace to turn in his arms and meet him face to face. I clung to his neck and the force and urgency of that kiss pushed me back one step, two until I'd covered the short distance back to his desk and he lifted me onto it.

Sometime later he broke away abruptly, gasping, and my awareness expanded beyond lips and tongue and pleasure and focused on the fact that I was sitting on a hard surface while one of Will's hands was on the back of my skirt, pushing my hips forward, and the other was knotted in the hair at the nape of my neck. My legs were apart, Will wedged tight between them and I'd locked a knee around his thigh, holding him into an unexpectedly intimate embrace.

Drawing in lungfuls of air I complained, "You said you'd be happy just to hold my hand for the rest of your life. That wasn't holding hands."

He reached behind him, unhooked my leg and took a pace backwards. "I intended that statement as a romantic gesture."

"So it's not true?"

"It's perfectly true. For just as long as you stay fully dressed. You look stunning, by the way."

My blouse had slipped off one shoulder, most of my hair had escaped its tidy bun and was hanging in damp tendrils round my face, my cheeks were red and I could feel the perspiration on my forehead. "Is that compliment meant as a romantic gesture too?"

He didn't answer, focusing on rebuttoning my blouse for me extremely slowly, with one part button to three parts wanton staring down it.

"Will?" I removed the remaining pins from my hair, and shook it out and his fingers came to a standstill. "Will?" His eyes were a deep, stormy blue now, and they were fixated on my mouth. "Will," I tried again. "Are you by any chance seeing what you said you saw last night? The bit in your bed?"

"Over and over and over again." He shook himself. "Right. I need to go and read Paradise Lost again or something else mind numbingly boring. See you tomorrow."

There was an ugly red mark on my shoulder when I woke the following morning, but it didn't hurt and it wouldn't show so I got dressed anyway and went to work as usual. It was only at the end of the day that I realised what it was for.

I was busy filling in Alfie's appeal form when a hand brushed my shoulder and Will's finger landed on the bruised spot hidden by my clothes. I was powerfully reminded of what it had felt like to be kissed there, and the renewed sensation curled across my skin and made me blush. When I looked up I caught him smiling.

There were seven grounds for appeal allowed in the Military Service Act, of which I thought only two would be of any use. Alfie could appeal if serious hardship would occur if he were called up owing to his domestic position, and on the grounds of illness or infirmity. Everyone knew that nearly as many men appealed against their call up as actually went to fight and I was reassured by the promises of two of the men I cared about most, so I filled in the form in my neatest handwriting with every hope of success.

Alfie's name, age, marital status and address went in, but I left his occupation blank because I wasn't sure that Will was actually paying him, and I wasn't sure that sweeping corridors and occasionally using a key would count as a job. I applied with the two letters of the grounds on which I was making the appeal and I asked for an absolute exemption.

At that point Will stepped in, or sat in, technically, as he extracted me from his chair and sent me to make tea, which I did, as badly as I could manage so he wouldn't get too used to it. He wrote a letter in support of the application in his beautiful copperplate script, periodically checking facts, asking questions and being generally irritating.

Dear Sirs

I am writing in support of the enclosed application for an absolute exemption from military service of Mr Alfred Drummond Esquire of 12 South Street, Poplar, on the two grounds listed in the application. The applicant is...

"Ivy, how do I spell intimately?"

"If you're trying to embarrass me again you're going to fail."

Intimately known to me and I am willing to furnish the tribunal with additional details with which they may not be familiar.

"How about overly familiar? You're overly familiar with me, why not everyone else?"

"You encouraged the familiarity as I recall, but very well."

Overly familiar. Mr Drummond has two younger brothers, one of which has sadly recently been reported as killed in action, and the other is...

"Where's your other brother Ivy? You never mention him, I can't remember his name."

I brought in the tea. "Philip. He's next oldest, after Alfie. He enlisted in the Post Office Rifles back in 1914 because he already had a job that Dad got him in the sorting office. Phil wrote to Mother for a while on and off, and then nearly two years or so ago now he stopped writing altogether and no one's heard from him since. Tom tried to find him but never managed it."

"Were you close?"

"Not like me and Tom. Philip always seemed different to the rest of us. I couldn't tell you why."

Presumed missing in action and has not been in contact with his family for some time. Consequently, the call up of Mr Alfred Drummond, Mrs Drummond's final remaining son would cause significant...

"Distress? Hardship? Anxiety? How would your mother feel if Alfie left do you think?"

"Relieved, I expect. Joyful."

"She can't be as bad as you think she is."

"Are you going to come and meet her at any point? Or my dad, are you going to meet him?"

"I sincerely hope not. I'll put distress."

Distress and considerable hardship. In addition, Mr Drummond, although not medically certified as unfit for duty, nevertheless behaves as one infirm of mind, being unable to form social relationships within the normal parameters and capable of only the most menial of tasks.

"I'm sorry, Ivy. That's a harsh thing to have to read."

"If it means Alfie doesn't get called up Will, you can write anything you like."

"Has nobody ever tried to treat him for anything?"

"They wanted to send him away to an institution once, before I was old enough to remember, but Dad didn't think Alfie was ill enough to go, so he came to school here, like the rest of us. Dad says as long as you set clear standards of behaviour and remind Alfie what they are he'll be fine."

In my opinion these circumstances make Mr Drummond unfit for service and I respectfully ask that you consider granting the requested exemption.

Yours faithfully, Lieutenant William Rawlings.

He sealed up both form and letter, addressed the envelope and handed it over with an expectant air.

"Thank you. I'm going to deliver this myself after school tomorrow so I won't be coming here. Will I see you over the weekend?"

"Are you planning on having any kind of crisis?"

"Not that I'm aware of."

"Then I'll see you back here on Monday."

I frowned most of the way home, and on Friday I mostly grimaced, while on Saturday I was practising my glower and by Sunday lunchtime I was working on my scowl. The sound of Charlotte's laughter pealing around the graveyard loud enough, if not to actually wake the dead, then at least to give them nightmares, did not help. "Tell me again."

"You heard me the first time. And the second."

"Yes, but I can't have heard you right. He said he could see the future, and that he saw you in bed together. How did he see it, exactly - tarot cards? Ouija board? Palm reading? Or did he just make up the stupidest thing he could think of to see if you'd fall for it?" She held her sides in an effort to rein in the effect of her hilarious joke, but her sides had expanded considerably recently, to the extent that she was now wearing an apron even outside the house in a vain attempt to hide it. "Oh, it's coming to me now, the mists are clearing. I can see you, Ivy Drummond, abandoning all sense and kissing me right now at the bottom of the stairs. Because that's such a romantic location."

"It wasn't like that."

"I'm only going on what you've told me, twice at least."

"That wasn't why I told you."

"Yes, yes I remember." She wiped her eyes, finished the rest of her apple and started on another. Mr Murphy had been unexpectedly generous this week. "Alright, what does your father think of him?"

"He's never met my dad. I did invite him in once, but he said he might come another time."

"Your mother then, does she hate him as much as she hates small children and cats?"

"She hates dogs too. No, he's never met her either, not properly. Said he didn't want to."

"That'd be the first sensible thing he's ever said then. How are you getting to go out with him if he's not coming round to the house when he collects you?"

"We don't go anywhere. He's never taken me anywhere in the evening except to work once, and I took him to the pub. I see him at school or I go round to his house."

"Then no. In my considered opinion, he doesn't love you, it isn't serious, I don't think his intentions are honourable and I think he's basically trying to get you to go to bed with him any way he can. Are you sure he's actually divorced?"

"He said his wife left him."

"That's not the same thing. It's really hard to get a divorce. I'm not sure if you still need an act of Parliament but his wife needs to prove adultery to divorce him and she also needs to have one other reason like, he's left her, or he's been cruel to her, or done something bizarre like kissed a horse."

"Thanks. That's exactly what I wanted to hear. I'm a horse."

"Good morning, girls." Mrs Carmichael appeared around the edge of a particularly ornate tombstone. "Having fun?"

"Mrs Carmichael - how did you find us?"

"I followed the laughter. You can hear it from right inside the church. It annoys your mother no end to hear you two laughing in the middle of Mass every Sunday, Ivy. Besides, there's a direct sight line from the little window near the vestry up to the trees where you sit. I watch you sometimes when Father Moran gets particularly righteous."

Charlotte had gone pale. "You can see all the way up here from inside the church?"

Mrs Carmichael eyed Charlotte appraisingly then held out her hand. "Yes dear. I'm Mrs Carmichael. You must be Irene Ransome's girl."

Charlotte shook her hand but I could tell her thoughts were elsewhere. "Yes. Charlotte. Pleased to meet you."

Mrs Carmichael stepped closer. "Then it's you I've come to see. About this." She stretched out and put her hand on Charlotte's stomach. "Have you felt her move yet?"

Charlotte nearly jumped out of her apron she was so surprised to be touched by a complete stranger, although I suspected it would happen more often as her pregnancy went along. Last time Mrs Carmichael had been pregnant she'd barely ever made it down the street without being prodded by someone or other. "Not yet. How do you know it's a she?"

The older woman smiled. "I was a midwife, and I've had eight myself. Lost two later, but I know a thing or two about babies. Ivy here has told me all about your situation and I'm here to help you. I have a proposition, although you may not like it."

"Did you find a room to rent Mrs C? That's amazing, thank you."

"Not so fast Ivy. It's not you I want to speak to. This is between me and Charlotte. We're going to need to speak frankly, dear."

"If you like." Charlotte put her own hand on her stomach. "What's your proposition?"

Mrs Carmichael linked arms with my best friend and piloted her off towards the church, leaving me standing like another marble angel, stock still on the hillside. I had to pick up the rest of the picnic and go home by myself, which meant I had time to develop my snarl.

Will was cluttering up the alley beside my house again, rather than having knocked on the door and waited in the parlour like a normal person.

"Don't you even think about jumping out on me, I can see you." The snarl was coming along nicely.

"The thought never crossed my mind. Can I help you with that basket?"

"I needed help carrying it half an hour ago. Right now I don't need you at all. What are you doing here?"

He shrugged, leaned against the wall. "Thursday was a long time ago. I missed you."

I booted open the gate and dumped the largely untouched and heavy picnic inside, before folding my own arms and fixing him with the results of my frown/grimace/glower/scowl/snarl practice. "I distinctly asked you if I was seeing you over the weekend. You made some insulting remark and said no."

"I'm sensing that was the wrong answer. Besides, that wasn't really what you asked me."

"It was."

"No, it wasn't, although I admit, it's taken me two nights to work it out. I don't sleep very well when I don't see you."

"Your sleeping arrangements are no concern of mine. My sleeping arrangements are no concern of yours. You're just trying to get me into bed."

"Not right now, no. Long term, I suppose so. Given that's the case I thought I should start answering some of those awkward questions you keep asking. Would you care to go somewhere," he indicated the alley with a sweep of one arm. "Slightly less stinking of egg?"

I squinted through the gloom. "It's Sunday afternoon. It's broad daylight. Don't you turn to dust if you go out in the sunshine? And on that subject don't bite my neck again. The bruise you left is taking ages to heal. You don't own me; you don't get to brand me whenever you feel like it."

"I've already promised I won't do anything to you that you don't want me to do. Come here and I'll promise again."

"No, because I'm pretty sure you could get me to do anything you wanted just by kissing me in the right way, whether I wanted to do it or not."

"That's good to know."

"Are you laughing at me?"

"I never laugh. I've forgotten how, remember? Are you ready to go now or are you going to argue with me all day?"

"Argue all day if I want to. I don't have to do anything you say, we're not married."

He sighed, "I'm acutely aware of that."

"Are you? Married, I mean. Are you still married?"

He squared his shoulders, raised his chin. "Here we go again, then. Yes, I am. But I'm working on it."

"I really don't care." I kicked the gate open, backed through without seeing it and was halfway to slamming it shut when Will said softly.

"Ask me again. The question you've been skirting around. The one so awkward even you can't say it. Ask me."

I caught the door, left just one width of a finger open to him, but I didnt speak.

"The answer is yes, I do," he said.

I sealed myself into my bedroom, securing every door behind me and then sat on Tom's bed with the wall at my back trying to make it not matter. It still did though. However much the war was changing the world, the fact that Will was married mattered to me. I was eighteen, still expected to go everywhere with a chaperone, to choose a man of whom my parents approved and then, once past the altar, to give up my job to go and run his house and bear his children. There was no sex before, outside or probably much even during marriage either, and the liberties I'd already granted Will were shocking. Divorce was a scandal, adultery a sin, and since I had so little control over the rest of my life my choice of husband was of prime importance. But a married man was out of the question, no matter how much he might love me.

Chapter Fourteen

I walked into the headmaster's office twenty-four hours later to find a letter waiting for me on the desk. The study door was open, but it was empty, so I sat on the sofa with a blanket and read. Will had written,

Ivy.

That conversation yesterday didn't go entirely as I'd anticipated and, since I've already foolishly admitted why I find it so difficult to speak to you face to face sometimes, I'm going to write down what I meant to say instead.

You want me to court you, I think. You're expecting me to meet your parents, I should escort you to some kind of tea party, a ball possibly. I'm not entirely sure. You're probably expecting me to stand in the road and profess my undying love to your bedroom window through the medium of iambic pentameter. Before I do any of that though, you should probably understand a little more about whom you're asking. I came to that conclusion while I was occupied in not seeing you over the weekend.

I am married. My wife's name is Clare and she lives in our house in Hertfordshire, which is a county somewhat to the north of London. We have no children.

Drink some more of that horrible tea you're sure to have made by now, exercise any restraint you might have over your temper, carry on reading.

I grew up in London, in the house you're familiar with, which belonged to my mother. We were very close. My father died when I was young and I was raised by my mother, and a phalanx of nannies, tutors and other helpers before I went away to boarding school. My mother's family was wealthy, but dead, and had left her with the residence you already treat as your own, as well as a larger property in Hertfordshire and assorted financial interests. She sold my father's business and consequently, I wanted for nothing. My mother secured me a teaching position not long after I left university and the years I spent studying the world around me, and then imparting that knowledge were the happiest of my life.

End of term holidays were spent in the country, which is where I was introduced to my wife. My mother had decided it was time for me to get married and the summer I turned twenty-one I was invited to make the acquaintance of the daughter of one of my mother's oldest friends. Clare was eighteen at

the time, the same age as you are now and I saw enough about her to like, to love even, to want to marry her. Ivy, I've done my courting. I've done the plays and the picnics and the long walks on the seashore and I've met parents and behaved properly.

The brandy is still in the cupboard if you need it, maybe you don't. I think you're the strongest person I've ever met.

I was married ten years ago. It was a big wedding, much of the county came. Clare's family was very well connected. We moved into the country house permanently and I settled down to enjoy the rest of my life. I barely recognise myself in that person when I think back on it Ivy, so much has changed.

Marriage didn't turn out the way I expected. The children that Clare so desperately wanted never arrived, and I know she came to blame me for the failure. The employment that so pleased me took me away from home and was incomprehensibly dull for her. As you've so correctly observed, very little happens quickly in geography, or in the life of a geography lecturer, it appears. I made maps, I amused myself, I spent a lot of time in research and I paid less and less attention to my wife. I don't think I was a very good husband, all things considered.

Three years ago, not long before she died, my mother decided it was time for a fresh start for both son and daughter-in-law, and she bought me a commission I'd neither expected nor desired. Clare supported the move, and between them I was left with little choice in the matter.

I completed basic training, at which I did not excel, and then, with war approaching rapidly for those with eyes to see it, an acquaintance of Clare's with a senior rank ensured that I was attached to the British Expeditionary Force in the summer of 1914 with informal instructions to survey the ground in France and produce a series of maps. High Command had already identified that the information they had on the terrain in France was insufficiently detailed so I was to land with the army, stroll around a little and be back in time for Christmas, along with everyone else.

Suffice it to say, that was another occasion in my life that did not go as planned. At Christmas, I was still in hospital. I had sustained quite severe burns to my back which took considerable time to heal – be warned, the scarring is extensive and repulsed Clare when she eventually saw it.

However, the physical damage was as nothing in comparison to the mental anguish I endured. From the minute I regained consciousness I was assaulted by the visions we've spoken of, far more bearable now than they were at first. It took some time to accept that the images I saw each time I met a new person or changed location in any way might be some kind of foreshadowing of future events. For many months, I struggled against it. I moved back to the country house after leaving hospital but I wouldn't leave my bedroom. I stopped eating. I didn't consider returning to work. I withdrew from society. Instead, I sought the advice of any doctor who claimed experience in neurological conditions, I tried more and more extreme cures and treatments and none of them prevented the daytime hallucinations, or the terror of the nightmares.

One morning, I woke to find blood on the bedsheets, a laceration on my forehead, a broken lampstand. Other days it was worse. My mother came to see me, ill as she was, because I couldn't leave my room to see her. I read the manner of her death in her face. I never saw her alive again.

Clare was sympathetic, at first, but as the months passed she became more annoyed, and then more afraid. I was no longer the man she had married. I didn't even recognise myself. The last night I spent in her company she had decided to come to my room, and, afterwards, while I slept, I caught her in the face with a fist and smashed out her front teeth. I woke to her cries and the horror in her voice as she asked me what was wrong with me.

I told her what had happened during the war. You've asked me many times why my wife left me. In the end, it wasn't because of the scars, or the hallucinations, or even the violence I'd shown her – it was because I told her what I had done on the battlefield and she was ashamed.

I'd join you in that brandy now if it wasn't only lunchtime as I write this.

Clare left the next day, going back to her parents. But I couldn't let her suffer for my misdeeds, so nearly a year ago, I packed a bag and came back here, leaving Clare with the house and the majority of my income, which is only fair.

I sought a post at the school of which my mother had been the greatest benefactor and I concentrated on trying to end whatever is wrong with me. Then I met you and everything changed.

I can court you, Ivy, if that's what you want. I can try. Half the time I feel I should push you away because I'm far too damaged to bring you any kind of happiness. The other half I just want to grab you and hang on. I've spent my life at the mercy of duty and convention, but I've seen too much to have any respect left for that now. If I had a choice I'd sell the London house and take you away somewhere to start again, somewhere no one knows us, a little house in the wilderness where I'd never have to go anywhere or see anyone but you. But you have responsibilities here, and not to me, and I still have a wife. I can't offer you anything, except that I'll always be there to hold your hand, for as long as I can.

I'll be at home by the time you've finished reading this. Let yourself in, you know where the key is. Or don't. Lock the office door behind you and walk home with Alfie. I leave it to you.

W.

I laid the paper down on the table carefully. It was a love letter, or would have been, if it hadn't contained quite so many references to his wife. I felt like rushing round and hugging him for the next twenty years and I also wanted to find his wife and kick her. But practical, capable Ivy, the Ivy who had been mature enough to look after her brother from the age of twelve, she knew that what Will was offering was impossible and she wasn't going to do either of those things.

I could never leave Alfie, Charlotte's baby, my parents, my one missing brother and the memory of the one already lost. And I wanted more for myself than to hide in a field with someone else's second hand husband. If it was an option at all after the war, I wanted a job and a family I could be proud of.

I locked the door and went home.

I badly wanted to check my decision with Charlotte, but by longstanding arrangement I only saw her on Sundays, unless there was an emergency – the other six days of the week she worked from dawn till dusk, and then fell into bed exhausted. I did try to see Mrs Carmichael on the way home to find out a little more about the proposition she'd offered Charlotte, but, although I could hear the children yelling through the door, she didn't answer.

The rest of that week went past as slowly as tectonic plates. I didn't see Will but I thought about him a lot, while I was cooking dinner or walking to work, or standing in the playground at lunchtime. Mostly these were dreams about what would have happened if I'd been eighteen ten years ago, on a summer holiday somewhere in Hertfordshire. Much of the time I just wanted someone else to talk to.

On Friday, another letter arrived for Alfie, which I thought might be his exemption, but it was an appointment with the Military Medical Board for an examination in a week's time, the first week of March, with a doctor I'd never heard of somewhere in Shoreditch.

By Sunday, the urge to go and talk to Will about Alfie, or about anything in actual fact was making me so restless I could hardly keep still. I practically ran round to Charlotte's house on Sunday morning and banged hard on the cottage door probably no more than half an hour after her mother had left for church. There was no reply and I guessed Charlotte was still in bed so I went to work with the door knocker until Charlotte's next door neighbour started flicking aside the curtains and staring at me disapprovingly. I went round the back but, unusually, the gate was locked. I paced up and down outside the house for the better part of an hour, while the late February sun teased the clouds, dancing out now and then to warm my face. I gave up and went to see Mrs Carmichael but she was out as well, and her house was locked and silent.

The desire to confide in someone, anyone was so intense I ended up aimlessly wandering the streets for a few hours before going home and preparing the most elaborate, time consuming lunch I could think of out of two leeks, an onion and the legs from several malnourished chickens, or well fed pigeons, depending on how honest that butcher had been feeling on Saturday.

About six o'clock, when we were sitting down to our evening meal, bread and dripping, because there was still a leak in the kitchen tap, a tremendous knocking at the back door pulled my father out of his chair with a groan.

Mrs Ransome blew in like a whirlwind, or at least a very stiff breeze. "Charlotte? Charlotte? Where are hiding her Hilda? I know she's here, tell her to come out and talk to me immediately."

My mother dabbed her lips leisurely and pivoted delicately in her chair. "Your daughter is not here, Irene. Have you checked the bushes in the park? The back of the pub? That alley near your house? There are plenty of places girls like her use, or so I hear."

"Mother," I remonstrated. "She's carrying your grandchild."

"Have you seen her, Ivy? I came home from church and she wasn't there – where did you leave her?"

"I haven't seen Charlotte today I'm afraid, Mrs Ransome. I called for her this morning but the door was locked and she didn't answer."

Mrs Ransome looked more distressed than I'd have expected from someone quite prepared to throw their daughter out on the street. "Then no one's seen her since nine o'clock this morning. Where can she have gone?"

"She's not here." My mother's voice was sweet, and all the more poisonous because of it. "I wouldn't have her in the house."

"That's alright Mother, Mrs Ransome wouldn't have her in the house either. You told her she had to leave didn't you?" I shrugged. "Maybe she left."

Mrs Ransome gnawed her lower lip. "She would have come here. You're her only friend. She has nowhere else to go."

I dropped back into my chair, the adrenalin subsiding. I was convinced that wherever Charlotte was, Mrs Carmichael had put her there, and she was quite safe, although why she hadn't confided in me I couldn't imagine. "Then we have a problem, don't we? She's your daughter," I extended a finger at Mrs Ransome. "And your daughter in law. Or as good as." I swivelled the finger to my mother. "And between you, you've left her homeless. I'll be surprised if you ever see Charlotte or her baby again."

My mother was unimpressed, which was her default expression whenever I spoke, but I was having the desired effect on Mrs Ransome.

"I didn't want her to leave," she burst out. "I only wanted Hilda to pay for the baby."

"I'm not paying for the baby."

"I am," said my father firmly. "Would you like me to come and help you look for Charlotte, Irene? I could do with some fresh air."

I suspected he'd be doing quite a lot of looking in the pub, but Mrs Ransome didn't know that and she accepted the offer gladly. I wasn't about to help her on with her coat, let alone anything else.

As soon as they'd left my mother tapped the table with her finger. "You know where she is, don't you Ivy?"

"Away from the two of you, by the sound of it. And good luck to her."

I slipped out but Mrs Carmichael's house two doors down was properly shuttered and dark, rather than just blackout shuttered and dark which looked the same but sounded different. Mrs Carmichael's children were not at home, which was much more unusual than their mother not being present and, at that point, quite reassuring.

When I went into work the next day, the fact that I couldn't talk to Will was almost painful and got worse as the day went on. I'd stopped going to his office after school and the single time I saw him was when he came into the classroom to collect his special class. From across the other side of the room he looked stiff and uncomfortable, and he managed not to look in my direction for so much as the briefest fraction of a second and I know, because I was staring at him the whole time.

I took Alfie into Shoreditch after work the following Friday, clutching a copy of his appointment letter until I located the large grey municipal building to which we were directed. There was a queue of men in the corridor, mostly around Alfie's age or older, all of whom were limping, bumping into things obtrusively or saying "pardon" a lot.

Three years on, and with conscription in full swing, everyone could see the call up papers for the death sentence they were, and medical exemptions were a guaranteed way to avoid the trenches. Unfortunately, both the army and the doctors they employed had realised that too, and there was a depressingly regular flow of men into and out of the consulting rooms at the end of the corridor, with sometimes barely more than five minutes passing before "come in" became "goodbye". Alfie's turn came quickly, and I opened the heavy panelled door hesitantly, to find a small, grey gentleman in a neat suit with slicked down hair and a trimmed moustache sitting behind a desk.

"Name," he said, without looking up.

"Alfred Drummond," I answered.

The man glanced my way, took a second look, put his pen down and smiled warmly. "Yours or his?" he asked.

"I'm Ivy." I walked over to shake his hand. "This is my brother Alfie."

Alfie just looked at the ground, and said nothing.

"Age?" asked the doctor. "Height?" Chest size?" He had to get up to measure the last two because I couldn't reach and Alfie wasn't telling. "Very well then Miss Drummond." The doctor favoured me with a cheery smile. "Is it flat feet?"

"No."

"Bunions?"

"No."

"Incurable deafness?"

"No."

"Is he mute?"

"No."

"Then what, may I ask, are the grounds for the medical exemption he's applied for? You'll have to give me a clue or we'll be here most of the day."

I sat on the single chair in front of the desk, Alfie hulking behind me. "He has a neurological condition."

The doctor's eyes twinkled. "Neurological indeed. That's a very long word for one as young and attractive as yourself. What kind of neurological condition?"

"What kinds are there?" I asked, managing to remain calm in the face of extreme provocation.

"An excellent question Miss Drummond. Excellent. And, may I say, you are asking exactly the right person. Neuropathy was my specialism before I was drafted in to sit in this office all day and look at bunions. What symptoms does your brother display?"

I was aware that Alfie was listening, although he might not show it. He was like a giant, man shaped sponge, just soaking up everything around him until one day, when he'd absorbed enough it would all come flooding back out, or so I hoped.

"He has difficulty in talking to people, especially people he doesn't know."

The doctor picked up his pen. "We all go through that stage. He'll grow out of it. The army will do wonders for his confidence."

"No, it's more than that. Alfie's only ever spoken to his blood relatives, and I don't think he's ever actually spoken to anyone else. Not his teachers at school, or our neighbours, or the greengrocer, or anyone. That's not common is it? He gets very obsessed by things. Natural things mostly like shells, and pine cones and sticks. He can spend hours alone, just arranging sticks."

The doctor had started writing again. "And there are no physical symptoms?"

"None. He's fit and healthy "

"And what about his mental faculties? Does he do anything particularly well? I've seen cases like this before where the patient often exhibits a certain skill in one specific area – for example, he has an excellent memory, or has a facility with complex calculations or can paint accurately after a single glance at the subject."

"None of that, as far as I know. He can read, but he's very slow. Will that be in his favour in getting an exemption?"

"I'm afraid, Miss Drummond, that there is no mental element to this test. The army doesn't want his brain, in fact, I sometimes think even having one is a liability. It's only bodies they're interested in. I can't grade him unfit on the basis of being a slow reader who's a bit quiet. What has been tried by way of a remedy?"

"Expensive treatment is beyond our means, I'm afraid, although my dad's always done the best he can."

"Electro convulsive therapy? Hypnotherapy? Sedatives? Stimulants?"

"Talking in a loud voice?" I suggested.

"Ah, I see your point," the doctor continued, writing on Alfie's notes.

"What do you think is wrong with him?" I asked, and the little grey man smiled kindly in response.

"I think he has a neurological condition. As I say, I've come across this before, and it's a condition which needs more research and more experimentation before a cure is found. I'm afraid your brother doesn't have time for either of those things."

"Are you going to declare him unfit for service?" I asked, a nasty twist of fear beginning to turn in my stomach.

"Not on this evidence," the doctor smiled at me again. "But I'll see what I can do."

"Thank you. And there was just one other thing I wanted to ask." I rushed on before I could think too hard about why I was asking. "Shellshock is a neurological condition as well isn't it? Do people who have it ever get better?"

"Of course, Miss Drummond, of course. Although there is an increasing pressure for shellshock not to be seen as a medical condition at all. Many people recover from it, particularly if they are not exposed to the circumstances which triggered it, but recovery often takes considerable time. Something which I too am short of today. It was a pleasure to meet you, Miss Drummond. Have a good day."

We were back out on the street five minutes later, and I went back to work feeling partly reassured by the doctor's vague promise, and more by his considerate smile.

Over the weekend I argued with my father, I roundly ignored my mother, I was impatient with Alfie and I expended large amounts of time in unnecessary cleaning. On Sunday, I finally managed to catch Mrs Carmichael, by the simple expedient of waiting outside her house all morning until she left for church. She would only give me a few hurried words when I asked her for Charlotte's location though.

"She's staying with Mrs Reckitt and her daughter in Folkestone. You remember Mrs Reckitt, her husband runs the White Star."

"I thought she was dead."

"Dead? No, Folkestone isn't that bad. Mrs Reckitt is one of my oldest and closest friends. Charlotte's gone to stay with her while she makes all the arrangements. She'll be in touch soon enough."

"Can I have her address so I can write to her then?"

"No dear, I'm sorry. She asked me not to say."

I wandered the churchyard randomly reading tombstones, and then I visited the library in search of an appropriate poem or book to study, but my heart wasn't in it. I sat in Poplar Park, surrounded by husbands, wives, brothers, sisters, whole extended families and innumerable friends as they enjoyed their Sunday afternoon. It was the most alone I'd ever felt.

A week passed, in which I tried not to feel like I'd lost everyone I'd ever loved and failed. On Friday, I had an envelope from Charlotte, except that it wasn't a letter, it was a wedding invitation. Pre-printed on a thin piece of white card with inaccurately scalloped edges, Charlotte's handwriting had filled in the blanks.

You are cordially invited to attend the wedding of Charlotte Irene Ransome to Frank Murphy at 5pm on Saturday 15th March 1917 in Folkestone Registry Office.

That was it, although she'd scribbled on the back.

Bring the fortune teller you love so much, I need him.

There was no forwarding address for a response – she must have simply assumed I'd be coming, and she was right. It was inconceivable that Charlotte had managed to find and fall in love with someone else under my nose in the short time that Tom had been dead, or even that she'd have wanted to. That meant that she was marrying because she had to – most likely forced into it by her mother's threats and by whatever pressure Mrs Carmichael had managed to exert. The only Murphy I knew was the one who ran the grocer's shop a few streets away, who had always had a soft spot for Charlotte, but was at least fifty, and probably already had a wife and children of his own. In any case, Charlotte couldn't bring up Tom's baby with someone else, I couldn't allow it.

I had no choice but to get down to Folkestone early, find my friend and try to stop this dreadful mistake before it got any worse. Briefly, I considered trying to accomplish all that on my own, before I realised that the invitation was meant for two. The words that Charlotte had written on the card kept me awake most of the night until realisation finally dawned, followed sometime later, and with a lot less brilliance, by the sun.

I made it until lunchtime before knocking on Will's door, which was a feat in itself, given the happiness and overwhelming sense of relief that had gladdened my steps all morning.

"Come in," he said, and I entered the room smiling because it had been so long since I'd heard his voice and it was exactly as impatient as I remembered. His sharp, pale blue stare flicked across me once and then flinched away, coming to rest on the paper in front of him and the pen that had ceased writing.

My smile died. "Oh Will," I muttered, and stepped towards him, my hand coming out into some kind of poorly managed caress.

He looked appalling, as bad as when I'd first met him. His skin was deathly pale, stretched taut over his bones and the smudged black circles under his eyes were so dark he looked like he'd been punched. He recoiled in his chair as I approached. "Stay where you are. What do you want, Ivy?"

I was at the side of the desk already, so I dropped the invitation into his sightline, which was still firmly focused on anywhere but my direction. Will bent forward, scrutinised it, and then pushed it away with the end of his pen. "What am I supposed to do with a wedding invitation?" His voice was dull, strained.

"Accept it," I answered, leaning my hip on the side of the table and folding my arms.

He edged the chair slightly further away. "Why would I want to do that?"

"It's my friend Charlotte's. The one who's having my brother's baby. I want you to come with me to Folkestone and stop the wedding."

"You're having another crisis then, and you want me to help," he sighed. "I'm sorry, Ivy, I don't think I can."

"Maybe not, but you're going to." I moved round the edge of the table until I was on his side, and then perched on the top.

Will stared somewhere past my left shoulder. "Why?"

"Firstly, you're coming because you promised. You said all I had to do was hold out my hand. Which one was it? Yes, this one I think." I held out my right hand for him to take. "And you'd be there, for the rest of your life. There it is then, off you go. Although I think it might be quite hard to tie my shoelaces, or use a knife if you're going to hold it all the time."

He pushed firmly back from the table, hands fisted on the arms of the chair. "You can't hold me to that promise, Ivy. Not after everything. You've made a decision not to see me anymore and I'm trying to stick to it, but it's not easy, and if you're going to come in here and start tormenting me then I won't be able to..."

"Secondly," I cut in, dropping my hand and taking a step backwards. "You're coming because that invitation is also addressed to you." I reached behind me on the desk flipped it over so he could read Charlotte's scribble, taking another small step backwards.

Will scanned it quickly, and then more slowly, and then finally, his eyes leapt to mine, wide and innocent. "Is that true?"

I smiled, broadly enough for it to hurt. "Oh yes. You are a fortune teller and she definitely wants you to come."

"The other part. The part where you love me."

"Oh yes. Although it took me a while to work it out, and it doesn't change much really. I'm still not running off to live in your shed and I'm not going to do anything I shouldn't while you're still married but…" I'd covered the short distance towards the door by now, backing away from the way his eyes had flared and darkened. "But I might be persuaded to wait for you until you aren't."

He rose silently from his chair, stalked across the room.

"And knowing how good you are at persuading me to do things I'm leaving. Right now." I twisted the handle behind me and escaped into the corridor.

I didn't speak to him again until the weekend, but the difference between not seeing Will last week and not seeing Will this week was the difference between sadness and happiness – hope. He haunted the corridors, but I ensured I never went anywhere without at least a dozen children in tow, or another member of staff and on Friday afternoon Billy delivered a note to the classroom addressed to me.

Ivy,

I'm going to assume that you know where Folkestone is.

We need to leave London on the twelve o'clock train to arrive before five and I shall be waiting for you with tickets in a carriage towards the front at that time. Depending on how long the wedding takes, or if we will actually be attending a wedding at all, we may or may not be able to catch the last train home. I've made arrangements to stay overnight just in case, but I suggest you acquaint your parents with the fact that you may be away, and that you pack something appropriate. I would have liked to discuss this with you, but you've been too busy having fun avoiding me.

Yours, Will.

Postscript— Folkestone is a coastal town in Kent.

Chapter Fifteen

On Saturday morning I rose early, read with Alfie, and then we went for a walk in the park to collect his afternoon's entertainment. Since the incident with David Andrews I didn't like to let him out on his own but he was clinging closer to me than ever these days and I doubted he would have gone out anyway. Then I made a fish dish for dinner (I put some fish and potatoes in a dish in the oven and left it to my mother to sort out, but technically, that counted as cooking). I left a note for my dad on the kitchen table, explaining that I'd arranged to meet Charlotte near where she was staying in Folkestone and that I wouldn't be back until Sunday morning. I'd no idea how Dad would react, since this was the first time I'd ever been away on my own but it being Saturday, he probably wouldn't notice until he got home from the pub, and he'd be in far too good a mood to care.

Then I dithered so long over the appropriate clothing to pack for a wedding that I was already late for the train before I realised that the arrangements Will was referring to had to include a hotel room somewhere and then I got so flustered I had to unpack and start again. By the time I arrived at Charing Cross I was in a flat out run, and only made the train by twisting the door open as it started to move and diving onto the carriage floor.

Will was in a compartment behind the engine on his own, with his hat over his face and his eyes closed, legs crossed at the ankle as he stretched out.

"Excuse me sir, is this seat taken?" I asked demurely, occupying the seat next to him and tucking my bag underneath.

"You're late," he remarked, without so much as opening an eye.

"You're," I searched for a suitable adjective. "Quite smart actually. You look quite smart."

He was wearing a dark grey suit of fine wool, a shirt with a starched collar and a pale blue tie.

"I don't approve of this trip. Just so you know," he said, ignoring the compliment.

I leant back on the seat. "Which part? The part where I stop Charlotte from making a terrible error or the part where you're taking me away for some kind of illicit overnight arrangement that I didn't agree to?"

"You can't interfere in somebody else's marriage, Ivy. It has nothing to do with you."

"It has everything to do with my dead brother."

"And I'm sure if he was here, he'd object. But who your friend chooses to marry has nothing to do with you. Ivy Drummond, of 12 South Street, Poplar. Or with me either."

"You're right. It has got nothing to do with you. This is between me and Charlotte. She's marrying a man she doesn't love, and I'm going to stop her."

"Lots of people marry people they don't love."

"You didn't though, did you? You loved your wife. You probably still do."

"Again, this has nothing to do with me. And if you're going to bring up my wife every five minutes I can just as easily get off at the next stop."

"I've mentioned the fact that you were married exactly once in the last five minutes, whereas you didn't mention it once in four months."

He pushed his hat back off his face then and sat up. "And are you surprised I didn't want to talk to you about it? The first time I answer your questions you cut off contact without a word and avoid me for three weeks. I waited for you, Ivy. I waited all night. I even stood outside your window, for goodness sake."

"Will, you asked me to run away with you and live in a barn or something and you know I can't do that."

"I said that was what I wanted, not what I expected you to do. I quite categorically recognised your responsibilities to your family. Besides, it was a house, not a barn."

"It sounded like a barn. In a field with no doors or windows, straw for furniture and turnips to eat. Possibly cabbage on a Sunday."

He relaxed against the seat again and closed his eyes. "It was a house. Two bedrooms, with a big fire in the living room to keep it warm and nothing but green pasture around it, very quiet so you could hear the birds singing in the morning."

I removed my hat, tried to brush the dirt of the carriage floor from my best skirt. "Yes, I can see it now. No running water and two miles to walk to the nearest well. Having to sweep out the enormous fire on my own every morning and restock it with logs I've chopped myself. The smell of manure wafting in through the windows from all that pasture outside."

He smiled faintly. "Long summer walks in the countryside. Sitting outside at night under a blanket counting stars. Reading. The smell of baking bread."

"Me in the kitchen baking the bread instead of paying for someone to do it for me. Reading the same book over and over again because it's too far to the nearest library and the lane is flooded for six months of the year anyway. Looking at the stars because there's a hole in the roof of the hovel."

He was grinning now, although his eyes were still closed. "Alright. You, teaching in the local school, beloved by every child in a five-mile radius. Me, writing long and fascinating books about the formation of continents to add to the library I've had shipped down from London. Paying someone to deliver logs. Waking up with you on a Sunday morning in the middle of our gigantic bed." He opened his eyes a crack to see if he was having the desired effect but I looked down my nose at him.

"Oh no. You're not going to embarrass me just by mentioning going to bed with you again."

He settled his hat over his face. "Good. Wear your hair down this evening."

That made me feel a touch warmer. "Why? We're coming back on the train with Charlotte tonight if we can, aren't we?"

"After what you've put me through over the last few weeks you've got exactly no chance of waking up in your own bed. You'll be sleeping in mine."

The fire in my cheeks hadn't heard about the coal shortage. "We need to have a conversation about making assumptions, Will. I said I'm not going to let you do that to me while you're still married."

"I'm not making assumptions. I can think of plenty of other things we can do together tonight, Ivy. You might even get to keep your clothes on for some of them, although I wouldn't count on it."

My ears heard him, but my body was also listening, and at that point it woke up and sent a flash of heat racing through me that was so intense I gave up and covered my face, vaguely murmuring something without consonants.

Will sat up straight and grinned broadly. "Easy. That was so easy. Have you gone the same colour everywhere? No, don't tell me, I'll find out for myself later."

"Stop it." I reached out and attempted to smack his leg.

"Are you alright in here miss?" the conductor tapped on the glass and then pulled back the sliding for into our compartment. "You look upset. I can come and sit with you, if you like?"

I was confused for an instant before I noticed him staring pointedly at my left hand and I realised that young, unmarried women probably weren't supposed to be sitting on their own with older men, laughing. Or well brought up young women anyway. "No, it's alright," I stammered, hoping the flush on my cheeks was invisible to the naked eye. "He's my... we're... err... travelling together."

Will handed over the tickets for inspection without comment. The conductor said "Indeed," and glared at him disapprovingly as he handed them back and resealed the door.

I sat up straight, put a bit of distance between me and the man in the next seat and chewed my fingernails, trying to work out if there was any possible way the conductor might have recognised me.

"Why does it matter what he thinks?" Will had put his back to the window now and was watching me intently.

"It doesn't."

"It clearly does. You could have said "he's my first and only true love, the man I adore with all my heart" or "we're not married but don't worry, he'll respect my stupid, self-imposed boundaries". Or I'd have been even happier with "what business is it of yours who I choose to talk to?" But instead, you're worried what some officious guard you've never met thinks. Why?"

I tried to explain it, but the argument seemed to falter under that critical stare. "I want to be proud of myself, Will. I want to stand next to you and say "this is the man I'm with" and not have anyone think I'm stealing someone else's husband or that I'm a common tart. I don't want any sordid secrets like my mother's."

He was shaking his head. "But you're not afraid of challenging convention in other ways. You want to work, even after you're married, and you go wherever you want, on your own if you have to, and you're certainly not scared of telling people what you think, particularly me. Why is this any different?"

I bit my thumb. "It just is."

"You've got your priorities wrong. I thought so. I brought something along that might help, but I don't want you to make a big thing of it, because it's not. Remember, it's how I feel about you that counts, not symbols and empty promises. This is just metal. Love is something else altogether." He fished around in his pockets until he caught something small and round, and then produced another, dropping them both into my hands. "These are my mother's engagement and wedding rings. You can wear them if it means you'll stop worrying what complete strangers think of you. I don't mind either way."

I opened my palm, poked at the plain gold band and the other one, the one that sparkled so brightly it looked like it was made from a fallen star. "Oh. Alright," I said, fighting to control the terrible swoop my stomach had just taken, poised now between joy and vomit.

He narrowed his eyes at me. "Is it alright? Are you sure you're not going to over-react and start crying or anything?"

"No. Go back to sleep."

"I'm not sleeping. I'm trying not to look out of the window. There are too many houses." He closed his eyes again, resumed his somnolent appearance.

I jammed both rings on my finger while he wasn't looking. "Although," I remarked casually, after giving him long enough to think I was just going to let that pass. "That was the most unromantic marriage proposal I think I've ever heard. If that's how you proposed to your wife I'm not surprised she left you."

"Oh dear God," he sighed.

"And now," I said. "You may kiss the bride."

So he did, quite thoroughly, and for such a long time we'd arrived in Folkestone and had been sitting in the platform for several minutes before I even noticed.

The town was heaving with soldiers. It was the main route to France for those crossing the Channel to fight and as we left the station and walked past the grand hotels, along the ornate colonnades and down towards to the seafront it was all I could do to keep from being separated from Will by the sheer press of people. He was uncomfortable, nervous even, his eyes straying to the buildings on either side of the road warily, jumping from person to person with a look of mounting horror. I relieved him of my bag, squeezed his hand firmly, trying to imagine what he must be seeing in the faces of those we passed, young men and boys about to set sail for an uncertain future.

Eventually I had to stop walking because Will was staring so fixedly at the ground he kept bumping into people and the arrhythmic twitching of his head was becoming disturbing. We stopped at the mouth of an alley or I did at least, Will made a good try at disappearing into it, finding some shadow to stand in like he was returning to his natural habitat.

"This is difficult for you isn't it? I shouldn't have made you come."

"Too many people," he muttered. "Terrible things."

"Go and find the hotel. Sit in the room for a bit. It's only three o'clock. I'll go and find the town hall and I'll see you there later."

It was a mark of his distress that this man, who had never once let me walk home alone in the dark, now left me standing on my own in an unfamiliar town where I knew no one. But I didn't mind. I liked the crowds, and the bright blue sky overhead, the salt tang in the air, the movement and the life and the energy all around me. I drifted aimlessly through the streets for a while, gazing through new shop windows, glancing at new faces, absorbing the suppressed tension in the air. Everything about Folkestone was that little bit too bright, the chatter too fast, the laughter too loud, like everyone was trying their very best to enjoy themselves and you could almost hear the town creaking under the strain.

The town hall was easy to locate, all cool grey walls and polished parquet inside and I was shown into a waiting room with a row of pristine brown chairs and scuff marks all over the centre of the floor. In common with everyone else who had ever been there I was too tense to sit, so I paced, and presently, the door opened on Charlotte.

She had on a dark blue dress which flared under the bust and a black jacket, much too big for her and flapping open at the front. At a casual glance, she didn't appear to be pregnant at all, but I knew what I was looking for and I could see how much she'd expanded over the last few weeks. She came towards me, smiling, but guarded. "Hello, Ivy."

I drew a deep breath.

"You remember Frank," she said, indicating the man who had followed her into the room. I hadn't recognised him because he wasn't wearing a white apron or standing behind a counter, but it was undoubtedly Mr

Murphy from the grocery shop in Poplar.

"Hello Ivy," he said, somewhat nervously.

"Anything you have to say to me you can say in front of Frank."

I looked at him more closely, at the barrel chest and the stomach running to fat, the balding head and the way he was already sweating. "No, I don't think I can." I marched into the corner and waited until she followed me. Then I hissed, in as close to a whisper as I could get while still being really angry. "What are you doing? You can't marry Mr Murphy."

Charlotte's volume was low, or at least, it started low and got progressively louder as the conversation went on. "Of course I can. He wants to marry me and I want to marry him. It's my choice."

"Of course he wants to marry you. You're eighteen and he's probably fifty at least. Have you told him about the baby?"

"He's old, but he's not blind, Ivy. He knows about the baby. That's why we're getting married."

There was a snick behind us as the door opened and Will came in, breathing hard and with an unhealthy sheen on his skin. He surveyed the room quickly, and went to stand at the opposite end next to the future bridegroom. "Mr Murphy," he nodded.

"Mr Rawlings," the other man acknowledged.

"If he knows about the baby then why does he want to marry you?" I continued.

"Because he's a very kind man, Ivy. And he's also quite lonely. His wife's been dead for years, he doesn't have any children and he lives above the shop on his own."

"You're marrying him because he's lonely?"

"No, I'm marrying him because he's got a shop."

"Nice day for it, Mr Murphy," said Will, overly loudly, I thought. "It's quite warm outside."

"That it is, Mr Rawlings. Very pleasant indeed."

"You're marrying him for his money?" I was incredulous.

"No. And also yes. It's a commercial arrangement."

"A commercial arrangement? A commercial arrangement? Marriage isn't a commercial arrangement. You can't go and sell yourself like a pound of apples."

"Nobody's selling. Nobody's buying. Frank needs help in the shop. He's getting older and there isn't anyone to look after him, apart from

Mrs Carmichael, his sister in law. All his family live here in Folkestone and he's got a cousin who runs the big grocery shop in town for him, but there's no one else. Mrs C's too busy to worry about Frank as well, she says. I need a home, and a job."

"Then why don't you go and work for the butcher and rent a room somewhere? You wouldn't have to marry him for it."

"You know that's not it. I need financial security and a place to bring up the baby."

"And for that you're going to sell yourself to an old man? Feed him porridge when he loses his teeth? Change his bedpan?" I may have been ever so slightly raising my voice at this point.

"How's business then, Mr Murphy?" asked Will politely. "Must be difficult to get the stock, with the war on, I imagine."

"Yes, Ivy Drummond," Charlotte may have been ever so slightly raising her voice too. "And when he dies my child will inherit the shop and the one in Folkestone and we'll have an income and security and I'll be a young widow. Frank's got no heirs. He wants his name to stay above the door. He's agreed. I've agreed. What's wrong with that?"

"Not as difficult as you "d think Mr Rawlings. I've got contacts here in Kent and I'm never short of good veg. But it's the fresh stuff you can't get hold of so easily. Lettuce and the like."

"You're not going to let him touch you are you? Or are you selling that as well?" I may have forgotten to whisper entirely at this point.

At the other end of the room Will was almost shouting in his continuing attempt to drown me out. "Did you come down on the train, Mr Murphy? Ours was half an hour late leaving, but the cost of the tickets was very reasonable for such a journey I thought. And the carriages were clean."

"You sound just like your mother. You're completely obsessed with sex. You look like her, you think like her. Why don't you just go and spread your legs for that skeleton in the corner Ivy, get it over with. He already thinks you're going to, that's the only reason he's still hanging around. Then you'll realise that there are more important things in life than who you sleep with."

Mr Murphy said. "Would you like a drink to help you with that cough, Mr Rawlings? I've got a tot or so of whiskey I keep by me for special occasions."

"I think I might, thank you," Will choked back.

"This isn't about money, Lottie. If it was about money you'd still be back at home where my dad said he'd support you and the baby. You wouldn't be hiding all the way over here in Kent, getting married where no one can see you."

"Frank is a very kind man, Ivy. I don't underestimate what he's giving me—it's more than I can ever repay, but it's not money—it's his name."

"So being Mrs Murphy is better than being Mrs Drummond?"

"I'm not going to be Mrs Drummond, Ivy. That's exactly the problem. You know what my options are. I want to keep this child." She put her hand on her stomach. "I will do almost anything to keep this child. How easy do you think that's going to be if I'm not married? I can't work, I can't afford to house it or feed it. I love my baby Ivy. I don't want to bring it up without a penny to its name. I don't want us to be pointed at in the street because I'm an unmarried mother, I don't want to see it go hungry or be bullied at school or blame me when it gets older for how my choices ruined its life. I need a husband. Frank is offering to take care of both of us and I'm more grateful than I can possibly say."

"Drink, Mr Murphy?"

"Your health, Mr Rawlings."

"I'm not my mother Lottie, and you aren't a thing like yours. This is Mrs Carmichael talking, not you. The world is different for us. The war is changing everything. You don't need to get married just because of what other people will say. There will be lots of unmarried mothers after the war, lots of young women in exactly the same position as you, and there's no sense in getting married to a man you don't love just for the sake of …symbols and empty promises."

"You don't believe that," said Will. "She doesn't believe that. She's desperate to get married because of what people will say. Look at her hand."

"This has got nothing to do with you Will Rawlings, as you've said on a number of occasions. Don't intervene." I snarled. "Lottie, I can look after you. I promised didn't I? Don't be talked into something you don't want to do. You've got other options. I can help you."

"You're not going to help me Ivy. I don't expect you to. I know you think you're not going to get married and you're not going to have any children and you're going to devote your whole life to looking after me and Alfie like the martyr you are, but it isn't true. From the minute you met him," she nodded at Will in the far corner. "You've talked of nothing else. I don't think you've thought of much else. You're in love with him and you've got the biggest engagement ring I've ever seen on your finger to prove it. I can't expect you to help me when you have your own life to lead. I have to help myself."

"Congratulations on your engagement then, Mr Rawlings," Mr Murphy remarked.

"We're not engaged. I've been trying to convince Ivy into a less... traditional sort of arrangement, but she just wants a ring on her finger."

"Don't they all."

"And what about Tom, Lottie? What about Tom? He's only been dead a few months. How do you think he'd feel if he saw what you're about to do? I'm here for Tom, I'm speaking up for him because he can't do it for himself. Don't go through with this, for Tom's sake."

"Tom's not here Ivy," she shot out. "I am not going to cry. You won't make me cry. If he was he'd be furious with me but he isn't so all I've got is you. Tom left me Ivy, he left and so I'm doing what you told me to do. This is what you wanted all along."

"I don't understand."

"You told me to stop breaking my heart. You told me to survive, so that's what I'm doing. Surviving. Now are you going to be my witness or not? Because I'm getting married. Frank, we're ready."

"Congratulations Mr Murphy. I hope you and Mrs Murphy will be very happy. It wasn't my idea to stop the wedding by the way, Ivy can be very stubborn."

"Do you know Betty Carmichael? My first wife's sister? Now there's a stubborn woman. Some might say deafeningly so."

Charlotte marched over to her fiancé, and fixed mine with an appraising stare. "You're the fortune teller then."

He inclined his head with a half-smile. "Mrs Murphy."

"You look after her. Or you'll have me to answer to."

"Mrs Murphy."

Charlotte got married. I couldn't stop her, in the end, so I pretended to smile although it made my brother just that little bit more dead. After the service was over and I had signed my name she said "Frank's opened the Folkestone shop. We're having a party for all his customers. Are you coming?"

Will's shoulders tensed but he attempted a smile, leant towards me and muttered in my ear. "Celebrate if you want to. Mrs Murphy is having a girl. She'll be fine."

"For a little while then," I said.

Mr and Mrs Murphy preceded us out onto the high street and quite quickly turned off it into a slightly less crowded part of town. Given that it was taking all my strength to steer Will though the crowds while he did his best to examine his shoes, I just hoped we'd get there as soon as possible so that I could make an excuse and get on the train home.

But as we turned into an unremarkable, unimpressive part of the commercial district Will came to an abrupt halt. Charlotte paused on the threshold of a large green shop about halfway down, with a striped awning and a couple of empty stands outside. She turned and then beckoned to me to hurry up.

From behind, a hand pincered my elbow, and a voice said overly loudly, and in a tone I didn't care for, "They're coming. You shouldn't be here."

His words hit me with the force and determination of a punch in the stomach, and had a similar effect. "What did you say?" I gasped, turning.

"They're coming." It looked like Will, sounded like Will even, but the man I knew was gone. His gaze lurched wildly across the street, each change of focus accompanied by a shudder and the scar that marred his face, seen so often I'd become blind to it, now stood out as an ugly red weal against the pallor of his skin. I could tell he was terrified.

I shook off his hand, scanned the skies, strained my ears for distant engines, the herald of bombs, "Now? Are they coming now?"

He stood unmoving, unable or unwilling to answer. I put my hands up, caught his face and turned it forcibly downwards. "Look at me, Will. Look only at me."

He blinked a couple of times and then he shook his head. "You can't be here."

"What do you see?"

"This one," he indicated a building with a flicking glance, and then centred back on me. "And this one. This one. This one. This whole street. On fire."

I released him, and surveyed the structures around us. They were shops, for the most part, the occasional tenement but recognisably shops, and not a cottage among them. They didn't fit the pattern I'd noticed before. I stood beside him, held his hand hard enough to hurt. "What else, Will? What makes this different?"

He swallowed, once, twice, pulled the next words out with an effort. "The man over there. Shopkeeper. Dead. That woman, that one, that woman too. Ah Ivy, that little boy. That boy." He broke off, staggering back against the wall.

"Are they coming now, Will? Do I warn the people? Do I get them away?"

He shook his head, answered something quite different. "I can't help," he said.

"Right. Stand exactly where you are. Close your eyes. I'll be back in a minute."

I ran for the shop and Charlotte, catching her just inside the entrance, whispering urgently in her ear. "Lottie. Will is ill and I've got to get him home. But listen." I fastened a hand to her arm to make sure she would. "He's seeing things. There's going to be an air raid here, right near the shop. The street is going to be bombed and people will die. I don't think it's today, not right now, but maybe tomorrow, or the day after, sometime soon. You can't stay here. The baby's in danger. Go back to London."

I left her staring at me in confusion and hurried back to Will. "Where are we staying? Do you know the way?"

A piece of paper came out of his pocket and into my hand, a confirmation letter from a hotel complete with directions and a listing for two rooms, one for a married couple, and the other in my name – his way of not making assumptions. I followed the seagulls until I reached the seafront and found the tiny, elegant hotel, all grand elevations and white stucco, and hastened upstairs, Will following docilely behind. He was silent, lost somewhere inside himself, but I had some fairly clear ideas on how to find him. The key I was given opened a large room on the top floor with a view out over the sea, a small bathroom and an even smaller balcony. Before the door was closed Will had kicked off his shoes and climbed in under the bedcovers fully clothed, curling into a ball. This wasn't quite how I'd expected the evening to go while we were on the train and while I wanted to help him, I was also out of patience with asking questions and not getting any answers.

I closed and locked any escape routes, removed all breakable objects from the bedside tables and shut the curtains, creating a prison to contain the darkness. Then, because my bag was missing and I was therefore without the seven different nightgowns it held, I slipped quickly into bed, fully dressed.

Will's body was hard with clenched muscle and tension and it took some time to unfasten enough of the buttons on his shirt to be able to pull it up and out of the way. I wrapped myself around him, melded my body into the rigid bends of his, and then I reached up, and explored the hidden damage to his back. From the top of his right shoulder, stretched in an asymmetric pattern down to his waist the flesh was ridged and hardened in places, smooth and rippled in others, a tactile map of the injury he'd suffered. The wound was already healed, but I stroked it anyway, hoping to salve the deeper hurt. Eventually the taut anguish underneath my fingertips released a little and I was able to ease the fabric off his shoulders and throw the shirt away. I put a hand on his side to steady myself and then I set my lips to his back and kissed as much of it as I could reach.

He breathed my name to the darkness.

"I love you," I responded. "You are safe here. I will not leave you." I smoothed down his arm until I found a hand and then interlaced our fingers. "Who have you told about how this happened?"

He took a breath, held it, indecisive. "Clare."

"None of the doctors, the nurses who looked after you at the hospital? None of the people you saw afterwards?"

"They made assumptions," he whispered. There was a silence. I kissed his shoulder, his neck, the place behind his ear.

"Tell me. I'm not leaving, I promise." I held his hand, and I kissed him, and he gave me his secret.

Chapter Sixteen

"We set out from Southampton, the summer of 1914, on a hot day with little wind. My boots were so new I still had blisters, but I had fifty men under me, all of them proper soldiers and I was conscious not to show any weakness. We landed in France, a crawling mass of humanity, and marched out across the countryside towards Belgium. The land was green then, before the trenches and the mud and I walked and made notes and tried to imagine I was back in Hertfordshire again. It was a long walk. I passed on the orders I was given, I did my best to learn names and histories but this was before conscription and the Pals Battalions, these were soldiers who knew what they were doing and I was an irrelevance to them. I calculated distances, I drew basic charts and diagrams and I didn't think too much about the battle to come. We were called to defend a canal, the Mons–Conde canal, a great conduit of water so foul you could smell it half a mile away. It wasn't a battle line, it was just us on one side and the Germans on the other and the water in between.

I was stationed some way behind the front line to begin with, back where the birds were still singing and the fields were thick with ripe hay. But there were more enemy forces than anyone had expected and the battalion was quickly moved up to support the rest of the troops.

There was a line of houses flanking the canal, lock keepers' cottages, farmsteads, so recently vacated that some still had food in their larders, vegetables still growing in their gardens. The firing was already underway and there were barricades between the houses to form a defensive position. We shot at them, they fired back, I kept my head down.

At dawn the next morning there was a call from further down the line, someone had seen the German artillery moving into position and I didn't realise I should have been frightened until the shelling started.

The noise was immense. The bombs that you heard on the night we met were nothing in comparison. My sergeant stood right next to me and shouted but I couldn't hear him. We were just within range of the big guns, but the snipers were taking the opportunity to strafe the lines and no one could move about very much. I spotted a cottage a little further back, a door to the left and two windows on the right, single storey, but with a high thatched roof and a barn next door. I ordered the men to regroup inside the house, so we'd have some protection from the rifles. I was trying to help, you see. I thought I knew best, I was trying to help.

Ten men went into that one house, more into the barn, and I came back outside again to mark the location of the German guns. I got the distance wrong. I'm good at estimating distance, I've been doing it all my life, but on that occasion, I got it wrong. I don't know how. So it was my fault. I tried to help, to protect those men but instead I put them within easy reach of the artillery.

The first shell hit the left hand side of the cottage, set the roof on fire, demolished the door. The men inside, they couldn't get out. I could see them through the windows, banging on the glass. There was fire inside the house and then the men were on fire too and they were screaming for me to get them out. I hear them in my dreams. And I didn't.

I heard the next shell whistle overhead, and I just stood there. I did nothing. The shell hit the house, it blew the windows out and the cottage and barn went up in seconds, I was struck by the flying glass and then the fire from the explosion caught up with me and I burned.

The pain was punishment, I think. I should've died with my men. But I was rescued, picked up and carried miles back to a field hospital and all because someone saw me lying on the ground and assumed I'd gone to save the men in the house, not that I'd put them there in the first place.

I got a medal and I couldn't tell anyone what really happened for fear they'd know how much of a failure I was, and a coward. These things I see, they are a punishment for trying to help, for getting involved. I ordered my men to their deaths because I thought I knew best, I thought I was doing the right thing. And now I have the visions and I can't help anyone because I'll make it worse, I'll cause more deaths, more suffering. I can't trust my own decisions. I know it's all in my mind, Ivy, I know you think I'm hallucinating, but my heart tells me that everything I see is true, and I daren't do anything about it." His voice faltered.

Mine replaced it. "You couldn't have saved them," I said. "It wasn't your fault."

Then I held his hand and waited until the silent, violent cries that convulsed him subsided into occasional tremors, and ragged, rasping breaths which stilled finally into the healing calm of sleep. I was prepared for nightmares so I stayed on guard for a long time. It was then I finally understood that nothing Will saw was real. The pressure of keeping the trauma he'd just related buttoned in had been too much and it had bled through the seams of his mind, surfacing in imaginary air raids, mistaken visions, nightmares. I wasn't sure what had triggered the crisis he'd had in Folkestone, but it was likely that the presence of so many soldiers had sparked off old memories.

I understood too, quite how ill he was, something I'd never seen before because he'd preferred to manage it on his own. The consequences of finally saying 'I love you' were that this was now my burden as well, my responsibility. I loved him – he needed me, and I loved him for it, but in the dark hours of the night I wasn't sure if that was what love was supposed to be. I wasn't sure his illness was a responsibility I wanted to take on.

Will slept beside me unmoving, all through that night and well into the next morning. The sounds of me getting up, going to find my luggage, coming back, deciding to wash my hair and dry it in the wind on the balcony, then getting dressed again, tidying the room and packing really, really loudly didn't wake him.

His eyes only opened when I was sitting with my coat and hat on, with the windows opened and the sunshine streaming in and the seagulls outside acting as a raucous alarm clock. He woke, smiled warmly at me, and then shot upright, a spasm passing over his face. "You're leaving, after everything you said, you're leaving me. How can this be happening again? Do I get to say goodbye, is that what you're waiting for?"

"You get to ask me what I want for lunch. It's nearly twelve, Will. If you don't get dressed in the next fifteen minutes I'm getting on the train without you." I was joking, but still, I couldn't quite meet his eyes.

He relaxed, grasped the covers. "Of course. Are you going to sit there and watch me?"

"Of course. You're not embarrassed are you?" I smiled, a more genuine attempt.

"Absolutely not. You can see me naked if you want."

"You're not naked."

"Sit there and find out."

I closed my eyes.

He carried the luggage back to the station and I dropped the rings back into his bag while he was buying sandwiches, not making a big thing out of something that wasn't. The train was crowded on the journey home and I sat next to a crying woman with two oblivious children and looked out of the window a lot. Will peppered me with concerned glances from the other side of the compartment. Then there was a bus ride through London with a confused elderly lady who kept asking me where she lived while I pretended to be interested in the state of my fingernails. When we got off in Poplar it was late in the afternoon and I turned in the direction of home and then paused.

"Thank you for coming with me. I'll see you tomorrow at school."

"No, I don't think you will."

"Excuse me?"

"I don't think I'll see you. I think I was right the first time. You're leaving. "

"I'm not leaving. I promised you I wouldn't."

"People have promised me that before."

I reached for the bag he was still holding. "I'm not leaving, but I do need to think. Goodbye, Will."

He held out his hand. "You can do your thinking with me. Out loud. I'm not letting you walk away. We can talk through this. Just don't walk away."

"I have to get home, Will. Alfie needs me."

"Not as much as I do. Not right now. Please, Ivy. If you love me at all."

I followed him home against my better judgement. He unlocked the front door, but only made it as far the doormat, because there was a letter on it. He stopped short, and I had to wait while he bent down, scrutinised the handwriting on the envelope then flicked it open and read it. Whatever message it contained screwed his face up into a grimace before he crumpled the paper into my hands with a resigned sigh. "It's your decision," he said. "I won't pressure you any further."

I read:

William,

What a surprise it was to receive your letter on Wednesday. A tremendous, if unwelcome surprise. I had never thought to hear from you again, following the manner of our last farewell, but I suppose I should be grateful that you have stopped cowering in your bedroom and are regaining charge of your affairs. On that subject, some of the instructions you have left with the bank are most tedious, and I would be obliged if you would amend them — I have enclosed a paper with detailed revisions.

That aside, I must say I found the content of your communication rather disturbing. I assume your purpose in informing me that you were about to spend an evening in the company of another woman was not to inspire jealousy or resentment — our marriage is a financial arrangement, as it has always been. Rather, I imagine you were attempting to supply me with evidence of adultery, to add to the grounds of desertion you have already manufactured. I am writing to inform you that no matter what your assumption, I have no intention of providing you with a divorce.

I cannot imagine why you believe I would wish to endure that particular scandal and shame. I am well provided for, I have a respectable position in society and, as long as you never return, I am perfectly content. You are free to pursue whatever rancid little trollop you like as long as you do not let your dalliance become public knowledge.

You have already demonstrated that, despite your frequent and increasingly desperate attempts, you are unable to beget an heir, therefore I have no concerns that there will be any unforeseen consequences of your infidelity.

But I will not divorce.

Any woman in your bed deserves pity, as well as a very good dentist. Do not bother me with the intimate details of your life again — I would prefer to correspond with you through our solicitor.

Your ever loving wife.

Clare

I went home and found my mother waiting for me in the kitchen where, judging by the number of unwashed teacups and the expression of extreme annoyance, she had been for some time.

"Where have you been Ivy?" It wasn't so much as query as a threat.

"Charlotte's wedding in Folkestone. She's married Mr Murphy the grocer, so there's no need to concern yourself with worrying about Tom's child any longer, it's gone. It's Mr Murphy's baby now. "

"I read your note. Was there even a wedding or have you just been with a man?" She meant every possible connotation of that question, and I hated her for it. I'd hated her every single day since I was twelve years old and I'd spent my entire life trying to prove I was as different from her as possible. Unfortunately, in this particular respect, I'd failed.

"Yes mother, I spent the night in bed with a man who wasn't my husband and I'm quite tired, as I'm sure you can understand. Now I'd really like to go and see Alfie so if you could just shout at me tomorrow instead I'd appreciate it."

Alfie was inside this twig den, so I lay on his bed and told him about Charlotte, forced down the aisle by convention and economics, about Will, trapped in a marriage he couldn't legally escape, and about our mother, who appeared happily married and behaved like she was single. Alfie and I came to the conclusion that none of them was a very good advertisement for wedlock, or one of us did, the other played with sticks. That night I made toad in the hole (not a real toad, it just tasted like one) and I slept like someone with no worries at all.

A letter arrived before Alfie and I even left for work. It didn't contain Alfie's exemption, but invited him to attend a military tribunal heading on Friday, most likely because they wanted to see for themselves what the doctor had already told them. I spent the rest of the week attempting to tutor Alfie in how to answer the difficult questions the tribunal might ask, such as "what is your name?"

When it came to it, Alfie was completely silent. On Friday morning at around nine thirty Alfie, my father, mother and I were waiting in a cold echoing hall, facing a pair of closed wooden doors. The building we were in was squat and low, a requisitioned municipal facility somewhere between a court room and a classroom, where the feeble light that managed to worm its way in from the outside was pale and thin. There were at least thirty other men and their relatives bundled into the same space, all of whom were appearing in person because their cases might set a precedent, or were particularly difficult to determine, or because they were conscientious objectors, whom everyone thought deserved to get a hard time.

Alfie was dressed in his best, and only suit, and kept his eyes fixed to the floor, avoiding contact with anyone else in the same situation. I'd been telling him all morning that all he needed to do was answer a few easy questions and we could all go back home but I wasn't sure the message was getting through. I squeezed his hand again, and hoped this wouldn't be too upsetting for him.

The door opened a crack, and a man called Alfie's name so we all went through. On the other side was a large, dimly lit room full of people with an unoccupied table at the far end, and two smaller tables in front of it. The table to the right contained a man in uniform with a thick pile of papers in front of him – the military representative, there to put the army's case should it be required. The table to the left was where Alfie was to sit. But sitting in the front row, within touching distance of Alfie, was David Andrews. My stomach dropped the minute I saw him, and took in the nose which hadn't quite set back into the same position, the half-closed eyelid that didn't seem to open properly any more, the broken teeth. His air of confidence and the expression of triumph as he regarded me were profoundly disturbing. Will was sitting in the row behind, frowning.

After positioning Alfie correctly, I took a seat behind him, flanked by my parents.

A hush descended on the room, marred only by the scrape of a wooden chair, the occasional cough and then a door at the back opened and three men entered. Two I didn't know, the third was Mr Andrews.

His gaze fell heavily on Alfie, lingered unnecessarily long on me and my father. The chairman of the tribunal opened proceedings, gave names and dates for the record and called the first case. "Alfred Drummond?" he bellowed.

Alfie stared at this hands and said nothing.

"Are you Alfred Drummond?" demanded the portly, red faced old man behind the table, spittle shimmering faintly in the air. Alfie sat as if he hadn't heard. Mr Andrews leaned over from the seat next to the chairman and whispered something I didn't catch. "Alfred Drummond. Are you Alfred Drummond? Are you deaf? Is he deaf? Answer to your name, young man."

I was on my feet and at Alfie's side without pausing for thought. "He's not deaf." I flicked a glance at Mr Andrews, who was staring at me with a look of cold disdain. "Sir. He's not mute either, he just doesn't like answering questions."

"Are you Alfred Drummond miss?" the chairman snapped, glaring.

"No, sir."

"Then why are you addressing this tribunal?"

I lifted my chin. "Because my brother needs someone to speak for him."

Mr Andrews muttered something else I couldn't hear in the ear of the chairman, whose cheeks matured from red to claret. "If this young woman has a father or husband present capable of controlling her, would he kindly tell her to sit down."

My father stood, tapped my shoulder. "Sit down, Ivy," he said.

He took my place at Alfie's left hand side. Elbowed out, I flushed but remained standing until, to my surprise, Will strode past me to Alfie's right hand, throwing me a warning look that ended at my empty chair. I sat, humiliated.

"Names?"

"Jack Drummond. Alfie's father. I will represent him." My dad sounded nervous, I thought, but his voice was loud and clear, and I felt a surge of pride in him.

Next to him Will said, "William Rawlings. I wrote in support of the exemption request." I noticed that he was ignoring the chairman and had locked gazes with Mr Andrews. "He knows who I am."

The chairman continued, "Very well then, gentlemen. I have a note here from Doctor Edwards recommending that Alfred Drummond is examined by the tribunal in person since, while he appears to be medically fit, he may demonstrate a neurological condition that makes him undesirable for active service. Mr Drummond, are you able to answer as to your son's mental deficiency?"

My dad replied, "I am. Alfie has trouble with other people. He doesn't like speaking much, especially not to anyone outside his own family and he struggles to understand how to behave properly. He's not a bad lad, he just doesn't understand."

The chairman consulted a paper slid across the desk from his left. "Has Alfred Drummond ever attended any kind of mental institution? An asylum? A specialist school for retarded children?"

My dad was shaking his head, "No, I always wanted to have him by me. He's not mad, he's just different."

The chairman made a note. "So he has no medical condition then, and has been raised at home and attended his local school."

"Yes."

"And what has he done since he left school, Mr Drummond? If he struggles as much as you say I assume he is not capable of steady employment?"

Dad shook his head, albeit reluctantly. "He has a job."

Another piece of paper arrived in front of the chairman. "He is employed at South Street Elementary School I see. Where you," he jabbed a finger at Will. "Are the headmaster I am told."

"I employ Alfie Drummond," Will admitted calmly.

"And this is not an exempted occupation is it?" the chairman demanded.

"Alfie is our caretaker." Will shook his head.

"Then why was this fact left out of the form? This paper makes no mention of any occupation and yet by your own admission Mr Drummond is in paid employment. I assume this is a deliberate omission made in an attempt to mislead this tribunal," the chair thundered.

Dad glared at Will. Will answered, slightly less evenly. "There was no intent to deceive. I have served myself and in my opinion Alfie Drummond is not fit to fight. He would be a danger to himself and the rest of his battalion."

Mr Andrews was scribbling furiously now and it took a few seconds before the response came back. "Your military opinion is not worth a great deal though, is it Mr Rawlings? You were discharged yourself with a nervous condition after only a single engagement if I have it right."

"I was injured. My service record is not in question here, and it is dishonourable of Mr Andrews to have brought it up. Alfie Drummond is not capable of combat; you only need to look at him to see that. There can be no benefit in sending him to the front."

"Your service record is entirely material to this tribunal, Mr Rawlings. You have shellshock. That's not an injury in my book. You'd be going back to the front yourself if I had anything to do with it. This tribunal dismisses your evidence. Kindly sit down."

Will dropped into the seat vacated by my father, passed a hand over his eyes. "That's what happens when I try to help," he whispered, half to himself.

I took his hand. "It's not your fault."

My mother noticed the handholding, glanced at me sharply.

The chairman continued. "To summarise. Alfred Drummond has no medical condition, has never been hospitalised, has received a standard education and is gainfully employed in an unrestricted occupation. But unfortunately, he doesn't like answering questions and is shy with people. Is that a fair description of your case, Mr Drummond?"

My dad didn't try to say anything, but put a hand on Alfie's shoulder. The chairman carried on anyway. "In fact, I believe that, far from being detrimental to Alfred Drummond's mental state, a period spent on active duty might be beneficial. He has recently been in trouble with the police?"

My dad just nodded miserably.

"I am apprised of the circumstances. Captain Andrews here, who has been an active member of this tribunal for many months has rightly declared an interest in this case and has excused himself from the decision making process. But I only need to look at the victim of your son's criminal behaviour sitting in the audience to determine, sir, that your son shows violent tendencies, and is quite out of control. He could better use his aggressive nature in the service of his country and therefore, since he has not been declared medically unfit, and there are no other extenuating factors, this tribunal dismisses the request for an exemption and orders that Alfred Drummond reports to the recruiting officer in Bow on Monday."

I dropped Will's hand and sprang to my feet. This was my fault, what was being done to Alfie was happening because of me, and that realisation had me up and shouting. "No. You can't do this. We've lost Tom and Philip already. You can't send Alfie away too."

The chairman's colour went from claret to port. "Many other families are in the same position, Miss Drummond. The war places a heavy responsibility on all of us. It is your role as a dutiful daughter to support your parents. Your brother can serve his country in other ways. Now sit down. Next?"

If I hadn't been distracted by Charlotte on that night in November and gotten lost, Alfie would never have been out on his own, and would never have punched David Andrews. If I'd have been thinking about Alfie instead of myself after Tom's death, I'd have realised David had retaliated and that Alfie was terrified. If I hadn't been busy dancing with Will, Alfie would never have been left alone long enough to attack David with his broom handle and land us all here. I lost my temper, I forgot to say "sir" or be dutiful and respectful or any of the other things I was always expected to be.

"No," I yelled, storming over to the table and screaming into Mr Andrews" face. "You did this. You've been out to get Alfie from the start. You're an evil, spiteful, vindictive old man. You think everybody respects you but they don't. You're ridiculous. You see enemies everywhere. You're laughed at behind your back and what's more, you're a coward and a hypocrite. Why has David never been called up? Why did he never enlist? You're very good at sending off other people's children to die but never your own. Did you have a word in the ear of this pompous idiot? Did you pay someone at the War Office? This tribunal is corrupt and I demand an appeal."

The court erupted. "Mr Drummond," yelled the pompous idiot. "Remove your daughter at once."

My dad was busy trying to get Alfie out of his chair and away but he said, "I agree with every word she says. Remove her yourself."

Mr Andrews half rose to his feet and shouted back at me. "You leave my son out of this. He's deaf in one ear – he can't do his duty, no matter how much I want him to. The war is not an excuse for settling petty squabbles. Do you think that any one of us here enjoys this, you silly girl? Someone has to take the difficult decisions. Someone has to maintain discipline, and it certainly isn't going to be you, or your useless, liberal father."

"No leave to appeal," intoned the third member of the tribunal, who looked like he'd only just woken up.

It was Will who came for me, grabbing my wrist and hauling me out of the room with brute force. "Ivy - think. You're upsetting Alfie."

I shook him off in the corridor outside and marched to the far end where only strangers could see me cry. Alfie was going to leave me, like Tom and Philip before him. Charlotte had married and taken her baby with her, my mother's loyalties lay with her priest and her God in that order and my dad was brilliant when he was around, but he wasn't around often enough. The world was moving on and leaving me behind with nothing left to hold onto. My family, everything I loved, had slipped through my fingers and I was powerless to stop it. I made a decision.

On the other side of the room my parents were standing awkwardly with little to say to each other and even less to say to Alfie, shock having apparently robbed them of all conversation. Will had hold of Alfie's shoulders and was talking to him urgently while Alfie's gaze had stuck somewhere near Will's knees. The conversation distinguished itself from the general blur of discussion as I got closer.

"Then you will learn how to clean your boots and wear your uniform properly and after that it will be marching and stopping when you're told to. That's very easy and then weapons training, and then." Will noticed me and stepped aside so I could hug my brother. "Alfie will have twelve weeks of basic training to do before he even makes it as far as the boats at Folkestone. I was just explaining what sort of thing he will learn. I've done it, it's not too bad. Just following orders. I think it's best if he stays in his routine for now Ivy, don't you? If Alfie and I just go back to school. I need you to sweep the floors and see to the fires Alfie, and then lock up, same as always. We'll do what we always do, alright? Nothing to worry about."

I finished my embrace and stood back, smoothing down Alfie's shirt and trying to look as brave and as confident as possible. "This will be fine, Alfie. I promise. We'll just take it step by step. Tomorrow you and I can go to the forest with a picnic and we'll take your bag with us so you can do lots of collecting."

"They're bound to send him home during training, Ivy," said Will. "They'll send him home if he can't cope. Don't give up. This isn't the end of the world."

I patted my hair back into place, readjusted my shawl. "It is for me. The end of one. The beginning of another." Very deliberately, I held out my right hand.

Will cocked his head to one side, considering. "Take the rest of the day off Ivy, you're a mess. I'll look after Alfie."

I waited, hand outstretched. Will shrugged, stepped up, took it. I manoeuvred him the two steps forward that meant he'd be forced to meet my parents.

"Can we appeal Ivy? Despite what they said?" asked my dad, sounding much as if he already knew the answer.

My mother addressed Will. "I don't believe we've been properly introduced."

I said, "I don't think so, Dad. Will says Alfie will have to do three months of training before he goes anywhere so we haven't lost him yet. Will can go through it with him this afternoon."

My dad nodded at Will. "Thank you for what you tried to do."

Will attempted to drop my fingers but I wouldn't let him and he was pressured into an awkward handshake with my father.

"Dad. Mother," I said. "I'd like you to meet Will Rawlings. He doesn't want to meet you because he's already married and he doesn't want to give you the impression that he's ever going to marry me. He's not. His wife won't give him a divorce, you see. But I love him enough that I don't care about that any more. As of today, I'm leaving home and I'm going to go and live with Will as his wife. I'll take Alfie out over the weekend so he won't see any difference but from Monday I won't be coming back to South Street ever again. Will and I are going to be moving to the country somewhere and Alfie can come and live with us when he gets home from training, or after the war, whichever comes first. That's alright Will, isn't it?" I cast an eye up and caught the first dawnings of a smile across his face.

"Absolutely not," snapped my dad.

"Perfect timing Ivy, as always," my mother's voice was bitter. "Thinking about yourself when you should be worrying about your brother. Alfie hasn't even left and you can't wait to go running after the first man who shows an interest like a common whore."

Will ignored them, enveloping me in a soft blue gaze that shut out the rest of the world. "Are you sure?" he asked. "This is your decision. Willingly or not at all."

I smiled. "I'm sure. As long as you go home and tidy up first."

He threw back his head and laughed and it was like the sun had come out briefly in the middle of that iron grey day. "Right then, I've got work to do. Alfie, you're with me, let's go back to school. Mr Drummond, it would have been a pleasure to have met you under different circumstances. Mrs Drummond, if you ever call your daughter a whore again you will not be welcome in our home. And Ivy – that was fabulous – I can't think why I didn't ask you to introduce me before." He swept an elaborate bow, kissed the back of my hand and then linked arms with Alfie and left.

Dad scratched his head. "What just happened?"

Chapter Seventeen

Dad disappeared to the pub shortly after we returned home, leaving me to suffer my silent, brooding mother, who stationed herself in the corner of my bedroom as I got out every bag I could find and prepared to pack.

Clothes first, everything that wasn't too threadbare or darned. It wouldn't do to start a new life wearing the patches of the old one. Underwear. Stockings. Nightgowns, although it was quite possible I wouldn't be needing too many of those. I blushed to myself.

"Don't do this, Ivy," my mother chimed in, a discordant harmony from the corner of the room. "Don't throw your life away on a man you barely know."

"I know him well enough, thank you."

Winter boots. Summer shoes, the shoes I was already wearing. Spare aprons. Socks. Wool, knitting needles, sewing kit.

"You might think you do. You might imagine you're in love with this man, but you're making a big mistake. He isn't free to marry you. Stay away from him."

"It's a bit late for this conversation isn't it, Mother? A couple of years too late at the very least. I've made my mind up and I'm not changing it now."

Hairbrush, rolling rags, hair pins. Again, something I was unlikely to get much use out of since Will seemed to prefer it down. Items of a feminine nature. I'd have to find somewhere to hide them in my new home.

"I've been where you are now, Ivy. I've made the same decision you're making and it ruined my life. I've regretted it ever since."

"I really have no idea what you're trying to talk to me about, Mother. If its sex, I've already spoken to Charlotte. Mrs Carmichael can teach me about babies, although that's not going to be a problem. I don't think you and I have anything left we need to discuss."

"When I was sixteen, I fell in love with a man who wasn't available Ivy, although he said he loved me and I believed him. It was a terrible decision, and it ruined all three of our lives. There's no happiness in loving something you can't have, Ivy. Ivy?"

Letters. Tom's letters to me were under my pillow. The letters I'd sent to Tom were still on the table in the parlour in their box, where they'd been waiting since the postmen arrived with the news of my brother's death in January. I went to fetch them and my mother had mercifully stopped talking by the time I'd returned. Memories. A picture that Philip had drawn of the four of us against the background of the forest that long ago time at my grandmother's house. A keepsake of Alfie's I could collect later, should I need one. A few books, although Will had implied he had a library. My grandmother's necklace, a brooch, a pin with a shiny paste stone.

"Did Philip never mention any of this to you Ivy? Did he never write?"

"Mention what, Mother?" I'd forgotten she was there.

I looked at the little pile of bags on the bed. It wasn't much to show for my eighteen years. I hoped the next eighteen years might be a bit more memorable.

"You don't love me very much, do you Ivy?" my mother asked, and I'd almost have thought she sounded sad, if I didn't know her better.

I tied the last few buckles, hefted the weight. "I love you as a mother, of course I do." I paused with my hand on the door knob. "I just don't like you very much as a person."

I was making an Indian recipe for dinner that I'd always wanted to try, mostly because we'd had a small jar of curry powder in the back of the larder for the last five years and I'd used absolutely everything else. The butcher sold me a rabbit he'd most probably bitten to death and then I went to Mr Murphy's for onions, because the shop was open again and people were queueing out of the door.

I caught snatches of conversation as I waited.

"She's so brazen. Swanning around like she owns the place, but the baby's never his. Do you think he knows?" said a woman I didn't know to another I didn't recognise.

"Mr Reckitt in the pub says it is apparently. A secret courtship down in Kent by all accounts and kept quiet because her mother didn't approve of the age gap."

"I'm surprised Mrs Murphy approves of the age gap, a pretty young thing like that. No, I don't believe it. The baby's not his. I wonder whose it is."

Charlotte nodded at me from behind the counter. She still had two months or so to go, but her apron would barely tie up the back and she looked hot and tired.

"Congratulations on your wedding, Mrs Murphy." I said politely.

"Nice of you to come, Ivy. Is the fortune teller feeling better?"

"I expect he's feeling very pleased with himself at the moment, thank you. I'm sorry we left so suddenly. How are you feeling? Three large onions please."

"Spectacular. Who knew that working in a shop would be so busy? I'm on my feet all day. Are you free on Sunday? How about these, big enough?"

"Yes, perfect. But no, Alfie got called up and he's leaving on Monday. I'm spending Sunday with him."

"Oh Ivy, that's terrible. No, no they're free."

"I don't know how he'll even get through the training but there's nothing I can do about it."

"Give him my love then. Next?"

I was out of the door as she moved on to someone else.

Dinner was yellow. It was a strange meal, full of innocuous chatter and then awkward silences, as the three of us remembered at various points how few more meals like this there would be. Alfie's impending absence cast a pall over the evening and the empty chairs around the table were a constant reminder that their ranks were soon to swell. Will had done a good job with Alfie though, because he ate with his usual gusto and betrayed no worry.

Both my parents frowned at me at regular intervals, but didn't dare voice their disapproval for fear of spoiling my brother's last few days at home. The minute Alfie was settled in bed I picked up my bags and left through the front door, circumventing any lectures awaiting me at the back.

The walk to Will's house was the longest journey I had ever taken. I found it was far easier to leave one life behind than to face another, and by the time I climbed the steps at Clock Barn Lane my nerves were rattling through me with the force of a steam train.

The house was in utter darkness, but the door was on the latch and once inside I saw that candles had been lit and placed at intervals all the way up the stairs. I locked the door behind me, hung my coat on a newly free peg, put my hat on a suddenly empty space on the stand, placed my shoes underneath and then picked up my luggage and followed the flickering light upstairs. Just over the threshold of the bedroom I paused. Will had been busy. The room was tidy, the papers that had littered every surface whisked away somewhere else, the bed made and turned down, the floor shining in far corners where it had been cleaned. The map on the wall was covered in a sheet, and a fire burnt merrily in the heath, supplemented by a few more candles. Will was crouched low over the desk writing something by the light of a gas lamp and he didn't look round as I entered.

"I won't be a minute. I've cleared the wardrobe on the right and the chest of drawers in the corner if you want to unpack. Tea in the pot over there." He waved a free hand towards the fire.

I poured some tea, more noisily than usual because my hand wouldn't stop shaking, and then, since Will showed no sign of making any sudden moves, I began to sort and hang my clothes. I'd relaxed by the time I felt his hand on my shoulder, the arm that came round my waist and pulled me back against his body, the breath that warmed my ear as he breathed, "Welcome home."

Just as quickly he let go and with deft movements took every single pin out of my hair and ran his fingers through it, spreading the strands out across my shoulders with a satisfied sigh. Then he took my hand and I followed him towards the bed. "Are you nervous?" he asked quietly, turning me to face him.

I moistened suddenly dry lips, nodded.

"We can stop at any time."

His right hand slid into my hair, this thumb against my cheekbone and his left sought my waist as he leaned in to kiss me. This at least was safe and familiar, the feel of his lips on mine, his open mouth, his tongue. I put my arms around his neck and kissed him back, but a few minutes later he withdrew, took half a pace away and fixed me with a stare that seemed to reach deep down inside me and pull on something hidden. His hands came up to my throat and one by one, he unfastened every button on my blouse, sliding it free of one shoulder and then the other, pulling it off my wrists until it dropped in a whisper to the floor. His fingers found the waistband of my skirt and the hooks came springing open, the material falling away from my hips. He held out a hand for support as I stepped out of it, now clad in stockings and underwear and my long cotton vest, hanging shapelessly from thin shoulder straps to the top of my thighs.

He knelt at my feet. My heart beat wildly, pumping blood to my cheeks, my chest, anywhere else that felt like becoming flushed and embarrassed. His hands glided up my left leg from ankles to knees, higher, as his thumbs hooked the top of my stocking and sinuously removed one, and then the other. His expression was intent, his gaze unbreakable, and I'd never been able to look away when he was staring at me as he was now, like I was the only thing he'd ever wanted to see. His fingers stroked up the outside of my legs, reached under my vest and stripped off my underwear.

I made a helpless little noise which drew a faint smile, quickly lost and he stood, let me go for long enough to shrug off his shirt, kick off his trousers. He nodded behind me towards the bed and I swallowed hard, took a deep breath, and clambered on, which was complicated by the way I was trying to pull my vest as low as possible so that he wouldn't see anything he shouldn't.

I lay down in the middle, arms and legs straight, my fingers clutching the hem of the dingy grey cotton that remained of my modesty and I shut my eyes tight. The bed dipped as Will lay on it next to me. I felt him pick a stray lock of hair off my shoulder. "Are you sure about this, Ivy? You look terrified."

"I'm sure," I quavered, licking dry lips over and over. "But could you just get it over with?"

His mouth met mine softly, and I could feel the pressure of his chest as he leaned down. "No," he murmured against my lips. "I don't think I could."

He kissed me once, deeply, and his mouth moved on, working its way down the side of my neck, making me shiver despite my nerves, and then he placed a line of kisses along my collarbone, until he reached the strap of my vest. A hand curved underneath it, pushed it down and off my shoulder and he chased down the bed after it, kissing the uncovering skin along my arm until the strap was somewhere near my elbow and my breast was exposed. I blushed hard, knowing what he was seeing.

But his lips came back up again, found the hollow of my throat and paused there while his right hand worked its way under my other strap and smoothed it lower. Then his mouth brushed skin and released as he sat up and his fingers operated in tandem to peel off the remaining fabric, over my forearms, wrists, folding it over at my waist. He paused then and I lay more than half naked on the bed in front of him, my breathing fast and shallow, heat warming my cheeks, imagining what he was going to do next.

He picked up where he'd left off, pressing open mouthed kisses from my neck slowly downwards, between my breasts while the balance of his weight shifted and his hand slipped under my vest and cupped the mound between my legs. I was ashamed of the way I jumped, ashamed of the gasp that sliced through the silence in the bedroom and ashamed most of all by the uncontrollable rush of wetness in the place under his hand. He didn't move, but the tight, warm press of his fingers down there drew a shudder from my spine, an arch from my hips that pressed me more securely into his hand.

His tongue was on me, stroking a wet line across my chest, circling a diminishing, concentric pattern around my breast that ended with my nipple in his mouth. He sucked. I moaned, or groaned or made some kind of indistinct sound at the speed with which the tender skin hardened as he teased it with tongue and teeth. Spirals of warmth coiled through my stomach, went lower and my legs separated. His middle finger moved then, sliding easily between the folds of skin and coming to rest inside the most secret part of myself.

That finger explored me once, leisurely, seeking something and then settled on a single place and stroked it. My hips came up off the bed, the muscles in my legs locked and then relaxed as he did it again. His mouth released my chest and the room filled with the soft, wet noises my body made as his finger rubbed it, circled it, tormented it with a gentle friction and I panted against the sharp pleasure of his touch. He bent across me, and his tongue found my other breast already taut but he simply flicked across it a few times rather than taking it into his mouth and really tasting it like I wanted him to.

I pushed my body towards him blindly, fingers groping for something against the sheet and he took the hint, dropped his head and suckled on me hard. A shiver broke over my chest, rippled down my back and I raised my hips rhythmically to meet the pressure of his finger. Then

I lost his warmth at my side as he moved down the bed and the fingers of his free hand touched my inner thigh.

I stopped moving, let him reposition my legs wider and braced myself for pain but his hand continued working and I felt his lips brush against me there once, twice, before he took his finger away and replaced it with his tongue. I lost any power to feel shame, or nerves, or embarrassment at that point. My hands clenched into fists and I cried out, a throaty and guttural sound while his tongue lapped against me and his finger penetrated deep inside. I writhed beneath his patient, determined attention; no one had ever touched me this way before; no one had warned me what to expect. Will's mouth and the fingers he now had thrusting into me, stretching, flexing, filling me up, moved faster and harder, and my body responded, strove towards a crescendo only just out of reach.

Conversationally, as if his face wasn't buried between my legs, he said, "When you came into my office that morning Ivy, this is what I saw. This is what I could only show you, not tell you. I saw me doing this, exactly this. And you were doing... Hang on a second, I think if I just..." His fingers twisted, curled and hit something different as his tongue descended, lashing at the throbbing place he'd been licking with pinpoint accuracy and the sensations overtook me and I shouted out, tipping over the edge. "And you were doing that," he said.

I flopped back again the sheets, shaking as Will's knees nudged mine wider and with a hard push, he drove himself inside me. This time my cry was more pain than pleasure.

"Open your eyes, Ivy." When I did I found him braced above me, one arm on either side, his blue eyes shining in the darkness. "I love you," he said. "Trust me."

But he was rammed in so tight that every small movement caused a wince and it took several long minutes before the pain faded into discomfort and the discomfort eased into familiarity. Will fumbled behind him until he managed to hook my knee and then lifted my leg, changing the angle of entry as he sheathed himself fully inside me with a groan. I tensed, tried to relax, to accept the weight pressing me into the bed, the grind of his hips as he rocked back and forth. There were lines of strain on his face, effort etching the muscles in his shoulders, while his thrusts became deeper, more powerful, and he entered me harder, withdrew more quickly. I lay back and let him get on with it, until one of the adjustments he kept making brought him into contact with something that widened my eyes and sent a shudder through me. That fleeting smile passed over his face, and then he gathered me to him, tucked his chin into his chest, and concentrated on hitting that same spot as forcefully, and as many times, as he could. I spread my legs as Will pounded into me, until I writhed beneath him and called out his name, while his whole body shook, jerked a final few times and he collapsed.

Will planted a kiss on my forehead with a "thank you" and then rolled off me, breathing hard.

I lay quietly, wondering whether it would be impolite to slip out to the bathroom for a wash so instead I pulled the sheet up to my neck and waited for a clue. "So, bad day?" he asked.

"Oh. We talk afterwards?"

"What did you expect?"

"I sort of thought you'd do that to me for a bit and then we'd go to sleep."

He lay on his side, propped his head on his hand and twitched the sheet off me again with thumb and forefinger, grinning. "We talked before, the only thing that's different between us now is that you don't have any clothes on and I get to do this." He reached out and deliberately grazed my breast with his palm. We both watched the nipple harden. "Besides, this isn't afterwards, this is between."

I turned onto my side too, remembering that there wasn't a part of me he hadn't already seen, in some cases at quite close range. "You want to do that again, then?"

"No."

"No?"

"No. Not exactly like that. Not if it's me doing it to you, as you so charmingly put it. Next time it's my turn to lie flat on my back enjoying myself and it's your turn to be on top doing all the work."

I think I would have been cross if he wasn't so self-evidently pleased with himself. "Are you saying I didn't do it right? What should I have been doing?"

He grinned. "You don't have any idea what I'm suggesting do you?"

"That I shouldn't have been enjoying myself? It was quite difficult not to."

He waved a hand dismissively. "Oh no, you can definitely shout louder than that. Now come here so I can hold you. After we do that with each other – it's usually a joint effort, you see – after that, there will be talking and holding, it's the best bit." He flipped over on this back and pulled me in so that my head rested comfortably in the hollow of his shoulder and my body was cuddled at his side.

"This is the best bit?" I was dubious.

"Don't be ridiculous. The sex is the best bit, or it will be, given some practise. But you might enjoy this too. Let's start again, I said "bad day" because I thought you might want to talk about what happened this morning, and you were about to say?"

"Is Alfie going to die?"

His amusement dropped away and his arm tightened. I found I did want to be held. "I don't know Ivy. I see you at the front door of this house, holding your key, and you're very sad, you've been crying and you're thinking about your family, that you're all alone in the world now, that you've lost everyone. I don't know when it happens, or if it happens, but that's what I see."

"I wasn't asking about what you see, what do you think? If Alfie goes off to fight will he survive?"

"Contrary to popular belief, I'm not a fortune teller. Twigs and dust, that's all I've got. What did you think of the thing in his room? It's beautiful isn't it?"

"It's a big pile of sticks."

"Is that what you really think? I expected better than that from you. You look at what Alfie's made and you see sticks, because that's all he's capable of, right? Did it occur to you that there might be something on the inside, or did you think, well, Alfie made it so it's just going to be a big pile of sticks?"

"I didn't realise knowing Alfie for four months gave you the right to criticise how I look after him. I do apologise. Next time you inspect the standard of care I'm providing I'll try to do better."

"I've spent quite a lot of my time with your brother since he started at school, while I allow you to swan around a classroom pretending to be a teacher. He's an artist. He can do things with wood I've never seen with almost no instruction. I showed him once how to use the tools and he got it straightaway, it's a gift. But all you see is a big pile of sticks. What happened to "there's more to see in life than facts and figures", and "go and read some poetry?"

"It's easy to criticise when you don't have to deal with it every day."

I pulled the sheet away from him, swathed myself in as much of it as possible and sat on the side of the bed. "This isn't the best bit, Will."

He threw an arm around my waist. "I'm sorry. I'm sorry. Don't leave. Please."

"I'm not going anywhere, it's a bit late for that. Why do you always think I'm going to leave you?"

He wouldn't let go. There was such vulnerability in his eyes, the scars exposed on his back a physical manifestation of how hurt he'd been that, looking at him in the firelight, I wasn't sure why I'd ever been intimidated by him in the first place. "Everyone I loved has left me. My mother, my wife, and you left me as well only last weekend."

"I'm in your bed, you're still married to your wife and your mother died. I don't think that's a fair accusation to level at any of us. I'm not leaving."

"You're not lying down either. I don't really understand why you're here in the first place, Ivy. This isn't what you wanted. Being with me isn't going to make you proud of yourself, I can't marry you. I would if I could though. If I could get a divorce. You know that don't you? I know the public symbols, the respectability, is important to you and I'd give you that if I could. I'd give you anything you wanted. But I'm also expecting you to have had a change of heart by morning."

I let the sheet drop, twisted round so I could run my fingertips across his chest. "This is a gigantic bed, Will. This room is nearly bigger than my house. You live here with all these rooms, all on your own and you have so much space. That's what your life is all about – space, and distance. You grew up here, but you went away to school and you've lived in the country and travelled. You teach geography for a living, you make maps, you're very good with distances, you said it yourself. Whereas I've never been anywhere at all. I've lived in a house with six people in the same space as this bedroom, all of us together, I went to the local school, and I've walked the same streets over and over again. I'm the daughter of a postman for goodness sake, I do the same round every day of my life. But I've lost it all. By Monday I'll have lost all three of my brothers and my best friend married the grocer – I don't think you can imagine what it's like to have so many people around you and to lose them all. That's why I'm here. You need me. I can help you."

He held himself steady as my fingers drew absent minded patterns across the flat lines of his stomach, inched lower. "I don't want you to help me, Ivy. I want you to love me."

"I do, Will. But not in the way I was expecting. That's what I realised this morning. I want the ring and the church and the romantic gestures, but I also want the sort of love that always walks me home on a dark night, that supports my decisions even when they're wrong, the sort of love that's content to hold my hand for the rest of its life. You'll do that, won't you? You'll always be there."

He reached down, released my tightly gripped fingers one by one. "Ivy," he said. "I'm going to show you the best bit."

Chapter Eighteen

I woke early the next morning. That was annoying because I'd only gone to sleep early the next morning as well and I was consequently tired which made being sore, sticky and badly in need of a bath all the worse. Will was mumbling in the depths of whatever dream he was having and I'd been woken with a misplaced elbow in the ribs. I stroked his back, trying to avoid the fresh scratches on it, and whispered in his ear until his consciousness faded and then winced my way to the bathroom.

My legs were shaking, the muscles trembling with the unaccustomed exercise because Will had kept me sitting on top of him for long enough to appreciate the position, and then to start enjoying what it could do for me, and then to start yelling at him to go faster and harder while he alternatively laughed and attempted to comply. I soaped away the blood stains, swilled his taste out of my throat, washed off the residue of the things he had done to me, and the things I had done to him in return. Then, wrapping a towel around me, I went downstairs to light the range for hot water.

I washed my hair, cleaned my teeth and attempted to follow my usual routine which was difficult, because the house was unfamiliar, I seemed to have forgotten to pack quite a lot of essential items and there were no mirrors. At first, I thought it was just the bathroom that was lacking in shiny surfaces, but a quick check of the other bedrooms, inside the wardrobes, on the dressers and in fact anywhere else I looked over the next hour revealed that there were no reflective items anywhere on the top floor. Downstairs there was no glass, no silver, no metal apart from the very tarnished cutlery, no way to check what I looked like whatsoever. I ended up trying to put up my hair in the parlour mirror holding back the black drape that covered it with one hand and stabbing myself with hair pins at regular intervals with the other.

I did the best job I could to appear decent and then walked back to South Street and realised I'd failed. My mother was sitting at the kitchen table when I opened the back door, with Alfie already dressed and eating probably a week's worth of meat for breakfast. "There's a mark on your neck, Ivy," she observed dispassionately. "Go and fetch a scarf or put on a different blouse. I assume you don't want everyone to know how you spent the night."

"Good morning, Alfie. When you've finished your breakfast do you mind coming upstairs and showing me what's in your bedroom?"

"What precautions are you using?"

"Mother. Is that an appropriate topic for the breakfast table?"

"How are you going to keep yourself from getting pregnant?"

"Aren't you contravening some kind of scripture by even asking that question?"

"I'm asking because my mother, your grandmother, never asked me. Or are you happy to be an unmarried mother, bringing shame on the family, begging for food on the street?"

"It won't come to that. Will would stand by me if I had a baby, which is more than I can say for you. Alfie, I'm going up to your bedroom, come and find me when you've finished."

Alfie's room was as neat and tidy as I'd taught him to keep it, except for the big pile of sticks in the corner, which I tried hard to see as something more special. I walked around it a few times – it touched the ceiling now and appeared to be woven together at certain points, the twigs bent out of shape, manipulated into some inexplicable design that made no sense until I gave in and crawled on my belly inside. What Alfie had made took my breath away and refused to give it back.

Although it was dark, the twigs allowed in a net of light that illuminated some elements of the structure and left others in shadow. It was possible to stand, if not move around freely and as I scrutinised a series of carefully arranged sticks towards the top of the pile, just above eye level, the light fell in a different angle and the face of my grandmother emerged out of the wood. What was the end of a few small branches, some woven together twigs and two carefully placed knotholes in one direction, became from the other a woman I had known when I was small, captured and preserved through the skill of Alfie's hands. It was beautiful beyond words, a likeness created entirely from wood but with a grace and an accuracy that belied the rough medium.

The time it must have taken my brother to select and arrange all the constituent parts, rebuilding over and over until the pattern was just right could probably be measured in years rather than months. But my grandmother's face was not alone.

Towards the middle of the stack the sticks converged in a larger grouping, smoother, wider, with a large forehead and the deep-set eyes of my brother Philip. He stared out at me from the middle of Alfie's creation, frowning into the distance, the sculpture having captured not only his features but the permanent sense of dissatisfaction he radiated, particularly when his family was near. I crouched on the floor to examine the final convergence in the wood, somewhere near my knee and therefore a more recent addition. It was Tom. My laughing, lost brother, the expression suggested by bark and branches one of happiness as the light set off something shining in the depths of the eyes and made then sparkle.

I stayed in the darkness of Alfie's mind for some time, trying to equate the expressive majesty of the art in front of me with my mute, clumsy brother. He had chosen to communicate eventually, and the manner of that communication was cheap, fragile, easily picked up and easily lost. It took me several hours to work out what it was that Alfie was trying to say, had been trying to say on his own, in his bedroom, for as long as I could remember. Watching him collect wood, studying each fallen limb and keep or discard it, the realisation came to me and I spoke to him for the first time since I'd left his bedroom and we'd travelled to the forest.

"This is where it started for you isn't Alfie? Not here precisely though, was it, but it was a forest. When we were all children, going off to stay with Nanna Kate in Kent and spending all our time playing in the trees, so far away from London and the people and the noise. I remember that time too. So did Tom, it was in one of his last letters, how he felt when he stood in the woods somewhere in France and it reminded him of us, playing together as children. I remembered it when Tom died, that time you jumped out of a tree and hit Philip on the head.

Maybe that's it, in times of stress or sorrow we remember our childhood, that time when we were safe and happy, here among the trees. I think that's what you're doing too isn't it? We stopped coming to the forest when Nanna Kate died and I can't remember exactly, but I think that's about when you started collecting the sticks. They're special though Alfie, aren't they? I think they remind you of Nanna Kate, and when you're putting them together you're remembering that she died. Philip and Tom too, am I right? Although we don't know that Philip's dead, but I agree with you, I feel he is too. I've certainly been behaving as if he's dead. The sticks in your room are a memorial to all the people who have died, is that what you're trying to say?

Every one of those sticks, all this wood, is how you show them that you love them isn't it Alfie? Building Nanna Kate, and Tom and Philip, that beautiful shrine you've got in your room is how you tell them that you love them and remember them, even though they're dead. I expect that's why you punched David Andrews back in November as well – because he had one of these branches, one you wanted, and by breaking it he stopped you showing how you felt.

Am I right Alfie, do you think? Do I understand you now?"

And my fabulous, talented, tongue tied and violent brother, who had never known his own strength or his own gentleness either, looked directly at me for the first time in years, and he smiled. Just quickly, just for a fraction of a second, he smiled, and I saw that somewhere deep down, Alfie had heard every word I'd ever said. Then he returned his attention to the ground and carried on searching.

We were a long time in that forest. I didn't get a word out of him but Alfie's silence had become more expressive somehow, like there were words in it if I could only learn how to hear them properly. There was a picnic, and we talked about our brothers, our parents, our lives and loves and what might happen in the future. And if the only voice was mine then it didn't matter, Alfie would answer in his own way, eventually.

My mother had prepared something elaborate for dinner when we arrived home, which was a surprise since I was sure she'd forgotten where the pans were kept, but I ate without tasting, spoke without much thought and less import. All I could think of was Alfie going away. It was a huge temptation just to go to my room when my brother went to bed, but Will would never forgive me if I left him again, so I put on my coat reluctantly.

He was upstairs on the bed reading when I arrived home, pretending to relax, but I could detect the nervous tension in him, his foot tapping uncontrollably against the empty air. Judging by the cursory glance I'd given the house on my way upstairs he'd occupied himself with cleaning for most of the day.

"Do you want dinner?" he asked, chucking the book aside.

"Can you cook?" I was quite surprised.

"I live on my own. Its cook or starve. How was your day?"

"I did what you said. I saw what Alfie made. I understood it. I don't want him to go away."

Will opened his arms to me silently and I took refuge in them.

Sunday consisted of a lengthy stay in bed, because my mother had decided to take Alfie to church for the first time in years so I wasn't needed at home, and because Will spent several hours teaching me why sleeping in his bed was preferable to sleeping in my own. Nevertheless, I was waiting at South Street for Alfie when he returned. Sunday afternoon passed in labelling his clothes, showing him how to pack and unpack the few belongings he'd take with him, emphasising the importance of writing home, although as far as I knew Alfie hadn't put pen to paper voluntarily since he'd left school.

My dad took him into the yard, abandoned long years of patient instruction about forbearance and not retaliating, and showed him how to fight, where to aim, how to hurt. My mother stood by impassively but I couldn't help repeating, "They'll send him home," to anyone who would listen.

After dinner Alfie went to his room and disappeared inside his memorial while I sat on the bed and read aloud anything I could find. I lay next to him while he fell asleep and it was past midnight when I left South Street, to find Will waiting patiently in the alley ready to support me as I stumbled home.

Alfie left early on Monday morning. My dad and I walked him to Bow, found the recruiting office and handed him over. There was a strange sense of unreality about it, as if nothing was quite solid. Our feet tapped the pavement, sounding out the void beneath it, the walls were blank and flat and as insubstantial as paper, the face of the recruiting sergeant stiff as a marionette. Alfie went along docilely as always, standing, sitting, walking, doing exactly as he was told. He looked at the floor and didn't answer to his name. I went through the motions, my body obeying the commands it was given while in my head I heard the creak of treetops in the wind, the susurration of leaves, watched the interplay of light and shadow between the branches.

It was only around lunchtime, crawled into Will's bed on my own that the tears came. Around three I surfaced from the flood of sorrow to walk aimlessly around the bedroom in search of the keepsakes of Alfie's I'd not managed to collect. I found the box with Tom's letters instead.

It was a small thing, still wrapped in brown paper and tied with string and with "Drummond" stencilled in untidy black print on the front. I hadn't thought too much about it since the postmen had dropped it off in January, but there it was, unpacked from my travelling case and placed on the bedside table by a thoughtful hand. I picked apart the knots, pulled the string hoping that there might be something left of Tom still lingering around the papers he'd kept, his smell maybe, an annotation, a drawing.

The box was full of paper, maybe ten letters in all, but they weren't the ones I'd written to Tom. They were all addressed to Philip and all from my mother. I opened, and read.

16 May 1915,

My dearest Philip.

There's no need to take that attitude with me. I promised to explain and I will. I've thought hard about what to tell you since your last letter and, although I haven't discussed this with your father it seems to me to be the right thing to do. Despite your protestations, you are in great danger and should anything happen to you, it would be a comfort to me to know that there were no lies between us.

Before I respond in full however, I must have your solemn promise that you will not tell Jack that I have told you. It would destroy him to know that his children are aware of what is his most carefully guarded secret and the source of much unhappiness within our marriage.

If you promise, I will explain,

Your loving mother.

23rd May 1915.

My dearest Philip.

Thank you for your last letter. I will hold you to that promise and in response to your last question – Tom has not been told, although if he asks I will tell him too. Ivy already knows part of it, and I am surprised she has never given you any inclination. She is very good at keeping secrets, it seems. I'll have to watch that.

Alfie I will never tell, this would only upset him.

You remember your grandmother, Nanna Kate, you used to call her when you were very young. You won't remember your grandad, my father Robert, because he died before your sister was born. We spent many summers at their home in Kent before my mother passed away too. What I am going to tell you will require some history – it will be too hard a story to hear if I do not soften it first with the background.

It is the story of my life, so forgive me for wanting to paint a flattering picture.

I was born in Kent, second eldest of four, the same as you, although my siblings were all sisters and one died young. We lived in the house you've visited, a cottage on the edge of a large estate, where my father was head gamekeeper and my mother was in service, before she married.

While my sisters spent much of their time running wild in the woods behind the house I was clever, and interested in the world around me. I read everything I could get my hands on, often staying later after school just to have access to the library. My greatest desire was to become a teacher, and my mother encouraged me in that. She was a great believer in following dreams, no matter how impractical and she spent much of her time so engrossed in her own imaginary world that my sisters were allowed to do as they pleased, and there was very little discipline in our house.

I was sorely disappointed when I left school and followed my mother into service, recommended by the high esteem in which my father was held for breeding copious pheasants. Life in the big house was a scullery maid was hard, but I made a close friend of a similar age—Irene Sturgeon—Ransome as she is now – the mother of Ivy's little friend, Charlotte. I have not been close to Irene for many years, following the circumstances of my wedding and I have never encouraged any more than a commercial relationship between our families, so if you do not recall her I will not be surprised.

I had been working at the house a full year before I happened to meet one of the younger sons of the family—I believe there were seven in all—while about my daily chores. I was pretty, in those days, although you will find it hard to believe; I looked much as your sister does now, I think.

This son, James by name, was a year or so older than I, and did not take after the rest of this brothers, He was small, with a sweet, sensitive face, nothing like the tall, broad, athletic children who comprised the rest of the brood. James enjoyed reading, as did I and we struck up an unlikely friendship, when was greatly furthered when I was unexpectedly promoted to maid and spent more time above stairs.

Over the course of several years – and make no mistake this was no passing fancy or summer romance – James and I fell in love. That love has been the most enduring aspect of my life and continues to this day.

I will leave it there until you let me know whether or not you wish me to continue, now that you have some idea where my story may be leading.

Your loving mother.

30th May 1915

My dearest Philip,

There were more questions in your last letter than I can possibly answer in one try, and you will have to be patient while I tell this in my own way. You have asked for the whole truth, and this, then is what I will give you, although it will be painful for you to hear.

James and I became engaged in the summer of my sixteenth year. It was a secret engagement, obviously, since the son of such a wealthy family, even a seventh son, could not marry a maid. James and I spent a great deal of time at my parents" cottage in the woods, which my mother, oblivious as she was to the dangers of such a liaison, encouraged. We made plans to run away and be married but those plans never came to fruition. I often wonder how my life would have been different if James and I had managed to legally wed. I doubt I would be living in London for a start, I have always much preferred the countryside.

In fact, a few misplaced words by my father to his master one day put paid to any plans that James and I might have had, and James was promptly sent away.

So, to answer your questions. No, I have never loved the man you know as your father. Yes, your father knows about James. Yes, I have always loved all my children, and all four of you are my children - that idea you had about Irene was quite off the mark.

I remain, your loving mother.

7th June 1915

I resent your last implication Philip. My mother, although lax in her ways would never knowingly have permitted the kind of inappropriate behaviour you are suggesting under her roof, and my father would have put a stop to it had he had the slightest suspicion that something was wrong. I was not pregnant with Alfie then, as you so bluntly suggest.

I meant only that my mother did not see that I was in love with a man who was not and was never going to be available to me, and she did nothing to discourage me from seeing James. I have always sworn that I would not make the same mistakes with your sister and I have always demanded the utmost obedience and discipline from her. In many ways, I have been stricter with Ivy, and harder on her than I have ever been with my boys, and this is a direct response to the way my mother was with me. I wish to protect your sister from the experiences that I have had to live through, and am even now struggling with.

So no, you are wrong. I did not have that kind of relationship with James with my parents" knowledge. James was sent away, and it took another year before he was able to write to me and let me know where he was. They had sent him to a seminary, where he was in training for the church.

I was never particularly religious and I perhaps have less faith now than I did then, which you will doubtless find difficult to credit, given the amount of time I spend at church. There are good reasons for that.

James also, was not especially devout but belief isn't necessarily a prerequisite for the priesthood these days and James had to abide by his parents" decision or be cast out without a shilling. He endured the training and complained bitterly to me about the sacrifices he was making for the sake of duty and honour. I am sure he thought that in time, his parents would relent, and he might be released from the career they had chosen for him.

But at length, he could stand it no longer, and he sent for me to come to London. I had a difficult choice to make. I desperately wanted to re-join my sweetheart, who had proven himself devoted over the course now of two long years. James had promised to marry me once we were both in London and away from our families, but I had a sense that this course of action might not be the wisest move. I confided in Irene. Her advice was to go.

She herself had tired of the drudgery of service and was smitten with the idea that she could move to London and find a much easier, better paid position in the city, where life was more exciting. Irene had two distant cousins already living in London, sisters Betty and Laura who you would know now as Mrs Carmichael from two doors down and Mrs Murphy who used to run the grocers shop and died young.

But again, Irene's advice wasn't free from self-interest so I turned to my mother. She also told me to go. Silly, foolish woman that she was, she advised me to follow my heart, to leave home and throw myself on the mercy of love, in hopes of a happily ever after. I think she thought it was romantic.

So I sought out my references, gave notice and left home.

Your brother is calling, and I must get this letter to the post.

I will continue shortly,

Your mother.

14th June 1915.

My dearest Philip. It's a good thing the penny post is free now Philip, as

I don't think your last letter was worth the price of a stamp. I am going as fast as I can.

Irene and I arrived in London in the autumn; it was quite a change from Kent. The streets were dirty, the people rude and the lodgings we rented with all the money I had been able to save were about the size of my bedroom back at home. But Irene was beside herself with excitement and spent much of her time walking the streets, seeing the sights, and amusing herself with the new opportunities available.

But I had good references and more experience and I quickly found a place in a large house in Westminster. The best Irene could do, when she finally bestirred herself to find employment, was as a general maid of all work for the Rawlings family over in Clock Barn Lane. We had to move here to Poplar as the rents were cheaper and that was all Irene could afford.

It was about this time that I met Jack Drummond. He was a postman even then, and a healthy, active boy with a cheerful manner and an easy smile and he had the round which covered our house, delivering whatever letters my mother happened to send. I opened the door to him once or twice, after which time he came round more frequently, often with a poor excuse – a misdirected parcel, a sudden need for a drink of water, a request to borrow a pencil. Irene used to tease him unmercifully, because she knew he had a soft spot for me. It was more than that though.

James and I did not get married. He never had enough time away from the seminary, we hadn't saved enough, the formalities were complex and if I am honest, the simple pleasure of being together again distracted me from something that had been very clear before I left home. Newly independent, with no watching parents and an income of my own, and being in London, free to see the man I loved was too much for my resolve.

It was at this point that my relationship with James became physical.

I can only imagine what you must be thinking as you read these words. We are none of us blameless Philip, and all I can say in my defence is that I loved James at the time, and I still do. Do not think too harshly of me.

Your loving mother

21st June 1915.

Philip, Your assumption is correct. But let me explain how that came to be. James and I were together many times before I discovered I was pregnant. My mother had given me no instruction in the matter, and I was quite far along before I realised what was happening. Even then there were women who could have helped me but I will not speak to you of such things.

Suffice it to say, James and I faced a choice. James approached his father for permission to marry me, or at least, for support, and his father refused to help. James could not support me on his own, he was without paid employment, had no skills to allow him to get any at short notice and, besides that, I don't think he was bold enough to go so directly against the wishes of his father.

Jack Drummond stepped in. Jack is the bravest, most compassionate man I have ever known who has shown his family nothing but love and devotion all these years. You have been angry with him for some time I think Philip, and one of the reasons l had to explain this whole story to you is so that you understand Jack better.

Jack and I had a very frank conversation. Jack was in love with me, he said, and he was quite sure that, given time, I would come to love him too. At that moment, I was so desperate for help, and so disappointed with James" lack of action that I agreed. I explained to Jack that although I wasn't in love with him, I was prepared to see if it was possible.

Irene was furious; she said I was taking advantage of Jack's kindness and that I would never be able to love him in the same way that he loved me. In hindsight, she was right, but at the time I didn't believe her. Irene was my bridesmaid, only because she was continually trying to dissuade me from marrying Jack, right up until the point that we left the church. Then she walked away and refused to have anything more to do with us, a situation with which I was quite content.

I know that James and Jack had words, and came to some kind of arrangement, although the details are unclear. James" mother, I think, gave him enough money to buy us this house, but James has never been able to see his children, except in public places like church. I married Jack, and Alfie was our first born son.

Your mother.

28th June 1915

Do not call me such things Philip; I am still your mother. I will get the rest of the story over with, and then you may judge me however you wish.

I had every intention of keeping my promise to Jack, but after Alfie was born it quickly became clear that he was not the same as other children. His development was slower; he did not speak as quickly, there was something not quite right. I was distraught. I needed support, and, although you will not understand this, I turned to James for that support. Jack, although my husband, was still a stranger. James was my strength and constant companion. And Jack – I think Jack understood that. I don't think he blamed me. I don't think he was even annoyed until I fell pregnant with you and Jack realised that you weren't his son.

Now you know the truth. James is your father, and also Tom's father. James stood by my side, although I was married to another, and has loved me throughout. He completed his training and became a Catholic priest, taking up his post as close to his family as possible, because he said that he would never love another now that I was already taken.

My relationship with Jack began to sour though. After Tom was born he began going out the occasional evening, which increased over time until he was spending more and more time drinking. One night he came home and told me that he couldn't stand to live this way any longer. He forbade me from seeing James. He told James the same thing.

Jack has always treated all my children as if they were his own. He has never once begrudged you, Alfie and Tom your parentage and he has behaved at all times towards you with nothing but love and kindness. If he drinks, and spends time away from home, it is because I drove him to it. I never loved him as I had promised to, and although he loved you all dearly, he was disappointed in me. As I was in myself as well.

Jack took steps to ensure I was never close with James and it was during this period that Ivy was conceived. Ivy is Jack's only child, although she has never suspected it, and Jack has never treated her any differently to the rest of you, which is to his credit.

However, despite the birth of your sister, the reconciliation between us did not last. The marriage was already too damaged. Your father relaxed his vigil, and, after several years I began to see James in private again. He had waited patiently for me, but the experience of being denied access to me had changed him, and he is not now the man I fell in love with. He realises, I think, what it has meant to lose what would have been his wife and family, if we had managed to marry when we had the chance.

Your sister once caught me with James but I made her promise not to tell her father and, more than that, I made her agree to look after Alfie and help out around the house. I made sure she never had the time or the opportunity to go gallivanting with boys of her own age, and so I have managed to keep her safe from the same kind of trouble that I fell into. From the same kind of love.

Love, you see, has destroyed all our lives. Jack has turned to drink, James is aggrieved and resentful of anyone he believes has a chance of happiness and

I am here, explaining to you why the man you have always known as Father Moran, our local priest, is actually your father. That was why I took you to see him one last time the day you went away. That was the cause of the tears in his eyes that piqued your curiosity. That was why he told you he loved you. I'm sure he does, but he has never been able to show it.

Write to me the minute you read this.

Your loving mother.

7th July 1915.

Philip – did you receive my last letter? Why have you not responded?

14th July 1915.

Philip,

You have not replied to my letter, please contact me as soon as you can.

28th July 1915.

Philip. My dear son. You asked me for the truth and I have told you. I hoped you were old enough now to understand. Please respond.

Chapter Nineteen

There were no more letters in the box. Philip must not have kept the rest, but I'm sure there were many more - to my knowledge my mother had written once a week to Philip since he had enlisted, and it was two years now in which he had not replied.

I understood the cause of his silence. I sat in bed, poring over the papers in my hand, re-reading and struggling to link the woman I knew, for whom I had no respect and quite a lot of anger, with the thinking, feeling person revealed in these pages.

A light tap on the door was followed by Will bearing a tray with tea and cake. He set it on my lap, kissed the top of my head and sat on the covers next to me. "How are you feeling?"

I shuffled the papers back into the right order and passed them over to him to read. "I hardly know."

I drank, and ate, and thought while Will read.

In the end, he said, "Does your mother know you have these? They weren't meant for you."

"No, but I'm not planning on raising the subject with her. She doesn't need to know."

"Maybe you should talk to her about it. You don't get on with your mother very well; talking to her about this might help."

"She tried to stop me leaving home you know. She didn't want me here with you."

"Shocking," he said. "What mother wouldn't want her eighteen-year-old daughter living in sin with a married man who has a history of mental health problems? Can I get in?"

I nodded, and he tumbled his clothes into an untidy pile and slid under the blankets, putting an arm around me as I snuggled into his side. "She loves Father Moran though; the same way I love you. I understand her choices."

He tightened his arm. "I wouldn't want you married to anyone else, pregnant or not."

"I can't get pregnant though, can I?"

"No. Clare was pregnant a few times but all were lost. The doctors she consulted said there was something wrong with me. You're not worrying about it, are you?"

"No, I have too much else to worry about. How long do you think it will be before Alfie comes home?"

"We'll have to wait and see. You sound a bit more positive."

"I am. I've always been worried that what you said about me being an only child meant that all my brothers were going to die, but now I see that isn't true. I am an only child in a way, because none of my brothers have the same father. I'm the postman's daughter."

"Do you believe that I can see the future then?"

"What you see is very real to you."

Will was silent for a while, stroking my arm absently. "Ivy, where did you get those letters?"

"They were delivered with the notification I got about Tom's death. I never bothered to open the box because I thought they were just old papers that Charlotte or I had sent him. But they're all Philips"."

"That seems a little unusual don't you think? The post office is usually quite careful about returning personal effects. I'm surprised they mixed up one brothers" post with another's."

His words gave voice to a feeling I'd had since I opened the box and realised what I was reading. I flung out of bed, threw on Will's discarded shirt and went downstairs into the hall, fumbling though the pockets of the coat I'd had on the morning the letter from Tom's well-meaning chaplain had arrived.

The letter was still crumpled back into its envelope, creased and torn from months in my pocket. I scanned it once, climbing the stairs while an old alarm sounded for the last time in the back of my mind and then dropped away, unheeded. The words on the page confirmed what my heart told me. Messages were always delivered in the end.

Back in bed, Will read the paper I handed him and then very carefully, and very gently he said. "What do you make of that?"

"Philip's dead. I don't need a telegram from the War Office to tell me that. Tom was looking for him, and he was close. The Post Office Rifles and the Poplar and Stepney Rifles fought together at the battle of High Wood. It was in the paper. Tom and Philip were in the same place at the same time; Tom knew that, he went out looking for Philip. I think Tom found him. Tom wasn't brave, you see. No, I don't mean that. I mean Tom was brave, but he wasn't reckless, he knew he had Charlotte and a baby to come back to. That's why I was so angry when I read this letter the first time. I couldn't understand why Tom would have been so stupid as to voluntarily go over the top to save a soldier he didn't know and had never met. He loved Charlotte too much to risk himself unnecessarily. But read this bit. "Heard a colleague shouting for help". That was Philip. Tom heard Phil shouting for help, recognised his voice and went to rescue his brother. The same as I would have done.

Tom got to Philip before he was shot. They were together when they died. And they're buried together somewhere as well. Both my brothers. Somewhere in a field in France."

Will caught me in his arms, held me while tears leaked from my eyes, and soaked his shirt. Then he found my right hand and gripped it in his, held it tightly throughout that long, lonely night.

In the morning I parcelled up both Philip's letters and the one from the chaplain and put them with a covering note into a box.

Dear Mother,

In this box are many letters, most of which you wrote to Philip early last year. They have been sitting in the parlour for four months. The letter you won't recognise is about Tom's death. I found it upsetting to read but the conclusion I draw, from Tom's letter and the fact that Philip's were delivered back to us by the War Office, is that both my brothers are dead, and that they were together when they died. I think Tom found and attempted to rescue Philip and I think their belongings were muddled before being returned.

I have read all the letters you wrote and I understand your explanation, perhaps better than Philip ever did. I love my father, but I have always been angry with you and I know that has come between us. Perhaps it is time for you and I to start again.

Ivy

I left the box by the back gate and went to work. I read with the children, I talked to Joyce Redpath; I smiled at Will when he came in to collect his special class although he didn't acknowledge it, but I felt oddly weightless. The certainty of knowing what had become of Philip was a release somehow, rather than the crushing sadness of Tom's death, and although Alfie was constantly on my mind I expected him back at any moment. I don't think I'd appreciated how much Will's gloomy prophecy had been weighing on my mind even though I didn't consciously believe it, but my mother's revelation had given me another way of seeing. Philip and Tom were both gone, but Alfie would be back eventually and I had a man who loved me, a new home and a future to look forward to. Despite everything, I felt the possibility of happiness floating just out of reach.

I knocked on Will's door at lunchtime, opened it without being asked. He was behind his desk, writing, as always, but I was arrested in the act of going over to kiss him by a raised eyebrow and a "Miss Drummond?"

I looked behind me involuntarily but there was no one else in the room. "You haven't called me that in a while. You've called me Ivy, and you've called me love, and you called me God once last night when I was on my knees doing that thing you like but "Miss Drummond's" a little formal isn't it?"

His face went slightly pink. "I think you should probably be Miss Drummond in working hours don't you? We don't want to give anyone the wrong impression."

"You're not, by any chance, embarrassed are you Will? And what impression would that be?"

"The impression that you're staying with me."

"You aren't running a guesthouse. I'm living with you. I'm sleeping with you. Not that there's much sleeping going on at the moment."

"I think our professional relationship should remain unchanged. I'm trying to protect you, Ivy. Life will be easier for you if no one knows – you can still be proud of yourself if what we do after work remains a secret. I'll be the headmaster and you can be the staff. Sort of. Will you think about getting some proper qualifications? I'm quite happy to support you."

"Thank you. I'll think about it. Headmaster. Sir. Should I be curtsying at this point? What do you want for dinner?"

"Can you cook?"

"Debatable."

"Then you shop. I'll cook. Now run along Miss Drummond. I'm very busy."

"Yes sir. Certainly sir. Do I have to call you that at home as well?"

"Ivy, if you get down on your knees and do that thing I like again, then I'll call you sir."

I fell into a comfortable routine over the next few weeks. Will would leave for work an hour before me and come home an hour afterwards and I saw him around school all the time. He seemed to have forgotten where his office was, he spent so much time out of it. He'd be in the playground as the children arrived, in the dinner hall at lunchtime. He stopped delegating assemblies to Miss Bird and there were rumours in the staffroom that he was actually doing some teaching. The only classroom he never came into was mine. In the daytime we behaved like strangers, but he made up for that every night, usually several times.

He wasn't an easy man to live with though, not really. I'd catch him staring into space when he was supposed to be reading, or he'd stop talking half way through a conversation and once or twice in the early dawn I'd stir to find him sitting on the edge of the bed with his chin on his hand. The burden of his memories was hard to carry.

I learned to interrupt his silences, knowing that he needed to talk more than he needed to think and I got to know every single detail of his time in the army, both the events that had scarred him and the steps towards recovery. He'd learned the names and history of every one of the men who had died under his command and he seemed to use these facts to torture himself on a daily basis. But I refused to let him dwell on it; lose himself in guilt and self-recrimination, so whenever that look stole across his face, thieving the light in his eyes I made him talk. When he wouldn't talk I distracted him with lips and mouth and body and when that wasn't appropriate I set him tasks. I cleaned that mouldering, dust stuffed house from top to bottom and Will followed after me, mending, painting, sanding, smoothing, repairing all the things that had broken or fallen out of place.

I forbade him from walking the streets after dark and I put up with weeks of interrupted sleep because of it, constantly talking him through his nightmares until they began to fade. I was tired all the time, my sleeping patterns so chaotic that my monthly cycle failed and I didn't bleed. It was a long time before the first morning came when I'd not been forcibly awoken in the early hours. The map on the wall stayed covered and garnered no more pins.

I gave up on cooking, but I became very good at devising intricate dishes for Will to execute, partly because he secretly enjoyed it, and partly because practically anything tastes better than a fish sausage. His culinary expertise needed work though, because eventually I found

nearly everything he cooked made me nauseous and once or twice I had
to sneak to the bathroom to throw up when he wasn't looking.

Clock Barn Lane was far enough away from South Street that I could
use a different grocer, butchers and bakers, so I never ran into Charlotte,
or Mrs Carmichael, or my mother and I shopped where I was a stranger
and consequently treated with mild suspicion or ignored.

Alfie didn't come back, and I had no word of him, but every time
there was a knock at the door or a letter arrived I'd jump, automatically
expecting news of my brother. There were some terrible days where
Will had to restrain me from searching out Alfie and releasing him from
whatever training camp had incarcerated him but mostly I spent my
time with a kind of vague hope that today would be the day that Alfie
came home. Being with Will was a welcome distraction, and he taught
me many things. How to write more neatly, how to dance, how to make
him laugh. But what Will and I mostly did together – apart from the
bits that involved panting and sweating – was plan.

We looked for somewhere to rent, either when Alfie returned, short
term, in less than a month, or long term, after the war. We debated the
merits of Scotland or Cornwall, we read guidebooks and discussed
villages; we lay in bed and plotted out the course of our lives.

And then, on the twenty fifth of May, Charlotte had her baby and
my world changed again.

There was a knock on the front door in the early hours of the
morning. I hadn't slept, because Will was having an unusually vivid
progression of dreams and I'd spent some time already trying to talk
him down, or pin him down in an effort to keep my teeth intact. He was
oblivious to all of it, and would have been wracked with guilt had he
been conscious. I threw on a long dressing gown and hurried down the
stairs, opening the door to my mother, whose much thinner and more
haggard face hadn't crossed my path since early April. By the look of
how flushed it was, and the heave of her chest against her dress, she'd
been running.

"Ivy," she gasped out. "Come home now. Tom's baby is coming and
Charlotte needs you."

I swung the door wide and let her in. "Wait in the parlour. I'll go
and get dressed."

I took the stairs two at a time, wondering what turn of events had
caused Charlotte to seek out my mother and why my mother, who'd

had four children herself and therefore had some experience in these matters, was looking so terribly worried. I pulled yesterday's dress off the floor where Will had thrown it, considered his restless, muttering form twisted among the blankets, scribbled a note and then lashed his hands together with the cord of the dressing gown I'd been wearing so he wouldn't hurt himself in my absence.

Then I clattered downstairs to my mother who was still standing awkwardly outside on the front door. "Why didn't you come in?" I asked trotting down the front steps.

"He said I wasn't welcome."

"He was protecting me. You're welcome. Next time, come in. What's the matter with Charlotte?"

The streets were dark, grey sheeted with rain and our boots sloshed through fresh puddles. "She went into labour the day before yesterday but she's not getting anywhere. Betty Carmichael's been helping her but Charlotte's too tired to push. She's been asking for Tom. Betty sent for me, I thought you'd want to help."

"Are they at our house?"

"Still at the shop, Mr Murphy's away in Folkestone apparently. Betty sent him a letter but he hasn't made it back yet. She was expecting him this morning."

"I didn't think you wanted anything to do with Charlotte. Why are you even involved?"

My mother was outpacing me in her haste, and I could only see the back of her head as she responded. "I have lost all my children Ivy, you included, although I did my very best to love you all. This baby is all I have left of my family. You were right. I should have been more involved, and earlier on. Now it looks like I've lost my chance."

"I doubt it, Mum. I'm sure Charlotte will be fine. Women have babies all the time."

"And lose them all the time. And sometimes they grow up and you lose them anyway."

"Have you had any word about Alfie, Mum?"

"No. I assume you haven't either."

"I'd have told you if I had. I'm not lost Mum; I'm only living round the corner. I know I've made choices that you don't approve of but I'm only lost if you want me to be."

She stopped outside Mr Murphy's shop and turned to face me, but her features were cloaked by the blackout and her thoughts were hidden. Then she clutched me to her chest in a hot, hard hug that was over as soon as it began. "I'm sorry, Ivy. For everything I've done."

As I passed through the counter and went up the back stairs I could hear the sound of Charlotte crying. She was lying on her bed, spread-eagled against damp, grey sheets, the enormous hub of her belly exposed and her legs and arms sticking out underneath like spokes. She was making a low, mewling sound that broke every now and then into a sob, which sounded uncomfortably like my brother's name.

I looked at Mrs Carmichael, appalled. Her sleeves were rolled up, her usually pristine apron smeared with stains and her ruddy face had taken on a ghostly pallor.

She said, "The baby's stuck. I can pull it out by force but there's a strong chance that it won't survive. If I don't do it, we'll lose Charlotte too. If she doesn't push I won't be able to shift the baby at all and we'll lose them both and she's too tired, poor girl."

I considered my friend on the bed and the niece that was my last link to my brother and I wondered at the impossibility of having to choose between them. But the words that Will had said to me in Folkestone, just after the wedding came back to me, and although I knew it was only the shellshock talking, it gave me hope.

"Get the baby out," I said. "It's a girl. She'll be fine."

Then I took Charlotte's hand.

"Tom?" she whispered at my touch. "Tom?"

"Tom didn't leave you, Lottie. He never left, not out of choice. He died because he went to rescue his brother, because he loved Philip and because he was brave, Lottie. Because he was very brave. And that's what you have to be right now. Open your eyes, Lottie. Look at me because I'm here for Tom. That's his daughter right there. You can feel her moving. You need to save her Lottie. You couldn't save Tom and I couldn't either but we can damn well save his daughter. Open your eyes Lottie. That's it."

"Ivy?"

"Yes. And Tom. And Philip. And Alfie. And all the other brave men who are still out there fighting. I'm here for all of them. It's your turn now, Lottie. Your turn. There's just as much courage needed from the ones who stay at home as those who go off to fight. This is your fight now. Your war. You need to be brave enough to fight for your baby."

"Ivy?" Charlotte sounded stronger now and there was more strength in her hand as she gripped mine back.

"Be brave, Lottie. Fight. Survive. Are you ready to push? Mrs Carmichael?"

"When I say three then, Charlotte. Ready?"

Charlotte said. "I don't think I can."

"Think about Tom. Can you see Tom, Lottie? Be brave for him. Fight for him like he did for you."

"One."

"Your baby's coming, Lottie. Any minute now you'll be holding her and all of this will be over. One last effort for her Lottie, that's all you need. Do it for her."

"Two."

"And do it for yourself as well. You want this baby. You want to show your mother she was wrong don't you? Fight then. If you want this baby you're going to need to push. Ready?"

"Three."

"Now."

Charlotte gave a tremendous, throat tearing scream, rising up off the bed as Mrs Carmichael grunted with effort and there was a wet slap as something gave under her hands. In my peripheral vision I saw my mother come in with a towel to take the baby.

"Give her a rub, Hilda," instructed Mrs Carmichael, but my mother had already turned the baby upside down and was doing just that.

"Clear the mouth," Mrs Carmichael was still busy with Charlotte. "One more push, there we go."

"Scissors, Betty," said my mother.

"In my bag. Keep going Hilda. She's not blue at least. She probably only needs a bit more, she looks a strong little thing. "

"Come on then, baby," said my mother. "Come on then, little girl."

There was a cough and a cry and a baby's wail filled the room. Charlotte did not react, she was prone on the bed, her eyelids flickering.

"What's the matter with her Mrs C?" I asked.

Mrs Carmichael was still busy between Charlotte's legs. "Loss of blood, tiredness and grief, I should think. If she's asleep I'll stitch her up. She'll thank me later. Hilda give the baby to Ivy, I need you to hold this together."

My new niece was pushed into my lap, yelling at the top of her voice and wrapped in a blood stained towel. I let go of Charlotte's hand, and comforted her daughter instead, whose hair was dark like her father's but with the smooth white skin of her poor exhausted mother, flat out on the bed. I attempted to soothe the baby while Mrs Carmichael and my mother finished with Charlotte and set out changing the sheets underneath her and disposing of the old ones.

"Your daddy would be so proud," I whispered to the child busy screaming in my arms. "Deaf, but proud."

It took some time for Charlotte to recover enough to sit up, and still more before I was ready to leave and it was around lunchtime when I was putting on my coat that a letter arrived for Mrs Carmichael.

"Hello, Mrs C," the postman greeted her with a cheery smile. "Your Peter said I'd find you here. He also said he's starving and when are you coming home. Letter for you."

"Thank you Robin," Mrs Carmichael took the envelope and flicked it open immediately while I put my shawl and shoes on and said my farewells. The she sat down on heavily on the foot of the stairs, one hand to her mouth. "Oh my heavens. Frank's dead."

"Mr Murphy?" I clarified. "How?"

Mrs Carmichael said slowly. "There's been an air raid in Folkestone. In the middle of the day yesterday. Lots of planes, not zeppelins. Ever one heard the engines and came out to look. A bright sunny day, no one thought to get out of the way. Mrs Reckitt says the grocers took a direct hit. Frank's dead and everyone who worked there. Customers. Lots of other shopkeepers. Children. Women. Poor Charlotte, and with a new baby as well. Where are you going Ivy?"

I was already half was out of the door. "I'll be back. I need to find a newspaper."

I scanned the front page of the paper for the facts: *Ninety-five people dead in Folkestone. One hundred and ninety-five injured. Twenty-three German planes carried out a daylight raid. Believed to have been turned back by rain cloud over London. Grocer's shop in Tontine Street took a direct hit. Multiple civilian casualties, particularly women and children. Eighteen soldiers killed in Shorncliffe camp, mostly Canadian. Concerns that this may signal a change in German strategy, and a move to planes rather than zeppelins. This is the first air raid by plane since a single bomber undertook an air raid on London in November which damaged a factory but caused no injuries. Cowardly behaviour of the Hun in targeting innocent children.*

I read the words there in the street and then took the paper home to Will, who was in the kitchen frying eggs, still wearing his pyjamas. He turned at my approach, awkwardly ran a hand through his hair. "I'm sorry about last night. Did I hurt you again?"

I put the paper down on the kitchen table, smoothed it out. "It was bad dreams, that's all. You didn't hurt me."

"Then why?" he asked, holding out his wrists to show the rope burns.

"I was afraid you were going to hurt yourself. Do you remember what it was you were dreaming about?"

"The usual. How's Charlotte? I take it she had her baby."

"Yes. It was a girl, like you said. She'll be fine, but Mr Murphy's dead."

"Yes. A shame. I liked him," he turned back to the pan, slid his breakfast onto a plate and carried it over to the table.

"You don't seem very surprised, Will."

"He was standing behind the counter in his shop. It was very quick, as far as I could tell."

"You knew."

"I saw it. And I went into his shop many times, I met him many times. I saw it a lot."

"And you didn't think to tell me so I could warn Charlotte not to marry him?"

"We've had this conversation. You warned her and she didn't listen to you anyway. What good would telling her have done?"

I stabbed the paper with a finger. "It was an air raid. Is this what you saw in Folkestone two months ago? Exactly two months ago in fact. Is this why you went catatonic on me and refused to speak?"

He scanned the page, set his plate aside untouched. "Yes. That's what I saw, although it feels different when it's in your head and not on a piece of paper. I saw what that street looked like afterwards. I didn't connect it with Frank Murphy though. All those people."

"Will," I said shakily, putting a hand flat on the table for support. "Can you see the future?"

He searched my eyes, his gaze hard. "Do you think I can? Do you believe me at last?"

"I don't know," I wailed. "You knew Mr Murphy was going to die and he did. You said Charlotte would have a girl – she did. You saw this air raid in Folkestone. You knew Mr Andrews would end up as a judge. You saved me from the bombing at Tanners and you said I was an only child and here I am, two half-brothers dead and the other one gone for weeks. For goodness sake Will, you even saw what I like best in bed. How much more right can you be?"

"But? There's a but isn't there?"

"But you have shellshock. You've been terribly injured. You see potential air raids and houses on fire everywhere and you're still having nightmares about things that happened three years ago. Mr Murphy was old and overweight, and he didn't look very healthy to me either. You had a fifty-fifty chance of being right about the sex of the baby. I should have thought the Germans were quite likely to bomb Folkestone anyway, given the amount of troops there, and you said yourself you'd been outside that factory for months before anything happened. I don't know whether it's true. I don't know whether to believe you or not."

He put a hand on my shoulder, squeezed it on his way out of the kitchen to get dressed. "It would help me if you did."

I went to see Charlotte, I played with the baby while she pulled herself together, and then, remarkably quickly, pulled her life together as well. She had a memorial for Mr Murphy, the following week, dressed herself in black from head to toe and then took over the running of her one remaining shop as if she'd been born to it. My mother looked after little Bethany in the mornings, and when she went off to her shift in the sorting office, Charlotte's mother took over for the afternoons. The baby had negotiated some kind of compromise between the three of them, although the fact that Charlotte was paying her mother by the hour helped. There were times over the next few weeks when, despite the mourning, I caught her smiling.

Chapter Twenty

Will and I calculated that Alfie would come home before the end of June, if he was coming home at all. Some soldiers managed to take leave before they were shipped off to the front, but whether Alfie could even make it back to Poplar on his own was a matter of some debate. After months of not worrying about air raids I found myself constantly looking to the skies, jumping at the slam of doors, pausing at the rumble of thunder.

Then, on the 13th of June, just before lunchtime, I was reading a particularly tricky passage with one of my most improved learners, when Will walked into the classroom. That was unusual because he'd only taken his special class out around twenty minutes before and they weren't due back for some time. He opened the door, stepped across the threshold, turned to face where I was standing and said. "They're coming."

It was the look on his face that stopped me cold. The cast of his features, the way he held himself told me how frightened he was, how terrified. But he was fighting it.

"They're coming," he repeated. "You shouldn't be here."

Forty children stared at him. A few sniggered. I was horror struck, horror punched, horror beaten round the face and left totally overcome by pure, naked fear, as I looked at the man I loved standing there and realised that I believed every word he said. I forgot the "Miss Drummond"; and the "headmaster" and the formality of the classroom and the fact that our private relationship wasn't supposed to be out in public and I ran through the desks to where he was standing, took his hand. There was a collective intake of breath amongst the children and an outbreak of whispering.

"I believe you, Will. Are they coming now?"

"They're coming," he repeated dully, his attention flicking around the room as he struggled to concentrate on me.

"Will, I believe you. You are not mad. A terrible thing happened to you in the war, but it wasn't your fault. You made a mistake and I forgive you, anyone would forgive you. Do I get the children out?"

He attempted to focus, failed, closed his eyes and did the single most courageous thing I'd ever seen anybody do. He smiled. He mastered himself, mastered the fear and the guilt and the self-doubt, beat it all back, opened his eyes and came out smiling. "They're coming," he said, confidently, clearly and in a whisper added, "Thank you."

Then he took charge. "Miss Redpath," he ordered. "Get all the children out. Not into the playground, it won't be safe. Take them to Poplar Park. Right now. Go." He turned to me. "I will fetch the school bell and ring an alarm then go to the top floor and help Miss Bird get the boys out. You clear the first floor, see to the girls." He was gone almost before he'd finished speaking.

I took a deep breath. "Children. Line up by the door. Don't take anything. Hold hands in twos and follow Miss Redpath. Don't run. Go now." My voice cracked across the room and the class rose as one and, pushing and shoving, headed towards the door.

Joyce caught my arm on the way past. "What's going on? Is this a drill?"

I replied grimly. "The headmaster says there's going to be an air raid. He's never wrong. Get them into the open."

I outpaced the children and raced for the stairs as the bell started to ring on the top corridor. The girls" classrooms on the first floor were already buzzing when I flung the door open and called to the teacher. "Message from the headmaster. There's going be an air raid. Take all the children to Poplar Park right now. Leave everything behind. There's no time to waste."

I waited until the class had started to move and then I picked up my skirts and headed for the top floor, against a flow of milling schoolchildren. Miss Bird was at the head of the stairs, flailing the bell with a mad urgency.

Will was a few paces behind her, herding children, and he called out my next instruction. "Clear the school, Ivy. Check every room."

"What are you going to do?"

"Save them," he said. "Every last one. Meet me in the park as soon as you can." Then he swept down the steps, students carried along in his wake.

I fought the crush to the far end of the second floor and began systematically opening doors. The woodwork room, science classroom, cooking facilities, boys teaching areas, store room and cupboards, nooks and crannies. I sent all the stragglers I could find running after their classmates, as the school began to fall silent around me and the children left. I checked the first floor, girls" classroom, the toilets, Alfie's cupboard, the staff room, the offices, as the last sounds of footsteps fell away. On the ground floor the reception classroom was already empty, the odd pencil rolling across a desk, open books on the tables, but there was no one left and the heels of my boots clicked lonely across the parquet floor. From somewhere outside music played, a dancing, familiar tune that I recognised but couldn't name. I trotted down the steps, did a final tour of the playground, checked in the back alley.

Above me the sky was clear and blue, and it was a warm, early summer day, the sun bathing me gently in the promise of heat to come. There weren't any birds, which wasn't unusual in the middle of London, but the sound of the living, breathing city around me seemed swaddled somehow, a background lullaby. I headed for the park, following the trail of chatter lingering in the still air, breathing as shallowly as possible, walking lightly and listening, always listening. I was nearly at the gates to the park, nearly within the sanctuary that had already accepted the children when I heard it. A low, far away droning, like thunder, only more organised, mechanised, a man made storm.

Children were standing in small clusters chatting, the older boys already starting some kind of raucous game, a few of the younger one still holding hands.

Will was moving from one group to another, addressing children by name I was sure he'd never noticed, exchanging words with the staff he'd always ignored. The relief in his eyes when saw me was palpable. Immediately, he found a nearby bench, stood on it, and, in a tone of command I'd only ever once heard him use he said. "South Street School. Be quiet and listen."

Against all my expectations, the children obeyed, stopped what they were doing and listened to a man who always seemed to prefer writing to teaching, a man who was now holding the attention of one hundred and fifty souls without breaking a sweat.

"Can you hear the planes?" he called.

A proper silence fell, a listening silence. The thunder that wasn't thunder rumbled across the park, killing any other noise that tried to compete.

"That noise is German planes. I've heard them before. They are coming. We will be safe as long as you do exactly as you are told. Get into your class groups and sit down. Teachers, I need a headcount."

The horde of children convulsed, reformed itself into seated, orderly lines, teachers moving among the rows and I thought, at that point, that Will had succeeded, that South Street School had been saved.

Joyce Redpath put up her hand. "I'm still short of twelve."

"Two," called one of the girls" teachers.

"Two here unaccounted for," came Miss Grafton, from the boys" staff.

"Who?" Will asked Joyce directly.

"Danny, Marigold, Eric."

Will glanced at me. "Did you check the study?" he asked, and I could tell by his tone that he was expecting me to answer in the affirmative, to make everything alright. I tried to remember going into his office, checking the hidden room behind the bookcase. I tried to remember if the little wooden door in the corridor that I'd missed for months before he showed me where it was had been open or not, but try as I might I couldn't remember. I shook my head slowly; panic mushrooming inside me, spawning an awful feeling of culpability, of failure at the thought that I hadn't done my job.

Without a word, he leapt off the bench, sped away through the park back in the direction we'd come, his black cape flying out behind him as he ran. I wasn't far behind although I was soon outpaced, running flat out into the thickening air, full of the drone of engines, the warning overhead.

But I called after him as I ran, because the questions I'd forgotten to ask now seemed louder in my head than the noise. I threw the words out but my voice was faint against the overwhelming din as the planes drew nearer. "Why do you have a special class, Will? What makes them special?" And then, the most important question of all, as he pounded up the school steps, barged the doors I hadn't locked with his shoulder. "What do you see about them, Will? What do you see?"

I was outside at the foot of the stairs when the first plane sundered the soft blue of the sky with its hard black body, the dirty smoke pumping out of its two engines, the wings scratching sparks from the sunshine. It was so low I could see the individual plates of metal riveted across its belly, hear the clanking groan as a hole in the undercarriage slowly opened, birthed a bomb.

But Will hadn't stopped; he was inside the building while I made it into the hall. From outside came the high whistle I'd only heard once before, on a night in November outside Tanners Steel Works, standing hand in hand with a stranger underneath a railway arch. "It's too late, Will," I shouted to him as he rounded the bottom of the stairs to the second floor. "There's nothing you can do to save them. The Germans aren't coming. They're already here."

The whistle rent the air, as if the very heavens were screaming and with a tremendous crash the house to the right hand side of the school was hit. I remembered I'd sent Billy round there with cake, once upon a time. I turned my head to see the entire facade slump forwards, the wall congealing in a puddle of brick in the middle of the road.

Will flicked a glance back at me over his shoulder, but didn't stop climbing. "The children are in danger because of me, Ivy. They're following my orders. They need me to save them. Let me do it. Just this once, I want to help."

He moved further away from me with every step, and as he did so I saw in him the shadows of everyone else who had left me - Tom, Philip, Alfie. I ran. I ran as fast as I possibly could, up the stairs, along the corridor, through his office to find the children huddled guiltily around the record player, the last notes of Alexander's Ragtime Band dying away. A few steps in front, Will ordered. "Get out now."

I said "Run," at almost the same moment.

Danny jumped, shot for the stairs, leading a charge of small bodies pushing past me. I took Eric's hand and Will swung Marigold into his arms as she'd started to cry. I made it into the corridor, thrust out my right hand behind me for Will to take and found Marigold's in it instead.

"Go, Ivy." Will said gently. "You shouldn't be here."

I took off down the steps, tugging both children behind me as the second bomb struck.

It hit the bell tower on the roof, which put up all the resistance of a flimsy, misplaced decorative item and shattered into plaster and splinters and the bomb carried on downwards. It penetrated the heart of the school, crashing through the ceiling of the boys" classroom, falling though chalk dust and paper until it burst open the floor. It smashed straight through the middle of the headmaster's study on the first level, and then drilled down until it came to rest on the smooth, warm wood of the reception classroom floor.

I made it to the bottom of the stairs, broke for the front door while around me the old Victorian brick shuddered, timbers shrieked and cried out against the violence of the intrusion, metal twisted painfully, glass pattered like tears against the floor.

The shell exploded.

Chapter Twenty-One

It took some time for me to finally decide that I wanted to wake up. It was quite pleasant to drift in the black well of semi consciousness, dimly aware that someone was holding my hand, that a familiar voice was talking to me, reassuring me that I was loved. I awoke gently, peacefully, lying on my bed in a cool, quiet room, safe and protected.

"Ivy Drummond, you'll be the death of me," my mother remarked.

That was not the voice I'd expected to hear.

"Mum?" I blinked my eyes open and instantly regretted it, because the light coming in from the small window on the left hand side of the bed where I was lying was retina blisteringly bright, and far too much for my sensitive brain. A headache sprang into being somewhere behind my left temple and I sank back onto the pillow with a groan. "Where am I?"

"Still in hospital obviously, and likely to stay in for a while longer. You look a fright."

"Thanks, Mum. My head hurts. Where's Will?"

"You've fractured your skull, or dented it anyway. The bandages only came off an hour ago. You've got one black eye and one red one and your face is scratched to pieces. I thought you were never going to wake up."

"I think I wish I hadn't. Where's Will?"

She sniffed disapprovingly. "He's not important at the moment. You are." She sniffed again, and I might have mistaken the cause. "Don't do that to me again, Ivy."

There was a splash of something against my hand. "You're not crying are you, Mum?" I couldn't bear to look.

There was a third sniff. "Don't be ridiculous."

"Mum?" It was far easier to speak to her with my eyes closed. "There was an air raid. I left some children behind inside the school. Will went back to get them out. Are they alright? Did they? Are they alright?"

"Yes."

"Are you sure?"

"Yes. Sixteen children left behind. Mostly the younger ones. Mr Andrews came running from the pub, and he took over, he did a fantastic job, saved so many lives yesterday. He told everyone where to dig, and he directed the rescue effort. We took the school apart brick by brick trying to find those children. Everyone helped, the whole street. Most of the little ones were nearly out of the front door under the lintel, it saved their lives. You and two of the smallest were just behind. They're all safe. The school was completely destroyed. No one remembered your Mr Rawlings though, Ivy, except Mr Andrews. As soon as they'd found you people were giving up, moving on to the next pile of rubble, but Mr Andrews insisted everyone go back and try to save the headmaster. He'd be wherever you were, Mr Andrews said."

"Where's Will, Mum?"

My mother said, in that blunt, forthright way she had, that many people would have called rude. "Dead."

I almost laughed at her, because she sounded so ridiculous. "No, he isn't. Where is he, I want to see him?" I threw the covers back, sat up, swung my legs off the bed and winced when I saw the ugly swelling on my ankle, felt the tightness across my stomach as stitches pulled.

My mother took my hand and squeezed it. "Mr Andrews tried to find him Ivy, we all did, we dug and dug but there was no sign. Nothing left at all. They've written to his wife. He's been declared dead."

"Unlikely Mum, impossible. He'd never leave me. He was the one always worried I was going to leave him, not the other way around. He promised to hold my hand for the rest of his life. Now where is he?"

"He's gone, Ivy. You won't find him and he's not important right now. You need to focus on yourself."

"How long have I been in hospital?"

"Since lunchtime yesterday, just after it happened. Nearly a day and a half."

"For a bump on the head and a sprained ankle?"

"It was a bit more than that, Ivy. You've a cut to your stomach, quite a nasty one – I stayed with you while they stitched it up. And it's very swollen Ivy, your stomach, much more than it used to be before you left home. Your chest too. I couldn't help wondering – but it's nothing to worry about right now, it can wait until you're feeling better."

"I'll feel better as soon as I see Will. Help me get home."

I struggled into a dress that my fingers were too painful to lace properly and stood, although my head span and I tasted blood at the back of my throat. By sheer force of will I hobbled into the hall to find Charlotte sitting primly outside, her golden hair a brilliant contrast to the black she was still wearing.

"Does she know?" she spoke over my head, addressed the question to my mother.

"She knows about him."

"I'm going home, Lottie. Help me get there. Please."

Charlotte nodded, and fastened a hand on my arm. "I will help you in whatever way you want me to," she promised.

There was a bus involved somewhere and I remembered walking braced between my mother and my best friend but nothing about the journey was real until I stood on the corner of Clock Barn Lane, the white house rising, tall and imposing as always, in front of me.

The key was still in its hiding place and my mother and Charlotte watched from across the road as I ascended the steps, turned the lock of my old front door. Once inside, I could tell the house was empty. Will's coat and mine were still on the pegs in the hall but there was fresh dust on the tiles. In the kitchen the range was cold and silent – it had been cleaned and swept but no fire was laid. The cups were washed, the plates on the dresser neatly in order, the sturdy kitchen table scrubbed and bare. I hauled myself up the stairs by the bannister, knowing that the confirmation I sought, the questions I'd been asking myself since I woke up could only be answered here.

The bedroom doors were all closed, save ours, and inside the desk was tidy, the books in order, the wardrobes untouched, clothes hanging neatly on their rails.

But it was the map on the wall I'd come to see, the map I'd only examined once, months ago and hadn't looked at since. From the time I'd moved in it had been covered, a symbol of the way Will was trying to move on with his life, or so I thought. Now I yanked the sheet off unceremoniously and took the closer look that I really should have taken before. I found my parents" house, the garden rendered in miniature, followed the road down past the White Star, turned the corner to where South Street School had once stood.

The entire area was covered in pins. I couldn't even make out the footprint of the school house, and many of the buildings around it bristled with so many pins there were more holes than paper. Will had been expecting the air raid. He had known, all this time.

In the middle of the map were pinned a few pieces of folded paper, with nothing on the front but a cryptic comment 'For when the day comes'. The handwriting left no doubt as to its author.

I sat on the edge of our hard and empty bed to read it.

My dearest Ivy,

I am writing this letter on the day of Alfie's tribunal, it's late evening, I've dropped your brother off back at home and I've been to the solicitors. I'm sitting here writing you a letter in the middle of a bedroom it took a mere four hours to clean, although there is so much paper in my wardrobe I doubt I'll ever see my clothes again.

I digress. This isn't an easy letter to write.

I am dead, my love. You are reading this letter, I'm not sure when, but you're only reading it because I have died in an air raid in the middle of my office surrounded by the children of my special class, as you call them. That's why they are my class. They are there when the bombs fall, the same as I am, they are going to die with me, because of me, and I've been trying to make that up to them in any way I can.

So many awkward questions Ivy, and you never asked me the right ones. You never asked me what I see when I look at myself - what the future holds for me. There's a reason the mirror downstairs is covered, a reason I've removed every other reflective surface in the house.

The day I woke up in hospital, when I was given a looking glass to see the scar on my face, the first thing I saw was my own death. I know exactly where it will happen, if not quite when. That was my first vision. It's why I've spent my time trying to prove whether or not the air raids I saw were real, it's why I drew this map, why I've walked the streets all these long nights.

You see Ivy, the houses that I see on fire, the people inside — I am one of them.

I should have died with my men on the battlefield. That was my war, my fight - I told you that in Folkestone last weekend, but I don't think you believed me. Did you never wonder how a geography lecturer with no experience in primary education and who didn't need the money came to be working at an elementary school?

The map on the wall will tell you. The school will be bombed, and I mean to be there when it is. It's why I spend most of every day in my office, waiting. The last three years of my life have been a torture for me, and I am too craven to want to face any more. I welcome death with open arms.

At least, that's what I thought until last November, until I saw your face in the firelight and I realised there might be another way for me. And there was, oh Ivy, there was. I have loved you since the moment I saw you, and even now you are on your way here to make that future a reality.

These last few months I have finally learned what it is to love. You have saved me, beautiful, precious girl. You took the pieces of the man I was and put them back together again. You gave me the courage to want to live again, to try again. Until the time comes, I will stay by your side, holding your hand, for as long as I possibly can. I hope when it comes, I can find the courage to face it, and to let you go.

Your key is in the lock. The front door is opening; I can hear it even from this desk in my bedroom. I hope you like the candles on the stairs, you will probably think they're another romantic gesture, but actually, I'm using them to hide the fact that I haven't got round to cleaning up the rest of the house.

The loose floorboard halfway up has just creaked. I've never heard anyone climb stairs so slowly. You must be very nervous. I'll sit here and carry on writing when you arrive so I don't make it worse.

Tonight changes everything. It's a night I thought would never come – hoped for, but never expected. When I saw that air raid in Folkestone last weekend I realised how little time I have left, you see. The planes are coming, as they have been coming for the last three years but so much has changed for me. I no longer want them to hurry, all I ask for is that they hold off a little while longer, so I can spend another day with you.

You are standing behind me. Carrying your bags, looking round the bedroom, wondering if you've done the right thing. I won't tell you, but this is your bedroom now, your house. I stopped at my solicitors on the way home and changed my will. This, and all the money I have that isn't already tied up elsewhere is for you to use, and for the use of your heirs after I am gone. I hope there will be many. Clare will not be pleased when she realises what I have done, but it seems I must die before I am free of her.

I hope that you will move on with your life, study for the qualifications you need, teach if you find it makes you happy.

You're drinking tea now, hanging up your clothes in the wardrobe.

I will leave you one last thing – I will give you our future together, although I won't be there to see it. I will find the house we spoke of on the train, the place you told your parents we'd be moving to. We can plan that life together, in whatever days remain and I will try to make as much of it as possible a reality.

You're humming to yourself. I think that probably means you're relaxed. I'm not going to tell you what I've seen — I'm not going to mention this letter, or the sadness that's coming. You don't believe that what I see is real anyway, and I do hope you are right.

I'm going to make you so happy in the time we have left, as happy as I am right now. You shouldn't be here with me Ivy, but I'm so glad you are.

I made it to the front door, but the age it took my mother and Charlotte to reach me could be measured by the movement of tectonic plates. I stood on the doorstep, my key clutched in my hand, and I knew I was not simply an only child, but completely alone.

Chapter Twenty-Two

There was shouting, I remember that much. I was doing most of it, screaming at my mother and Charlotte because they were there, screaming at Will because he wasn't. The Germans came in for quite a lot of my anger as well, and I probably yelled loudly enough for them to hear. This wasn't like Tom's death, or Philip's, which had happened far away and days ago by the time I found out – Will died on the street where I grew up, only yesterday, and his death was too new, too close yet for tears. Eventually, Charlotte helped me 'in whatever way I wanted her to' by slapping me round the face, and telling me that breaking my heart wouldn't do any good.

I went to our bedroom, to stand in front of the map, while the sun's light was swallowed piece by piece by the ravenous darkness and outside the window London disappeared into its maw. One hundred and sixty-two people died in that air raid, and four hundred and thirty-two were injured. There were people all over the city whose family, friends and colleagues would never be coming home, people in the same position as me, and while this should offer some comfort, I was much too selfish to think of anyone but myself. I grieved alone.

I am dead, my love. The words of his last letter haunted me, whispering through the darkness when I tried to sleep. How did he know? And, more importantly, was he right?

If I hadn't got lost, maybe everything would have been different. I looked at the map and I went through every single second we had spent together since that night in November and wondered if there was something I could have changed, something I could have done better that would have saved his life. The conclusion I came to was this – Will left the battlefield long before I met him, but he was still fighting a very personal war, struggling to survive the aftermath of that conflict. And I only told him that I was on his side half an hour before he died. It didn't really matter whether he was right or not, I should have supported him, in the same way he supported me.

For a long time, I'd confused love and marriage, and held out for something he could never give me. When I finally decided to go to bed with him, I'd confused that with love too. I'd never believed him, never trusted him, never been there for him unconditionally - Will always thought I was going to leave him, and I very nearly had. I'd told him I loved him many times, but until now, until this moment, until I'd lost him, I'd never really understood what it meant. I needed to tell him I loved him properly at last, before I could say goodbye.

I also needed to do it right now, because as soon as his wife arrived and they finally dug his body out of the rubble she'd take him away for burial wherever she saw fit. It was still dark as I left the house, my mother asleep in one of the bedrooms, Charlotte gone home to take care of Bethany. I crept downstairs, avoiding the loose floorboard, and I flung on Will's old black coat, hoping that it would bring some comfort, although it still reeked of damp. I walked the two miles back to school, through streets which were supposed to be sleeping, but I could feel the crackle of tension thrumming through the walls and I doubted many people had closed their eyes that night.

I rounded the corner, passed the back alley where the gate was undamaged and still closed, although most of the wall around it no longer existed. As I approached the front of the school the road became clogged with debris and I picked my way through fallen brick, across blackened timbers, over a crust of glass. A picture book flicked its bright pages at me in the strengthening breeze. The air smelled of wet plaster, and a rivulet of water dampened the pavement, escaping from where the children's toilets used to be. Only when I was near the entrance was it safe enough to look up, and see the damage that had been done.

The school was hollow. Its walls were still standing but all the windows were gone and through the holes I could see that the building had been cored, the central staircase missing and a tide of rubble washed in front of the doors. There appeared to be no way in, but I noticed multiple footprints in the dust, cavities in the pile of stone, discarded beams, splintered where the ends had levered up obstacles that didn't want to move. The stove up in the second floor classroom was visible from outside in the street. I placed my hand on the sturdy red brick, by way of comfort, and I could feel the storm of tears gathering behind my eyes.

Then I saw him. A tall, familiar figure in a greatcoat, standing silent inside the building, his face tilted to the open skies. Dawn had pushed red fingers through the darkness but I'd have known this man in the dead of night. I stood on a pile of brick, clambered in through a window, my feet stirring up clouds of dust as I raced across the floor and threw myself into his arms. "Alfie, Alfie," I cried, hugging him tightly, while the sorrow inside dispersed slightly. "You came back."

I realised eventually that Alfie wasn't embracing me, but was locked in place, with his hands at his sides - he wanted me to get off him. I stepped back, but the words poured out before I could think about the best way to break the news. "Will died Alfie, Will is dead. The school was bombed and Will was still inside and he's dead somewhere under all of that and…"

I broke off abruptly because Alfie had walked away. I choked back a sob. I shouldn't have expected anything else, I knew Alfie couldn't deal with emotion but I felt raw, tender, like the outer layer of my skin had been peeled back, and his reaction stung me. He moved away, searching the ground for something and at length, he picked up a piece of wood, and carefully added it to a pile behind him. I swayed, thought I might fall, but I controlled myself and took a deep breath, "I don't think there are many sticks here Alfie, why don't we go to the park and see what we can find there?" Alfie was unchanged, had returned from his time away unaffected and now, more than ever, he was my responsibility, must be my sole concern from now on.

Alfie paused, his head down, and once again I had that sense that he didn't want me near him, and, more than that, Alfie wanted me to be quiet. When he moved again he reached for a green canvas bag, almost the double of his collecting bag at home, and from this he removed a hammer and some nails. The hammer had his name on. I wondered how many soldiers came back from basic training carrying tools instead of weapons.

While he laid out the wood he had collected I rummaged inside the bag, finding more equipment, a saw, a plane, a water bottle and a letter, which I skimmed. Alfie had a week's leave and then he had to report for duty in Folkestone, but he had been assigned to the Labour Corps, as a result of the unfit medical rating that he had been recently granted following reassessment. It meant he would not fight, and might not even go to France at all, but would spend his war making things for the army. I reached out to touch his arm, but he was already standing again, very still, in the same spot, eyes down, focusing on something I couldn't see. It came to me slowly. Alfie was listening.

I looked behind him on the ground to see what he was making and it was not the twisted sculpture I was expecting but something long and thin, and quite recognisable. The tears came then, when they brought the least relief, and I smeared them with my hands, frantically looking through the wreckage for what Alfie had spotted.

We were standing where the reception classroom should be, and above me, the first floor was spiked with timber joists, floorboards hanging between in impossible angles, the ruins of walls leaning precariously above. Half buried in the frozen torrent of stone that poured down the centre of the school there was one, much larger slab of wood, tilted to rest on its upright partner, forming a small triangle beneath. The sun was rising, and as the dim glow brought definition to the chaos, I could see that the wood was panelled. There was only ever one room in this school with panelled wood walls, walls so close together that one could rest on the next without falling. Within the space at the bottom of the wall the light glanced on carved feet, the turned legs of a desk.

The ring of Alfie's hammer shattered the quiet, but all the houses abutting the school were damaged and deserted and there was no one to complain. When Alfie's deft fingers had finished their work he held a ladder. He paused again, to listen. I could not hear what he heard. I had not spent a lifetime listening instead of talking, using my ears instead of my mouth. An intense rush of love for my brother wobbled my legs, and I was grateful for the first time in my entire life that he was born the way he was, born for this moment, for the unique skills he had that no one else could match.

My mother told me Will was dead, she dug in the rubble of the school for him. Charlotte told me Will was dead, she had been twice bereaved already. Will himself told me he was dead. But there is more to life than just facts and figures, so much more to feel and wonder at, so much more to understand. I'd heard lots and lots of stories about people being killed in air raids, but almost none where they got miraculously saved, and I wanted this to be that sort of story. I screwed my eyes shut and I prayed to the God I hadn't believed in for six years for a miracle.

Alfie took some time to find a stable location to rest his ladder, and when he did he climbed laboriously up it, reaching the first floor and balancing carefully between the joists. He pulled the ladder up after him and used it as a bridge, spreading his weight across the skeleton floor as he approached his target. He put the ladder across the cascade of stone, crawled gingerly over it, although his movement stirred up an enormous cloud of dust, which filled the gaping cavity inside the school and made me cough. I waited for the dust to settle, but once it had been released, it took advantage of its freedom, choking the air until my eyes watered and I couldn't see my brother. The pile of rubble creaked and groaned, complaining in a low pitched rumble that I could feel through my soles. It started to move. A brick tumbled towards me, a wedge of plaster began to slide, a timber rolled and then the whole mountain of debris was moving, throwing up so much dust that I couldn't breathe.

Then Alfie came striding down the tumbled stairwell, riding the fall, slipping and sliding but still on his feet, although he was overbalanced with the weight of the burden slung over his shoulder. He went past me without stopping, made for the opposite end of the building, mounted a desk and dropped out of a window while I followed blindly.

In the back alley, Alfie laid down the body he was carrying, then propped himself against the back gate, heaving for breath.

Will was dead. He had no obvious injury but he showed not a flicker of consciousness, his chest still. I knelt in the dust, ran a finger down the face I had once touched, and held and kissed, in its agony and its ecstasy, and I found it warm. I pulled his head into my lap, my tears falling freely now, splashing his face and with the water from Alfie's bag I wet his lips, tipped enough down his throat that he awoke with a start, coughing reflexively. He couldn't, or wouldn't open his eyes but he raised a shaky hand, groping for the bottle and I supported him while he drank.

"Said go," he murmured, and I had to bend close to hear.

I stroked his cheek. "I came back. I always come back."

"Safe?"

"The children? Yes, all safe. You saved them. But I thought you'd died. I thought I'd lost you, Will. I read the letter you wrote—'I am dead, my love"—and that's the last letter of yours that I am ever going to read. You are forbidden from writing to me ever again. From now on, we are going to discuss things face to face. Forever. Til death do us part, and it won't." I shook his shoulder, needing some vent for my relief, and anger, and joy and a mix of other feelings too complex to name. "No matter what you see, or how bad things get, I'm not leaving you. I love you. Don't you ever keep anything from me again."

He grimaced, and his eyelids flickered, and he croaked, "Dead. Thought I was dead. But then Alfie, and dust." His eyes opened a crack, and he squinted, but pushed my outstretched hand away weakly as he struggled up, levering himself into a sitting position next to my brother. He reached over, touched the back of Alfie's hand and murmured, "Thank you."

Alfie's response was to locate his saw, and begin polishing it on the tail of his shirt.

I tried to hoist Will up. "Let's get you to hospital then. Does it hurt anywhere? Do you think you can stand?"

He shook me off, his voice stronger now, and he bent his legs, flexed his shoulders, wincing. "I'm not going to hospital. Ever again. I've survived worse than this. Sit with me."

"You need medical help Will, not idle conversation. You've been stuck under a pile of rubble for two days."

"I was stuck under a desk. Sit with me."

I sighed, lowered myself to the ground. "Your wife is on her way here, by the way. You were declared dead when no one could find you and they've sent for Clare already. Although as it turns out your office was the safest place to be. If you'd been even a few seconds behind me coming down those stairs most of the school would have fallen on you." I took his hand, and then, feeling how much it was trembling, I pressed myself into his side and wrapped my arms around him, holding him tight. "I'm glad for the visions, Will, despite everything. If you hadn't been exactly where they told you to be, Clare would be burying you and I'd be back at home with nothing."

"Clare thinks I'm dead?"

The tremors under my hands began to ease and I hugged him again. "Clare, my mother, Charlotte, Mr Andrews, everyone else who lives in South Street. They all tried to save you, but only Alfie succeeded."

"Clare thinks I'm dead?"

"Apparently so. I suppose this means I'll have to meet her, at last. She'll be on her way to Clock Barn Lane."

He took a deep breath, shrugged free of my embrace and coughed for long enough to be painful. "Not nothing," he corrected eventually. "That house is yours, and there's another. I may have neglected to mention it in all the excitement of thinking that every single second of every single day was the last I was going to spend with you. I bought a house so you could still have the future we planned. It's down near the coast, plenty of open fields around it, nice big oven for baking bread, backs onto a forest so you won't have to walk far to fetch the wood. There's enough room for Alfie too. It all passes into your name in the event of my death."

"You aren't technically dead, Will. Despite that letter."

He fumbled for Alfie's shoulder, boosted himself upright and leaned against the gate. "Oh, but I am. Clare would like nothing more than to have me permanently out of her life – and who better than Captain Andrews, pillar of the community, to sign my death certificate? Your parents might even approve of me if I bequeath you all my worldly goods."

I rose, took his hand and patiently explained, in the same tone of voice I used with my class, "You've had a nasty bump on the head, but the doctors can make it all better. Come with me to the nice, clean hospital."

He was frowning, but his mouth kept twitching towards a smile. "I can stand," he said. "But I can't make it down to one knee, I've been stuck under a pile of rubble for two days. If you want to marry me, you'll have to take me exactly as I am right now. No rings, no romance. No name either, I'll have to choose another one."

"That isn't funny, Will. If you won't go to hospital, come home with me and we can wait for your wife together. I don't need to marry you, what we already have is enough for me, especially now you're alive."

"It isn't enough for me, especially now I'm dead." He waved a hand to forestall my objections. "Hear me out, I'm thinking clearly for the first time in three years. I'm not dead. I was expecting to be, and I can't tell you what it's been like, waiting to be blown to pieces every five minutes. Knowing I was going to take innocent lives with me. Knowing I'd been selfish enough to let you love me anyway. But I'm not dead. And the only people who know that are you and Alfie, and I don't expect Alfie will tell. As long as I can make it out of London before anyone sees me I can stay dead which means I'm also divorced. I can move to the country, I can start again." He held out a hand for me to take. "I can marry you."

I struggled to follow his reasoning. "You want to pretend to be dead?"

He beckoned to me again. "Of course. I don't want to be that man any more, Ivy. Skulking around in the darkness, seeing horrors everywhere - unable to sleep for the nightmares and the guilt. Shackled to a woman I don't love, treating you as a stranger. I want to be proud of myself again, I want a new life. I want Will Rawlings to be dead. He was weak and afraid."

I stepped close, took the outstretched hand. "Will Rawlings was exceptionally brave. He faced his fears. He did his duty. He died saving the lives in his care."

"Eventually," he said. "Alfie can help me to Charing Cross and I'll take the coastal train to the cottage. As soon as the solicitor's sorted out my will it will pass into your name. You stay in London long enough to make sure that no one suspects I'm alive and then come down and join me. Alfie can live with us, exactly as we planned." I supported him through a few unsteady paces. "I'll say I was bombed out, lost all my papers and identification. We can get married in a registry office somewhere quiet, no witnesses."

I sniffed, "You really aren't very good at proposing, are you? Given that you've had some practice."

He leaned his head against mine, whispered into my hair. "You found me in the darkness Ivy, when I'd given up all hope of ever seeing the light. You've given me a new life. Come and live it with me."

When I could bear to, I stepped back a little. "Of course I'll marry you. But I'd stay with you anyway, because I love you. I finally understand how much stronger love is than anything else. Stronger than convention, than religion, stronger even than death." I tipped my head back so I could look him in the eye. "It's strong, the way I feel for you, and powerful. I know you, Will Rawlings. I know everything you've been through and I love you because of it. And I will carry on loving you, no matter what you're called, or where you live, or what the future holds for us." I closed my eyes, nestled back into his arms, and I wondered.

I wondered about the conversations I'd never had with my mother, about the things that could happen between a man and a woman, that I was now fully aware of, and could describe in some detail. I wondered whether Will's cooking was really bad enough to make me sick, and whether a few sleepless nights were really enough to stop a monthly bleed. Most of all I wondered just how much Clare had paid the doctors who had told Will her inability to have children rested with him.

He took a few deep breaths, before putting both hands on my

shoulders and pushing me firmly away. "Our future is..." His fierce, penetrating ice-blue stare bored into me, but it simply bounced off the tremendous welling happiness I felt, and, when it came, his reply sounded like he was doing some wondering of his own. "I can't. I don't. I don't see anything about you. There's nothing when I look at you now, no visions, no premonitions, no idea of your future." His expression relaxed into a wide, uncomplicated smile. "There's just you. Ivy Drummond. Whom I love more than life itself."

I slipped the black coat off my shoulders, handed it to him to put on, and then, with my arm on one side, and Alfie's support on the other, we shuffled and hobbled in the direction of the train station. "Let me tell you the future that I see then, for a change. There is a cottage in a wood, white washed, with roses around the door. If it doesn't look like that at the moment, then the man who currently owns it needs to get on with painting and planting over the next few months to make sure it does. The front of the house looks out over wide, sweeping fields, and you can see it from miles around, because there is always a light in the windows and the curtains are rarely drawn. No one in the cottage fears aid raids.

A husband and wife live there. The husband reads a lot, goes out for long walks, and writes long and detailed books about geography, which he never, ever discusses with his wife. He gets up early to light the fires and he has learned, after a long process of trial and error, to bake his own bread. He forgives himself. He heals. He sees nothing to trouble him and he sleeps soundly. He always has a meal on the table when his wife gets home from work. His wife is the headmistress of the local school and is actively involved in charity work, helping to support war veterans. She is proud of herself, and of her children. There are two, both girls, Philippa and Thomasina."

"No children have ever been more unexpected. Or unlikely."

I continued, ignoring Will's interruption. "No children have ever been more loved."

"No children have ever been more loved," he echoed. "Whatever their origins and parentage. Although their names will be the subject of future discussion, particularly if they are strapping boys."

"The house is always busy with people coming and going. The children's uncle, Alfie, who lives in a house he has built himself in the forest, is a welcome guest, although he is also the village carpenter, having learned many skills during the war, and is much in demand."

"The family owes a debt of gratitude to Alfie that can never be repaid, and he is welcome however, and whenever he chooses." Alfie didn't reply to Will, but I knew he was listening, as always.

I went on. "The children visit their grandparents in London regularly, and they also stay with their cousin, who has moved into the big white house in Clock Barn Lane with her mother, Charlotte, as it has far more space than the shop. Their laughter fills the empty rooms, but they miss their father, who always stays in the country."

"Their father misses them. And their mother. And her presence beside him in bed on a Sunday morning. He misses her every day she spends away from him, more than he can ever put into words."

"And they are happy, the husband and wife in the cottage in the wood."

"Yes, I think they will be."

The End

About the author

Sally commutes into London every day and has been writing adult romance short stories and novels on the train for the last ten years on and off. This makes her a very popular person to sit next to, particularly when she is writing bedroom scenes. Sally started out in fan fiction, and then moved on to writing a parenting blog and she misses the instant feedback from readers that being part of a community offers. Sally writes contemporary and historical romance. Connect with her on Facebook or Twitter or email her at sallyannepalmerauthor@outlook.com